THE ENEMY WITHIN

DIETER SCHUMANN IS a wizard of the Celestial college. When he is denounced by a witch hunter as a heretic in league with the Chaos Powers, he is forced into a deadly bargain – to clear his name he must infiltrate a Chaos cult and identify its leader. But such a deal has its perils, not least of which is the corrupting influence of Chaos. Just how far will Dieter have to go to find the information he seeks, and can the witch hunter even be trusted to uphold his part of the bargain?

More Warhammer adventure from the Black Library

· GOTREK & FELIX ·

GOTREK & FELIX: THE FIRST OMNIBUS
(Contains the first three Gotrek & Felix novels: *Trollslayer*,
Skavenslayer and *Daemonslayer*)
by William King

GOTREK & FELIX: THE SECOND OMNIBUS
(Contains books four to six in the series: *Dragonslayer*,
Beastslayer and *Vampireslayer*)
by William King

Book 7 – GIANTSLAYER
by William King

Book 8 – ORCSLAYER
by Nathan Long

· THE WITCH HUNTER SERIES ·

by C.L. Werner

Book 1 – WITCH HUNTER

Book 2 – WITCH FINDER

Book 3 – WITCH KILLER

· BLOOD ON THE REIK ·

by Sandy Mitchell

Book 1 – DEATH'S MESSENGER

Book 2 – DEATH'S CITY

Book 3 – DEATH'S LEGACY

A WARHAMMER NOVEL

THE ENEMY WITHIN

RICHARD LEE BYERS

For Denise.

A BLACK LIBRARY PUBLICATION

First published in Great Britain in 2007 by
BL Publishing,
Games Workshop Ltd.,
Willow Road, Nottingham,
NG7 2WS, UK

10 9 8 7 6 5 4 3 2 1

Map by Nuala Kinrade.

A CIP record for this book is available from the British Library.

ISBN 13: 978 1 84416 444 8
ISBN 10: 1 84416 444 6

Distributed in the US by Simon & Schuster
1230 Avenue of the Americas, New York, NY 10020.

See the Black Library on the Internet at
www.blacklibrary.com

Find out more about Games Workshop
and the world of Warhammer at
www.games-workshop.com

THIS IS A DARK age, a bloody age, an age of daemons and of sorcery. It is an age of battle and death, and of the world's ending. Amidst all of the fire, flame and fury it is a time, too, of mighty heroes, of bold deeds and great courage.

AT THE HEART of the Old World sprawls the Empire, the largest and most powerful of the human realms. Known for its engineers, sorcerers, traders and soldiers, it is a land of great mountains, mighty rivers, dark forests and vast cities. And from his throne in Altdorf reigns the Emperor Karl-Franz, sacred descendant of the founder of these lands, Sigmar, and wielder of his magical warhammer.

BUT THESE ARE far from civilised times. Across the length and breadth of the Old World, from the knightly palaces of Bretonnia to ice-bound Kislev in the far north, come rumblings of war. In the towering World's Edge Mountains, the orc tribes are gathering for another assault. Bandits and renegades harry the wild southern lands of the Border Princes. There are rumours of rat-things, the skaven, emerging from the sewers and swamps across the land. And from the northern wildernesses there is the ever-present threat of Chaos, of daemons and beastmen corrupted by the foul powers of the Dark Gods. As the time of battle draws ever nearer, the Empire needs heroes like never before.

f Claws

North of Here Lie The
Dreaded Chaos Wastes.

Erengrad.

Here Be Trolls...

Praag.

Middle Mountains,

Kislev

Kislev.

enheim.

Wolfenburg

Talabheim

The Empire

Alldorf

Karak Kad

Nuln.

The
Moot

Sylvania.

Dracken
-hof.

Zhufbar.

Averheim.

Black
Water.

Black Fire Pass.

Karak
Norn.

CHAPTER ONE

DIETER SCHUMANN WRINKLED his nose at the distinctive stink of Altdorf, a smell composed of river water, waste of every sort, sulphur and smoke. He'd half-forgotten it during his years away, just as he'd forgotten how the city was never silent, even at night.

Trying to ignore the foulness in the air, he breathed slowly and deeply to clear his thoughts, and then his ears picked out particular sounds from the ambient drone. Marching feet tramped in unison, and with each stride, leather creaked and metal clinked.

Dieter cast about for a hiding place, settled on a narrow, shadowy space between two wooden buildings with wax-paper windows, and scrambled into the darkness. Heart pounding, mouth dry, he crouched low, making himself as inconspicuous as possible.

When the marching men came into view, he slumped in relief, for they weren't the watch after all. They were soldiers, outfitted with steel breastplates, helmets and halberds canted all at precisely the same angle over their shoulders. He wondered what business had summoned them forth from their barracks at such an hour. Maybe it was something to do with the marauders beyond the city walls.

He waited for the halberdiers to pass by, then crept back out onto the street, where he once again sought to settle his mind. It was more difficult now. His near-brush with authority, inconsequential though it had been, made him more aware of just how easy it would be for someone to look out of a window or step out of a doorway and catch him at his work. Still, he had no choice but to stand in the open. He needed an unobstructed view of the sky.

He whispered words of power and spun his left hand through a mystic pass. Magic stung the joints of his fingers and sighed through the air around him. Wishing he still had his telescope, he peered up at the stars.

At first they looked as they always did, and he wondered if he'd been too frazzled to cast the spell properly. Then, however, he spotted the rhythmic fluctuations as several luminaries brightened and dimmed in succession, defining an arrow to point him on his way.

Head still cocked back, he prowled onwards. Other stars flared and faded when it was time to turn right or left. As if to mock him, his course took him almost within shouting distance of the sixteen slender spires comprising the Celestial College, and he yearned to dash there and beg for succour.

But he didn't. He'd been told he had a shadow who would intervene if he attempted any such thing, and that no one would help him in any case, and he believed it.

The stars led him near the temple of Sigmar. He imagined all the witch hunters who likely resided within the sprawling complex, and despite himself, he hunched his shoulders and quickened his pace.

In time he crossed one of the countless bridges spanning the Reik. Most of the boats and barges were moored at this hour, but some still glided with lanterns aglow at bow and stern. On the other side rose the easternmost precinct of the city, which was to say, the largest of its many slums. Looking as if the first brisk breeze would knock them down, buildings leaned against each other like drunken revellers. The shadows seethed with rats. The district enjoyed an evil reputation, or at least it had when Dieter lived in Altdorf, and he watched for footpads as he skulked along.

But no one bothered him, perhaps because, in his torn, grimy clothing, he didn't look as if he possessed anything worth stealing, and eventually the stars stopped drawing lines for him to follow. Now the fluctuations swirled round and round like a whirlpool in the heavens. Underneath was a dilapidated building with shutters lost or hanging askew, tattered windows and a tavern on the ground floor. A hanging sign identified the establishment as the Axe and Fingers. Beneath the legend was a crudely painted illustration of a blade – it actually looked more like a butcher's cleaver than an axe – chopping the digits off a corpse-white hand.

Dieter took a deep breath, then went inside.

If the magic had guided him correctly, there should be one or more unsavoury characters lurking in this poorly lit, low-ceilinged place, and at first glance, the patrons, glowering, unkempt men and ageing, painted prostitutes, looked the part. The problem was that no one of them looked it more than the rest. Where, then, to begin?

He selected, essentially at random, a pox-scarred fellow sitting alone at the bar huddled over a tankard of ale as if he feared someone would try to snatch it away. Dieter claimed the rickety stool beside him, then said, 'I just came into the city. From upriver.'

The other man didn't answer, or even glance in his direction.

'I had to go somewhere,' Dieter persisted. 'I lost everything.'

The pockmarked man slowly turned his head to glare with cold grey eyes. 'It could be worse. For instance, I could break your back and stamp in your ribs if you keep bothering me.'

'I just hoped you could tell me where to look for work, but never mind.' Trying not to appear intimidated, Dieter rose and moved away.

He ordered a mug of ale of his own, sipped it for a time, then made another approach. That one didn't work out either, nor the one after that. It was rapidly becoming clear that this was a neighbourhood tavern patronised by ruffians both suspicious and disdainful of outsiders. Strangers were unwelcome, and no one cared to hear their tales of woe.

A newcomer graced with a glib enough tongue might have ingratiated himself even so, but Dieter had simply managed to irritate. A little more, and someone – maybe everyone – really would try to hurt him.

Damn it, he didn't have the training or aptitude for this task. He'd explained as much, yet here he was anyway.

'Can I bring you another?' asked a soft, somehow wistful soprano voice.

Dieter looked up at a slender blonde barmaid he hadn't noticed hitherto. She must have slipped into the taproom while he was feeling sorry for himself. Though she was younger and prettier than any of the prostitutes – probably he should say, the full-time prostitutes – the cut of her bodice was equally revealing, and the paint and powder on her face just as thick. Still, he thought he saw a trace of sadness in the features all but buried underneath.

'Yes,' he said. 'If I'm going to starve in the gutter tomorrow, I want to be drunk tonight.'

She hesitated. 'Are you sure? When your belly starts to ache, you may regret leaving all your money here.'

'No, I won't. I need to feel better, or, failing that, numb. So fetch me another and one for yourself, too, if you're inclined to keep me company.'

She was. The taverner looked on, but made no objection as she set the tankards on the round little table with its malodorous tallow candle and seated herself across from Dieter. He surmised she was allowed to fraternise with customers if it seemed possible they might end up renting her charms.

He paid for the drinks with two brass pennies. 'Thank you. My name is Dieter.'

'I'm the one who should thank you. You're treating me. And I'm Jarla.'

'Well, here's to your health, Jarla.' He saluted her with his ale.

After that, he lapsed into what he hoped would seem a morose taciturnity. He hadn't had any luck trying to babble his story to anyone who would tolerate it. Maybe it would work better to let her draw him out. It was, after all, a part of her trade.

'Are you truly in danger of starving?' she asked.

He shrugged. 'Altdorf is your town. You tell me. Can I find work?'

'People do. It's a huge, bustling city.' She hesitated as though torn between honesty and the wish not to demoralise him any further. 'But the guilds control trade and all the crafts, and if you're not connected to any of them, it can be hard to find a job that pays more than a pittance.'

He smiled bitterly. 'So much for me, then. I'm no guildsman. Obviously. Anyone could tell that just by looking at me. But I don't even know any. I never set foot in Altdorf before today.'

'Why are you here now? You're not old, but you're older than the boys who run away to the capital with nothing but a dream of striking it rich.'

'Maybe we should talk about something more pleasant.'

'If you like. But sometimes sharing your troubles makes you feel better.'

She had that wistful note in her voice again, and he wondered if she lacked a confidant of her own. Not that it mattered. He was here to solve his own problems, not inquire into someone else's.

So he launched into his story. If she wasn't the one who needed to hear it, maybe that person would be obliging enough to eavesdrop.

'I came here because I had to go somewhere. There was nothing left for me where I was. Even though it was a nice little village once.'

'What happened?' Jarla asked.

'Well, first, beastmen raiders came in the night. They caught us farmers by surprise, and even if it had been otherwise, we wouldn't have been able to defend ourselves. The creatures massacred several families in the first moments of the attack. The rest of us ran, and naturally many of us fled to the castle of our lord the baron. Our protector.' He infused the word with all the sarcasm he could muster.

'Didn't he help you?'

'No. Maybe he and his men-at-arms could tell there were a lot of beastmen. At any rate, they plainly wanted no part of them, for they didn't come out to fight. They didn't even open the gate to shelter us, for fear the raiders would rush in with us. They just watched from the battlements while the goat-men slaughtered us at the foot of the wall.'

Jarla covered his hand with her own. 'That's horrible.'

'Yes. It was. I saw my brother and his wife cut down. I don't know why the beastmen didn't get me too, except that I threw myself down on the ground and lay still. Either they all missed seeing me, or else each of them thought another member of the band had already killed me.'

'I'm glad you survived, even if your hamlet didn't.'

'Actually, it did. Or we believed it had. Many died, but not all, and even though there were barely enough of us left to manage the work, we did our best to carry on. Until we realised things were different.'

'What do you mean?'

'The beastmen left a taint behind. I don't know if they did it on purpose or if it's simply their nature to poison whatever they touch, but after that night, the crops were strange. The grain was stunted and had a reddish cast to it. The grapes were long as your finger and white as bone. The lambs and piglets were stillborn as often as not, or came into the world with too few legs or too many eyes. Then a human baby was born with a face on its belly.'

'Fortunately,' Dieter continued, again in a tone of bitter irony, 'this time the baron did take action. He sent for witch hunters.'

'What did they do?'

He snorted. 'What didn't they do? They said the fief must be cleansed at any cost. So they burned the fields and orchards. Slaughtered the livestock and any man, woman or child they suspected of changing under the influence of the contamination. They killed poor Wolfgang just because of his skin rash, even though some of us tried to tell them he'd suffered from it long before the beastmen ever came.'

'Everyone says witch hunters can be cruel.'

'Then everyone is right. They finished the goat-men's work and destroyed the village. We all had to leave, because, with the crops burned and the animals killed, we would have starved if we stayed.'

He sneered. 'But one good thing did happen. I got to see our proud lord beg. He depended on our crops and rents for his own living, so he begged the witch hunters not to be so severe, and then he pleaded with us to stay. We laughed in his cowardly face.'

'I'm so sorry,' Jarla said. 'But you're starting a new life now, and I hope it will be a good one.'

The host banged something down on the bar. Dieter glanced around to see the man staring in his and Jarla's direction.

Though he couldn't be sure, he thought the barmaid coloured beneath her mask of paint. 'We've been talking for a while,' she said. 'I need to go back to work. I mean, unless…'

'You're very pretty,' Dieter said, 'but not tonight. Maybe after I find work, and have my wages in my pocket.'

She patted his hand and stood up.

UNWILLING TO DEPLETE his meagre funds too quickly, Dieter nursed his ale until the crowd started to thin out, then took his leave.

He had no idea whether he'd accomplished anything at all, and, weary, his nerves frayed, felt a crazy urge to shout the fact to whoever might be listening in the dark.

Look at me! I'm terrible at this! You need to find somebody else!

But he didn't, because it would do no good. Instead, he looked upwards and whispered another spell.

Certain stars brightened and others dimmed. Some changed colour. The transformation was subtler than when they'd flared and faded in succession to guide his steps, and this time it was spread across the length and breadth of the sky. Still, after peering for a time, he picked out the message written there for those with eyes to see.

According to the divination, he had made progress towards his goal. And towards danger and ruin as well.

Under the circumstances, it was as favourable an augury as he could have expected. Feeling encouraged in a bleak sort of way, he trudged onwards to find a place to sleep.

DIETER PICKED UP his tankard, and his hand throbbed. The discomfort must have shown in his face, because Jarla asked, 'Are you all right?'

'Fine,' he said, though that was overstating it a little. As she'd predicted, he'd found employment, but it was a strenuous, low-paying job assisting a rat catcher. He had to wade through reeking sewers and crawl into other cramped, filthy spaces. He'd imagined himself fit – he still possessed the same lean frame he'd had as a youth, and, at home, had taken a walk every day – but even so, his new duties had bruised his knees, scraped his palms and planted aches in his lower back. And this afternoon, when he was picking up the carcasses of poisoned rodents, he'd discovered one was still alive when it bit him. His new employer had laughed until he choked.

But at least he could afford bread, and his allotted quarter of a vermin-infested bed in a doss house. Most importantly, he could afford to keep returning here to drink and talk with Jarla.

For, unlikely as it seemed, she did appear to be the key. All his divinations suggested as much in their ominous and uncertain way, and in addition, she was a little too willing to spend time with him, considering that he had yet to pay her to lift her skirts. His sorrowful, rancorous tale had snagged her interest, and now he had the feeling she was trying to determine just how deep his bitterness ran.

Unfortunately, she didn't seem to be in any hurry about it, and he was running out of patience, unwilling to go on living this wretched existence until some passing member of the watch happened to recognise him and take him into custody. It was time to push.

'You don't seem fine,' Jarla said. 'You've begun to make your way–'

He snorted. 'Is that what you call it?'

'–in Altdorf, but you're still unhappy.'

'You don't get over losing your family and home all at once. Maybe you never do.'

She sighed. 'I hope for your sake that isn't true.'

'You know, it isn't just the sadness of the thing. It's the unfairness and stupidity.'

'What do you mean?'

He lowered his voice. 'What's the difference whether a sheep has four legs or five, so long as the wool will make a proper thread? Where's the sense in destroying grain just because the colour's a little off? Why not grind some and try it? The loaf might taste just the same. For all anyone knows, it might taste better.'

She glanced surreptitiously about the taproom, trying to make sure no one was eavesdropping. 'Corruption will spread and destroy everything if allowed to fester. That's what everyone says.'

'"Everyone" meaning the lords and priests. Did you ever stop to think that it serves their interests to keep us terrified of mutants and daemons and such? It prevents us from noticing how our masters abuse us.'

'Some would say that's simply the way of the world.'

'Then maybe the world needs to change. Is it really too much to ask that we have barons who fight for the folk under their protection, and witch finders who don't punish the innocent along with the guilty? By the hammer, that infant with the extra face was horrible to look at, but what harm had it ever done to anyone? It didn't ask to be born deformed.'

'I confess,' Jarla said, 'I've had such thoughts. I suppose many people have. Everyone who's lost a child or friend or brother to the pyre.'

Dieter leaned forwards so he could speak even more softly. His back gave him a twinge. 'You hear about people who do more than think. They work to pull the bastards down.'

She hesitated. 'Yet people say it's impossible to oppose the Empire without serving Chaos, wittingly or not, for the one is our bulwark against the other.'

'But what is Chaos, anyway? Do we even know? Folk used to say it's magic, but the Emperor employs his own wizards, so what's the difference? Maybe Chaos is just the priests' word for anything different. Anything that threatens to knock the rich and powerful off their thrones.

Maybe, if we had our heads on straight, we humble folk would all be cultists.'

She studied him. 'That's… not something most people would dare to say.'

He decided it was time to back off. 'I shouldn't have said it, either. I'm sorry.'

'Don't be. We're friends. You can tell me anything.'

'Well, I appreciate that.'

'But it is just talk, isn't it? Your way of letting the hurt and anger out. You wouldn't really join such a sect.'

'Don't be so sure.'

She rose, circled the table, put her hand on his shoulder and leaned down to whisper in his ear. 'Then finish your ale – take your time about it – and meet me in the alley.'

Tense and excited in equal measure, he waited as long as he could bear, then made his own departure. Lightning flickered in the northern sky, thunder grumbled, and the occasional drop of rain plopped on his head. Jarla was waiting where she'd said she'd be.

'What's happening?' he asked.

'I'm going to take you where you say you want to go.'

He did his best to feign astonishment. 'Truly? That's… I mean…'

'Hush!' she said. 'No more talking until we get there. We've already said too much where others might overhear.'

He sucked in a breath and gave her a nod. 'All right. Lead on.'

They kept to the alleys and enclosed passageways so narrow and dark that, left to his own devices, he might not have even noticed their existence. They turned often. From time to time, he caught a glimpse of the river, and once, of the burned, ruined structures surrounding the Bright College. Yet even so, in a matter of minutes, he was lost.

He supposed it didn't matter. In a pinch, he could call on the stars to guide him. But usually, he had a keen sense of direction, and now he felt muddled.

That wouldn't do. He needed to be as sharp as ever in his life. He breathed deeply, hoping the cool night air would clear his head.

It didn't. Instead, his legs seemed to fall asleep as if he'd been sitting motionless instead of walking. He stumbled once and then again.

Something's wrong with me, he realised.

He tried to think what to do about it, but found himself too dazed and addled. He croaked Jarla's name and crumpled into the mud.

CHAPTER TWO

THE KNOCKING, NOT thunderous but sounding in a succession of rapid, insistent staccato bursts, jarred Adolph Braun from his slumber. It would have been remarkable if it hadn't. His employer, a master of the Scribe and Bookkeepers' Society, slept upstairs, but a journeyman had to make do with a pallet in the shop on the ground floor of the house, just a few paces from the front door.

Adolph felt more irritated than alarmed as he threw off his blankets, rose, and groped his way around the writing desks and stools that were all but invisible in the dark. It was true, he led a dangerous double life, but he was cunning about it, and wasn't worried that retribution had come calling, not at his master's staid and respectable house. His chief concern was to silence the pounding before it woke the old man, and the old man's ire.

He fumbled with the bolt and cracked open the door. A flare of lightning illuminated Jarla standing on the other side.

His irritation evoked a tension in his arm and the back of his hand, as if it were urging him to lay it across her face. 'Damn you,' he whispered. 'You know I can't entertain a whore here.'

'Please,' she said, her voice as soft as his, 'I need you. There was a stranger. He started coming to the tavern, and saying the kind of things we listen for. So I befriended him to see if he was really the sort of man we need.'

He grunted his comprehension. One good thing about her job – about both her jobs – was that they brought her into contact with men who felt inclined to confide in her, and occasionally she found one with the proper mix of boldness and virulent dissatisfaction to join a cabal such as theirs. 'Go on.'

'Well, at first I had a good feeling about him, but tonight everything started moving too fast, and he was the one pushing it along. Supposedly, beastmen attacked his village, but all of a sudden, he suggested that perhaps Chaos isn't as awful as most people think, and then raised the subject of treason and forbidden cults. He even said right out, right there in the taproom, that he wished he could join one. Who would be so reckless?'

'A spy,' Adolph said, feeling sick to his stomach, 'trying to draw you out.'

'That's what I suspected, and once I did, I realised there were other funny things about him. He talked more like a city man, maybe even an educated man, than a peasant from some little hamlet, and if he really was a farmer, his hands should have been callused. They weren't. They were blistered from–'

'Shut up!' Adolph snarled, and she flinched. 'I don't care about his hands. How much does he know? Where is he now?' A terrible thought struck him. 'By all the voices whispering in shadow, if you let him follow you here–'

'I didn't! I leaned over him and slipped sleeping powder in his ale. Then I told him I'd take him to a cult and led him around back streets and alleys until he passed out.'

Adolph felt some of the tautness go out of his limbs. 'I guess, once in a while, you aren't completely worthless.'

It was kindly meant, and it annoyed him when she flinched again. If she didn't appreciate it when he tried to be nice, then what was the point?

Not that this was any time to ponder the perversity of women. 'What happened next? Did you kill him?'

'No. I didn't know if I should.'

He sneered. 'Meaning, you're too squeamish.'

'Meaning, I need you to come and help me decide what's best to do!'

'All right.' Confronted with a crisis, she'd performed better than anyone would have expected. But now she was buckling under the pressure, and it was plainly up to him to bring the matter to a satisfactory conclusion. 'Just let me put on my shoes and get my knife.'

JARLA WASN'T ESPECIALLY strong, but she'd managed to drag Dieter behind a section of fence and into someone's tiny, neglected, weed-infested garden, where passers-by were less likely to notice him.

Despite her newfound suspicions, she found it a relief to find him lying unharmed in the drizzle. He looked like just another of Altdorf's homeless paupers sleeping outdoors, but that didn't mean someone wouldn't steal his clothes, or hurt him simply for the amusement it afforded, or that the rats wouldn't decide to nibble his flesh.

Adolph crouched to inspect their prisoner more closely, and it struck her that the two men looked as if they ought to switch roles. With his burly physique and coarse, choleric features, Adolph should have been a drudge, while a man with a thin frame and intelligent face like Dieter's should spend his days writing documents and adding up sums in a ledger.

Adolph grunted. 'Let's get this done and get away.' He pulled the curved, single-edged knife from the sheath on his belt.

But Jarla hadn't fetched her lover simply to kill Dieter while he lay insensible and helpless. She could have done that herself, whatever he thought, or at least she hoped she could. 'Wait.'

Adolph glowered at her. 'Why?'

'What if he isn't a spy? I could be wrong.'

'True. You generally are. But from what you told me, this seems to be the exception.'

'I don't want him to die if he doesn't deserve it.'

'We have to do what we have to do to protect ourselves and serve the Changer,' Adolph said. 'It doesn't matter who deserves what.' He scowled. 'Did you spread your legs for him? Did you like it? Is that why you're baulking all of a sudden?'

His spasm of jealousy evoked the usual mixed emotions in her. On the one hand, he'd known from the day they met what she did to earn her living and serve the god, so what was the sense of getting angry about it? But on the other, when the resentment flared, it showed he really did care about her after all.

'No,' she said. 'It's nothing like that. It's just… if he's a spy, who's he spying for? Who has he talked to, and what did he say? Shouldn't we find out?'

'Well… maybe.'

'So we need to question him.'

'That would mean waiting for him to wake up, and we're in danger every moment we linger here. On top of that, suppose we try digging answers out of him, and he lets out a yell?'

'It wouldn't matter how much noise he made if he was in Mama's cellar.'

'It's too far away. How are we supposed to get him there?'

'You're strong. You could carry him. I'll help. He's a drunk friend, and we're taking him home.'

'No. Too risky.'

Unwilling to surrender but uncertain what to say next, Jarla hesitated, and at that moment, Dieter groaned. Adolph wrenched himself back around and poised his knife against the thin man's throat.

DIETER WOKE COUGHING and retching, and the convulsions jammed his neck against something hard and unyielding. After a moment, the object pulled away, affording him the space to twist his head and expel the burning foulness from his throat. Through tears blurred his vision, he saw that he lay on a patch of earth that, despite the weeds overtaking it, still displayed forlorn, fading signs of orderly rows and cultivation. Once, it had been somebody's garden, bounded and protected by a fence. Light rain pattered on the ground.

Fingers grabbed him by the hair and jerked his head back around. A square face scowled down at him. The hard object pressed against his throat once more, and this time he felt that it was sharp – a blade, which had already nicked him when he coughed. He began to feel the sting of the little cuts, too. He was lucky the spasms hadn't killed him.

That seemed to be the only bit of good fortune that had come his way. He strained to remember what was happening, but the pounding in his skull, the vile taste in his mouth and the nausea still churning his guts made it difficult.

'I wanted to kill you in your sleep,' said the man with the knife, 'but Jarla wanted to question you. You're awake now, so I guess we can spare a moment to try it her way. But struggle, or raise your voice above a whisper, and that's the end of you, understand?'

'Yes.' The mention of Jarla's name helped bring his thoughts into focus. He recalled their final conversation in the tavern, and the circuitous creep through the alleyways that followed. He'd thought he'd fooled her, but now could only assume he'd somehow roused her suspicions, whereupon she'd rendered him helpless with a drug or spell, then run to fetch one of her fellow conspirators.

'Who are you?' asked the man crouching over him.

Dieter was frightened enough to tell him, except that the truth was damning. 'I already explained to Jarla who I am. I don't understand. Is this some kind of test?'

The knife pressed his raw, smarting neck a little harder. 'You don't have time to play games.'

'I'm not.'

'Get over here,' the big man said. 'Hurt him. Break his fingers or something.'

'Me?' Jarla asked. When Dieter shifted his eyes, he could see her standing off to the left, hugging herself as if she were cold.

'No, the Grand Theogonist!' her companion snapped. 'Of course, you. I can't do it. I have to hold onto him and be ready to stick the knife in if he struggles or squeals.'

Jarla's features clenched with a mixture of reluctance and resolve. She trudged forwards, knelt down, and took hold of Dieter's wrist.

As EVERY WIZARD knew, the energies required to fuel his sorceries fluctuated from place to place and time to time, and that was the problem. The man in the dark hooded cloak needed to act quickly, and it was just his bad luck that his immediate surroundings had little power to offer. The ambient forces wouldn't support the manifestation he intended.

That left him with a choice. He could go somewhere more accommodating, or he could try to raise the raw energy he needed. As time was of the essence, he'd opted for the latter.

Accordingly, he strode along the twisting little side street seeking a fellow pedestrian. Damn it, people claimed Altdorf never slept, even late at night. So where was everybody?

He rounded a bend and spied a yawning youth emerging from a doorway. Perhaps the boy had apprenticed to a trade that required him to report for work well before dawn.

'You,' the magician said, and the boy turned in his direction. The warlock whispered a word of power and fixed his quarry with his gaze. Fortunately, this particular cantrip required only an iota of mystical force to power it, and the lad froze like a rabbit before a serpent. Only for a heartbeat, but that was all the time the sorcerer required to dash across the intervening distance, whip the dagger out from under his mantle and drive it into the youth's torso.

Even late at night, on a deserted little street with a paucity of lamps, it was dangerous to commit murder right out in the open, but the warlock had no time to worry about that. He kept on stabbing. The boy grunted every time the blade rammed home, and fumbled at his attacker as if he hoped to shove him away. But he no longer had the strength.

Finally the youth collapsed and lay motionless. Working as quickly as he dared, given that a slip could ruin the magic and imperil him in the process, the sorcerer carved sigils on his victim's brow and cheeks. Then he dipped his forefinger in blood and daubed additional symbols on a wall.

The act of desecration cracked the barrier between worlds, and power flowed through. The mage could feel it rising like floodwater full of drowned corpses and filth. He shuddered in mingled ecstasy and revulsion.

Since he needed a clear head for the conjuring yet to come, neither emotion was useful. Drawing a deep breath, he did his best to quell them, then declaimed words of power and flourished the gory knife in mystic passes.

The glyphs he'd written sizzled and steamed, eating their way deeper into the boy's face and even into the brick wall. Faint but ominous sounds, suggestive of a reptilian hissing, whispered from the empty air.

Then, abruptly, the creature appeared, its brightness driving back the dark and making the warlock squint. He watched for any indication that it meant to attack, for such defiance was always a possibility, no matter how able the summoner.

Happily, the entity wasn't inclined to resist. Rather, writhing this way and that, its body throwing off heat, it simply awaited his commands.

DIETER CLENCHED HIS fist, and Jarla pried at it, trying to get hold of one of his fingers to bend and snap. He had the feeling she was reluctant, and wasn't yet exerting her full strength. But if he continued to resist, she would. It was only a matter of time.

Curse it all, he was a wizard, in theory, the possessor of extraordinary powers. Surely his magic could extricate him from this nightmare? But how, when the ruffian with the knife would no doubt slash his throat as soon as he tried to recite a spell?

'I told you to hurt him,' the male cultist growled.

'I'm trying,' Jarla replied.

'Idiot! How difficult is it? If you can't grab a finger, gouge an eye.'

'Please,' Dieter said, 'you're making a mistake. I'm not your enemy. I–' Something luminous and yellow streaked through the darkness above their heads, and he faltered in fear and astonishment.

The long, sinuous creature appeared to be a flying serpent either shrouded in flame or composed of that element entirely. Plainly, it was some minor spirit of

Chaos, although Dieter didn't understand why it had come. Jarla and her fellow cultist hadn't alluded to summoning it, nor did they need its help to control or kill their captive.

But whatever the reason, its arrival extinguished whatever feeble hope he had left, and he wondered if he should deliberately provoke the man with the knife into cutting his throat. It might well be a less excruciating death than the one the fiery serpent would give him.

Then, however, Jarla somehow sensed the creature wheeling above their heads. Perhaps she caught the all-but-inaudible hiss of its corona of flame. She glanced up, then screamed and lurched off balance.

Her outcry startled the other cultist, and his head snapped around. He looked where she was looking, and then, as the snake turned for another pass – to all appearances, studying the mortals on the ground – his eyes opened wide, and his face turned white. As though steadying himself, he swallowed, sucked in a ragged breath, then jumped to his feet. He apparently didn't care about immobilising Dieter any more. He wanted to be ready to dodge, run or fight if the serpent dived at him.

So, obviously, he and Jarla were just as afraid of the entity as Dieter was, even if that didn't make any sense either. The pair worshipped Chaos, and the unearthly reptile was a manifestation of that universe of blight and madness. Judging from its form, it might even serve their particular deity.

'What does it want?' Jarla whimpered, rising.

'Shut up!' Adolph said. 'Don't talk, don't move, and maybe it will go away.'

It didn't. Instead, as lightning danced in the clouds behind it, it opened its jaws and dived at Jarla.

She screamed and threw herself to the side. Fearful that the serpent's blazing mass was about to slam down on top of him, Dieter rolled.

Fierce heat swept over him and receded just as quickly. He looked up and saw that the snake, after missing its initial strike, had pulled out of its dive and was spiralling skyward once more. Its lack of wings notwithstanding, it flew with an agility no terrestrial creature could match.

The cultists bolted from the forsaken little garden. Proceeding more warily, Dieter rose and peeked out into the alley–

–to see that his erstwhile captors' flight had accomplished nothing. The serpent could fly faster than they could run and had manoeuvred to cut them off. At the moment, it hovered in the air ahead of them.

Its behaviour suggested it was more interested in Jarla and her ally than in Dieter. Was it possible that if he simply stayed put, it would kill the cultists and go away? It seemed worth a try.

Except, what then? He wouldn't be any closer to accomplishing his task. Indeed, if he allowed Jarla to perish, he might be forfeiting his only hope of ever succeeding. Whereas if he saved her...

That, of course, was assuming he could. His training had included some battle magic. Afterwards, serving the Empire as a journeyman wizard, he'd even fought in a few skirmishes. But never without a rank of soldiers standing protectively in front of him, and never against a foe like this.

Still, he decided to try. He stepped out into the alley, and, as the serpent whipped itself around and dived at Adolph, raised his hands to the heavens and rattled off an incantation.

Power shivered through him, and despite his desperate circumstances, he thrilled to its exhilarating touch. He thrust out his right arm parallel to the ground, and a dart of blue light streaked from his fingertips.

Down the alleyway, the serpent's fangs clashed shut in a burst of flame, and Adolph threw himself flat to avoid them. The creature dropped on top of him, and probably didn't need to do anything more to kill him. If it stayed where it was, and he couldn't struggle out from underneath the weight of its coils, its mere proximity would roast him alive.

Except that at that moment, Dieter's luminous missile struck it at the base of its wedge-shaped head. It hissed and turned to glare in his direction.

When he met its gaze, he shuddered, for its blank eyes somehow conveyed infinite malice and the promise of savage retribution. He yearned to run, but quashed the impulse, instead conjuring a second dart. When that one pierced the spirit, it sprang back into the air. Adolph rolled and slapped at himself to extinguish the flames now nibbling at his clothing.

The serpent hurtled straight at Dieter. He rattled off the first words of another spell. Dangerous to work so many in succession, dangerous to cast them so quickly, but, as was always the case of late, he had no choice.

He felt the heat of the onrushing creature's body. He recited even faster. Disembodied voices howled and gibbered, a warning of botched casting and magic twisting awry.

It didn't, though. Despite his haste and the fear gnawing at his concentration, he'd evidently got the spell right, or near enough, because a great wind roared, smashed into the serpent and tumbled it backwards. It shrieked, caught itself and, its aura of flame blowing out behind it like a comet's tail, attempted to struggle forwards once more. So far, though, it wasn't having any luck.

Dieter pierced it with another glowing dart. On his feet once more, black, charred patches on his clothing but essentially unharmed, Adolph snarled a spell of his own. Dieter couldn't make out the actual words above the scream of his conjured wind, but they had a vile, rasping quality that made his skin crawl.

Swirls of inky shadow writhed into existence around the serpent's body. Adolph grinned, then scowled when the black bonds vanished as abruptly as they'd appeared, and without seeming to trouble the spirit in the slightest. It was as if the aura of flame had burned them from existence.

Meanwhile, Jarla threw stones. Unfortunately, unlike arcane attacks, the rocks fell short or flew wild, deflected by the same wind that kept the snake away from Dieter.

Although it wouldn't hold it back much longer. The creature had started slowly but was steadily gaining ground, and the artificial gale would subside in a few more heartbeats anyway, when the enchantment ran its course. Once again, Dieter struggled against the panicky urge to flee.

He cloaked himself in a bluish shimmer that might, if he was lucky, stop the serpent's fangs like armour. He then focused his mind and reached high into the sky, where his form of wizardry lived. He needed a storm, and in fact, there was one raging, but unfortunately, well to the north, with only the fringe hanging above the city. But if his skills sufficed, perhaps that would be good enough.

He chanted, and the warp and woof of existence responded to his commands and entreaties. It was like hooking a fish, like seizing clay in one's grasp and moulding it, somewhat like a hundred mundane actions yet like nothing anyone not a wizard could ever comprehend.

The bellow of the wind started to fade. The serpent lurched closer. Adolph grabbed Jarla by the bodice, spat an incantation into her painted, terrified face, stooped and, to all appearances, tore her shadow loose from her feet. She thrashed, and he set the murky figure standing upright. Portions of its body stretching and contracting as it moved, it charged the creature of Chaos.

But the conjured servitor scarcely bothered the serpent any more than the dark bonds had. A single snap of its blazing jaws destroyed it.

The wind died entirely. The snake shot forwards, and Jarla, apparently at least partially recovered, wailed. Dieter kept chanting as his attacker surged into striking distance.

The shimmering haze he'd conjured to sheathe his limbs kept the serpent's first bite from penetrating, but it couldn't block the heat. It was like standing in a furnace, like the air in his lungs and throat had turned to smoke and embers. Somehow he held to the cadence and precise articulation his spell required. The serpent reared to strike again.

Then the world burned white and boomed as lightning, drawn far from its natural course by Dieter's magic, pierced the creature from above. The serpent vanished instantly. The blast hurled Dieter through the air to slam down on his back.

Gasping, blinking at after images and listening to the ringing in his ears, he knew that by rights, the thunderbolt, striking so close, should have done more than pick him up and fling him. It should have burned or killed him. But he'd had the power under control.

Jarla ran to him and dropped to her knees beside him. 'Are you all right?' she cried.

He sat up. 'I think so.'

Breathing heavily, looking as if he was starting to feel the sting of his singes and blisters, Adolph approached more warily. 'You're no farmer,' he said. 'Those were powerful spells you cast.' Dieter wasn't sure if the other man's tone reflected admiration, jealousy, or both.

Nor was he inclined to dwell on the matter. He had something more urgent to figure out: what he needed to say next.

'You're right,' he said. 'Like you, I know some magic, and also like you, I would imagine, I don't tell people about it until I trust them completely.'

'Right,' said Adolph, 'but who are you really?'

'Someone who truly does want to join your cause,' Dieter replied, clambering to his feet. 'Can the details wait until we're away from here? The fight made enough commotion that I doubt it's safe to linger.'

In addition to which, he could use the extra time to polish his new set of lies and fix the particulars in his memory.

Adolph scowled. 'You're right. We should leave before the witch hunters show up, and we want to go this way.'

They hurried onwards, not quite running, but striding quickly. Dieter struggled not to flag, to deny the weakness and fatigue that inevitably followed so much spell casting. At first Jarla too seemed to strain to keep the pace, as though she was still suffering from Adolph's mystical violation of her person. Gradually, though, she appeared to rally, and then she gave Dieter a tentative, inquiring sort of smile.

'I'm sorry I drugged you,' she said, 'and sorry we tried to hurt you, too.'

It had terrified him at the time, nor, in his secret heart, was he inclined to take his mistreatment lightly even now, but he forced a grin. 'You thought I was deceiving you, and on one level, I was, so I have only myself to blame.'

Forgiveness widened and brightened her smile. 'Adolph is right. The way you defeated the daemon' – evidently she wasn't sufficiently well-versed in Dark Magic to distinguish between true daemons and lesser entities like the one they'd just encountered – 'was amazing.'

'He and I defeated it together!' Adolph snapped. 'Don't you remember me casting my spells, you stupid whore?'

Jarla flinched.

They walked in silence after that, on towards whatever new dangers awaited. Dieter tried to draw encouragement from the fact that at least his situation was less dire than it had been only minutes before. Or several weeks before, for that matter…

CHAPTER THREE

THEY'D BEATEN DIETER with their fists, scourged him with a thin black whip, and left him dangling from a rafter with the weight of iron balls and chains hanging in turn from his ankles. Eventually he'd passed out, to wake bound and gagged on the cold dirt floor of a cell.

A rat came creeping, enticed, perhaps by the bloody smell of the lash marks on his back or the galls on his wrists and ankles. He heaved and thrashed as best he could until the rodent scurried away.

'That works for a while,' said a cheerful bass voice, 'but eventually the rats figure out a prisoner in restraints can't really do much to fend them off, and then they take their supper. I've seen it happen time and again.'

Dieter hitched himself around to face the bars and the corridor outside, where Otto Krieger stood. With the light of the torch in the wall sconce wavering behind him, the big man was little more than a shadow, but by now, fear and outrage had stamped every detail of his appearance into his prisoner's memory.

Krieger was broad-shouldered and barrel-chested, with a square, pleasant face and a smiling, ruddy mouth. Had he opted to wear something other than the sombre garments and ominous regalia of a witch hunter, a new acquaintance might have taken him for a genial, convivial fellow, with nothing brutal or cruel about him. Unfortunately, the reality was otherwise.

Krieger selected one key on a ring, inserted and twisted it in the lock securing the door, and the mechanism clanked. He entered the cell, bent over Dieter – who struggled not to cringe – hoisted him up and sat him on the wooden bench by the back wall.

'There,' the witch hunter said, 'that's better than the floor, isn't it? It's certainly a better attitude for a friendly conversation. Although for that, we need to take the gag out of your mouth. Promise me you won't try to cast a spell.'

With his back and joints throbbing, Dieter doubted he could have mustered the necessary concentration in any case. He nodded.

'Good man.' Krieger pulled down the knotted kerchief. 'You must be thirsty.' He produced a leather canteen and held it to Dieter's lips.

Until now, the witch hunter and his assistants hadn't given Dieter anything to drink, and the lukewarm water eased at least one of his miseries. He felt an irrational twinge of gratitude, and tried to quash it.

'Now, then,' Krieger said, 'let's talk about the evidence against you.'

'There isn't any,' Dieter said. 'There can't be.'

Krieger tapped the satchel hanging with his broadsword and wheel-lock pistol from his broad black square-buckled belt. 'I have the affidavits. Testimony sworn in Sigmar's holy name. A woman named Elfrida never fancied you – I don't know why not, you look all right – yet one night, she felt compelled to couple with you anyway.'

'"Felt compelled"? Meaning, I bewitched her? She was drunk! We both were! It was Sun Still!'

'Several witnesses saw you cast spells while in the company of a boy named Berthold–'

'I plucked pennies from his ears to make him laugh. It's not even real magic, just sleight of hand.'

'–and subsequently, he wandered off alone into the forest, where wolves attacked and killed him.'

'You can't believe I made it happen!'

'Several miners heard strange whispers in one of the shafts. Then a support gave way. A man lost his arm.'

'A terrible accident, but again, nothing to do with me. Since I settled here, I've done nothing but try to help my neighbours. Much of Celestial magic is divination, and I tell the farmers where to dig their wells and when to plant. I help the miners locate veins of ore and coal. I search for lost sheep and cows, and lost children, when necessary. Anyone will tell you! Why would I work to help *and* harm the village?'

'You do some small semblance of good so the town will tolerate a wizard in its midst. Then, having lulled everyone's suspicions, you can address your true task: spreading pain and despair to advance the cause of Chaos.'

'That's insane.'

Krieger rested his hand on the satchel. 'Your neighbours say otherwise.'

'Then it's simply because they have a morbid fear of any magician, and you played on it. Or because you bribed or threatened them.'

The witch hunter chuckled. 'I will admit that, once I hinted I might pay a modest fee for pertinent information, several witnesses came forward. While after I made it clear that in my view, only a Chaos worshipper would seek to defend another such, a couple of folk who at first seemed inclined to speak on your behalf thought better of it.'

Dieter could scarcely believe what he was hearing. 'Then you admit to manufacturing a case against an innocent man.'

'There are no innocent men, my friend, simply varying kinds and degrees of guilt. Certainly there are no innocent wizards. Sigmar teaches that all magic derives from Chaos, no matter how you scholars of the colleges try to obfuscate the fact.'

'That may be your opinion, but we have charters from the Emperor allowing us to practise our arts.'

'Until you get caught abusing them. Let's discuss the contents of your house.'

'What? My telescopes? My star charts? My staff? A wizard of the Celestial Order is allowed to possess such tools.'

'Arguably so, but what about this?' Krieger unbuckled the flap of his satchel and removed a child's toy comprised of a wooden cup and handle linked to a little ball by a length of leather string. 'Recognise it?'

Dieter did. It had been Berthold's. But he refused to say the words, as if that would make any difference.

'How about this?' Krieger produced a kerchief. In point of fact, Dieter didn't recognise it, but suspected it belonged to Elfrida. 'Or this?' The witch hunter proffered a little clay figure of a man with one arm missing. 'I believe they're the sorts of items a warlock might have used to lay curses on the folk who have come to grief.'

'You planted them!'

'You'd be surprised how many witches utter such slanders. You probably wouldn't be surprised that nobody ever believes them.'

Struggling for calm, Dieter took a deep breath. 'You must realise, you don't even have jurisdiction over me. I'm a mage of the Celestial College. If I'm accused of wrongdoing, my order is supposed to adjudicate the matter.'

Krieger shrugged. 'Technically, you may have a point, but we're not in Altdorf. I've spoken with the Graf, and, upright, pious child of Sigmar that he is, he's eager for me to bring this troubling case to a quick conclusion. That's why he allowed me the use of his dungeon.'

'Damn you!' Dieter said. 'What's the point of this? What is it you actually hope to accomplish?'

The witch hunter grinned and clapped his hands together. The smack resounded in the cramped confines of the cell. 'Finally, you said something intelligent. Good. I was beginning to wonder if I had the wrong man.'

'You do.'

'Now don't turn thick on me again. Obviously, I'm not talking about whether you really used sorcery to pry Elfrida's knees apart, or fed poor little Berthold to the wolves.'

'What, then?'

'Have you ever heard of the Cult of the Red Crown?'

'No. I assume you're talking about a Chaos cult? I've heard there are many such groups, but I've never bothered to learn about any of them. They have no relevance to my field of study.'

'It's a society devoted to the Architect of Fate, the Changer of the Ways. My colleagues and I have learned that the cult has a strong presence in Altdorf itself, and we suspect they're in league with a horde of mutant raiders who prey on caravans and other travellers on the roads leading into the city.'

Bewildered, Dieter shook his head. 'And you suspect this has something to do with me, miles and miles away in little Halmbrandt?'

'No, not yet. But I intend for it to. You see, I've made it my business to bring down the Red Crown, but it's difficult, because of the way they're organised. At the top is a sorcerer called the Master of Change. He only deals with his lieutenants, who aren't told one another's real names. Each of the lieutenants leads a coven, and none of the covens has any knowledge of the others. Do you see the strength of such a system?'

'I think so. You witch hunters can identify and attack a single coven and still accomplish relatively little in terms of crushing the entire cult. Because, no matter how you torture them, the members can't give up secrets they don't know. Although if you arrest the leader…'

'So far,' Krieger said, 'I haven't managed to take any of them alive. If need be, they turn their magic on themselves. I need a different strategy, and that's where you come in.'

'I don't understand.'

The big man grinned. 'It's simple enough in principle. I break you out of this prison. You run to Altdorf. You use your divinatory abilities to find a coven, and then you infiltrate it. Once inside, you ferret out the cult's secrets, up to and including the identity and hiding place of the Master of Change.'

'I don't know how to operate as a spy!'

'Sigmar has given you the gift of finding hidden knowledge. It's the essence of your art, and it's what's required.'

'There must be someone better.'

'You'd think so, wouldn't you? But believe it or not, there isn't. You have the proper skills, and in addition, you haven't been to Altdorf in years. Not many people remember you any more, even at the Celestial College. Your particular mentor is dead, and your fellow students graduated and moved on. That anonymity will make it easier for you to pass yourself off as something you're not. It would also make it easy for me to denounce you to your order and convince them of your guilt, but let's hope it doesn't come to that.'

Dieter took a deep breath. 'Let's say I do this for you. What happens to me afterwards?'

'I clear you of the charges against you,' Krieger replied. 'You regain your freedom. Your good name. Your life. Whereas if you refuse to do your duty and serve Sigmar, and the Empire in its time of need, I'll regretfully proceed with your torture, trial and execution. You'll never see the sky again until my assistants march you to the stake.'

'How can you justify killing a man you know to be innocent? How could you live with yourself?'

'Oh, I'd manage somehow. So what's it going to be?'

Dieter felt sick to his stomach. 'This whole idea is crazy. I doubt I'll even find the cultists, and if I do, they'll unmask and murder me. But you've left me no choice except to try.'

IN A SMALL community like Halmbrandt, even prosperous and aristocratic folk were frugal enough to extinguish every lamp and candle when it was time for bed, and the Graf was no exception. Groping his way down the murky passage, his abused limbs stiff and aching, Dieter nearly tripped over the vague shape of the body before he spotted it.

'What's this?' he whispered.

'One of the servants,' Krieger answered from behind him. 'I don't know what he was doing out of bed, but don't worry, he didn't see me. Just keep moving.'

'Is he dead?'

The witch hunter jabbed the muzzle of his pistol into the small of his prisoner's back. 'I told you to move. We're in danger every moment we delay.'

Dieter reluctantly stepped over the recumbent form and crept onwards, until he and Krieger finally exited the keep.

Krieger tossed him the sack he'd been carrying. 'Clothing. You don't want to wear wizard's robes any more. The bounty hunters and such will be watching for that.'

Dieter opened the bag. 'Did you kill that man?'

'Probably not. I just knocked him over the head. It was necessary to clear him out of our way, and if I did break his skull, Sigmar will reward him for giving his life to further our ends.'

'How does Sigmar deal with murderers, and wretches who bear false witness?'

'You don't have time for complaints and recriminations. You need to be well on your way to Altdorf before I "discover" your escape. I imagine a good many of your neighbours will offer to help hunt you down, and if they volunteer, I won't say no, lest they suspect I'm not as zealous as I ought to be.'

Dieter pulled off his tattered shirt. The night air was cold on his skin. 'It would ruin your whole crazy scheme if they caught me, wouldn't it?'

'Yes, but I guarantee that in the end, you'd regret it even more than I would.'

Dieter finished fastening his new garments, the attire of a peasant or common labourer. He was used to better, and the homespun felt coarse and scratchy, especially where it lay against the welts on his back.

'Do you expect me to make the journey alone?' he asked. If so, his career as a spy would likely reach a painful and inglorious end before he even reached Altdorf. Given a choice, no one travelled alone. The roads were too dangerous.

'No. There's a caravan camped just a few miles down the road. Hurry and you can catch up with them before they break camp and move on in the morning.'

'They'll want to be paid.'

'And I have a few coins for you.' Krieger threw him a pigskin purse that clinked when he caught it.

Dieter took a deep breath. 'All right. I guess I'm ready.'

'Not quite. I have advice you need to hear. Once I turn you loose, you'll suffer temptations. You'll wonder if you shouldn't run to the Celestial College and ask for help. Don't. I've built a strong case against you, and what's happening now – your escape, the attack on the servant – makes it stronger. Your colleagues are as wary of witch hunters as any other wizards. They won't risk compromising themselves to shield a fugitive who looks guilty, particularly a man no one remembers.

'You'll also,' Krieger continued, 'consider simply disappearing. Perhaps leaving the Empire altogether. You'll think a life in hiding or in exile wouldn't be much of a life compared to what you've lost, but it would be better than getting murdered by the Red Crown, or captured and burned when some roadwarden or watchman happens to recognise you. Once again: put such notions out of your mind. My men and I have ways of tracking you. Shirk the task you promised to perform, and we'll find and punish you.'

'I understand.'

'I hope so. Because I made it a point to learn about you, Herr Schumann. You accomplished some remarkable things before you made your money and retired here to study stars and clouds or however it is you pass the time. Granted, your achievements didn't involve spying, but they were impressive nonetheless. I'm confident you can do this job even if you doubt it yourself, and once you do, I'll make everything right for you. I swear it in Sigmar's name.'

Another man might have jeered at such an assurance from a knave who'd already proved himself so utterly dishonest. Or vowed that one day, he'd exact revenge on the bastard who had so abused him. But with his injuries paining him and Krieger's pistol trained on his torso, Dieter realised that such a declaration would only make him feel more helpless than he did already. So he simply stood and listened as the witch hunter explained how he was to make contact with him when the time was right.

ONCE AWAY FROM the Graf's dungeon and Krieger's pistol, Dieter's state of mind started to improve. He found himself calmer and better able to think.

Which, he decided, was what he ought to do. Together with his magic, a capacity for practical, logical deliberation had always served him well. Unfortunately, it was a difficult knack to apply when people were pummelling and flogging him, but that wasn't the case any more. He left the path, sank down on the ground, and gingerly rested his sore back against the trunk of an oak. His ordeal and exertions had so exhausted him that it was bliss to sit, and he felt a sudden pang of fear that he might actually fall asleep, and be discovered so, slumped and snoring, when the hunters caught up with him. He promised himself he'd get up and march onwards as soon as he finished his deliberations.

Krieger had done his best to persuade him he had no choice but to do his bidding, and while he was frightened, helpless and humiliated, his captor's arguments had rung true. But were they really?

Or, to put it another way, could Krieger and his helpers actually track him wherever he went? The witch hunter claimed as much, but maybe it was only a bluff. Maybe Dieter could shake them off his trail if he wanted to.

Did he? He didn't know. He valued the quiet, comfortable life he'd built. It suited him, and he supposed he was willing to take risks to keep it.

But maybe this insane task was more than risky. Maybe it was suicide, pure and simple.

Perhaps he should put Krieger to the test. Find out if he really could track him. If it turned out he couldn't, Dieter would know he at least had the choice to cooperate or flee, and then he could make a decision.

Unfortunately, it would mean a somewhat longer period of travelling alone. But even if he had the bad luck to encounter orcs, goblins or one of the countless other perils infesting the wild places of the world, perhaps his magic would see him through.

He rose, his stiffening limbs protesting. He swept his left hand through a sinuous pass and murmured an incantation. Waking abruptly, squawking and screeching, birds exploded from the nearby trees. They felt magic stirring, and it alarmed them.

Dieter winced at the noise. If any pursuers were within earshot, they were bound to hear. But he couldn't have anticipated the birds' reaction, nor could he do anything about it now.

Power burned through his body, and he grunted at the discomfort. Then that sensation gave way to a sort of tingling lightness.

The feeling meant the enchantment had taken hold. Secure in the knowledge that while it lasted, he wouldn't leave any scent trail, footprints or other signs of his passage behind, he tramped off at a right angle to the road and up a wooded slope carpeted with slippery, rotting leaves.

Away from the path, the branches crisscrossed thickly overhead, but not so thickly as to conceal the sky entirely. A scholar who knew every star and constellation could see enough to give him his bearings. When the sun rose, he peered backwards, studying the slopes he'd just traversed. So far, nothing was moving among the trees, nor could he hear anything but chirps and trills of birdsong. No doubt folk were searching for him, or would be shortly, but they didn't seem to be anywhere nearby.

Encouraged, he tramped onwards, desperately craving rest but only permitting himself to stop for brief intervals. Twice more he employed the same charm to break whatever trail he might be leaving, and at one point waded up a cold, gurgling stream to accomplish the same purpose. Afterwards, his shoes were soaked, and he wished he'd had the sense to take them off first.

Around midday, he reached a different road, narrow and rutted. No one had maintained it of late, and the forest was well on the way to overgrowing and erasing it. Still, it promised faster, easier travelling, and if he followed it far enough, it would take him to Grunburg. He could go to ground there and ponder his next move.

Or so he imagined, until Krieger, smirking, pistol in hand, stepped out from behind an elm a dozen paces ahead of him. 'Hello,' the witch hunter said.

Dieter felt a surge of rage and frustration. Hard on the heels of that came the reflection that Krieger only had one shot, and short-barrelled guns like the pistol weren't accurate beyond close range. The wizard decided he liked his chances. He drew breath to chant his words of power and raised his arms to commence the necessary passes.

'Don't,' Krieger said. He waved his off hand, and half a dozen of his men, scarred, vicious-looking ruffians in brigandines, emerged from cover. They had Dieter surrounded, and each was aiming a crossbow or arquebus at him.

Dieter lowered his hands.

'Good,' Krieger said. 'I imagine that's the first sensible thing you've done since we said goodbye in Halmbrandt.'

'How did you find me?' Dieter asked.

'I warned you I have watchers keeping track of you, and I promise, they'll stay on your trail no matter what sleights you try. But actually, I didn't need an alert from them to intercept you. I expected you'd try to run.'

'Then why turn me loose?'

'To get this out of the way. To prove to you there's no escape so the impulse won't distract you from your work. But you asked how I found you. Well, I knew you couldn't just vanish into the hills for an extended period of time. You have your talents, but you're no woodsman, and I didn't turn you loose with any food. You needed to make for another settlement, and you only had a few options. I looked at a map, figured out you'd pick up this road, and then it was easy for men on horseback to circle around and get ahead of you.'

The explanation brought back the sick, helpless feeling in the pit of Dieter's stomach. For all his magic, all the alleged insight and foresight of a Celestial wizard, he couldn't outthink his tormentor no matter how he tried. 'What happens now?'

'Something unpleasant,' the witch hunter said. 'You disobeyed me, and I have to punish you. Take him.'

Krieger's guards moved forwards. With their weapons still pointed at him, Dieter could only stand and wait until a pair of them gripped his forearms from behind and immobilised him.

Then Krieger himself advanced. He eased down the hammer of his pistol, holstered it, and then, suddenly, pivoting, putting the weight of his entire body behind it, drove a punch into Dieter's belly.

Other blows followed, to the stomach and the ribs, until Dieter lost count of them. Finally, breathing heavily, face flushed, Krieger stepped back, and his assistants released their holds. Dieter crumpled to his knees and retched.

'I hope,' Krieger said, 'you don't think you've been tortured, because you haven't. Up until now, we've simply been trying to get your attention. We can't treat you the way we treat ordinary warlocks, because you wouldn't be capable of doing your job afterwards. Of course, if you convince us there's no chance of you doing it anyway – and one more act of resistance will be enough to convince me – we'll have no reason to hold back. Then you'll find out what torture is really all about.

'So I'll ask you one last time: will you carry out your end of our bargain, without any more foolishness?'

'Yes,' Dieter groaned.

'I'm glad to hear it. I'm afraid the caravan is long gone by now, but don't worry about it. My friends and I will take you to Altdorf ourselves.'

CHAPTER FOUR

JARLA AND ADOLPH led Dieter down a short flight of steps to a door below street level. Adolph pounded on it, and then, as the wait for a response dragged on, growled, 'Come on, come on.'

Dieter sympathised with his impatience. In the wake of their encounter with the fiery serpent, he was just as eager to get off the street, even though he realised that for him, it would only mean heading into new danger.

Finally a small panel in the centre of the door slid open. Despite the darkness, Dieter could just make out the gleam of an eye on the other side of the peephole.

'It's us!' Adolph said. 'Jarla and me. Let us in.'

'Of course, dear,' quavered a scratchy woman's voice. Dieter heard a bar slide in its brackets, and then the door creaked open.

On the other side stood an old woman clad in a night-cap, nightgown, ratty slippers and a crocheted shawl. Her stooped, skinny frame looked fragile as an eggshell, she had the serene, gentle face of a perfect grandmother, and all in all, on first impression seemed as unlikely a Chaos cultist as Jarla.

Or at least she did until she caught sight of Dieter standing behind his companions. Then, where another person's eyes might have widened in surprise, hers narrowed, and just for an instant, her pale, wrinkled features seemed calculating and sly.

She ushered her callers into a dark space illuminated only by the red coals glowing in the hearth, then, moving with a quickness that belied her years, barred the door behind them. After that, though, she doddered. She used the embers to light a punk, which in turn served to kindle two stubby tallow candles and an oil lamp.

As the sources of light wavered to life one by one, they revealed that the old woman occupied a sizeable portion of the building's cellar or conceivably even all of it. Suffusing the air with their aromas, bundles of dried herbs hung from the ceiling, and pots of moss, mould and mushrooms sat on a table alongside a chopper, mortar, pestle, forceps and a lancet. Tattered, yellowed anatomical diagrams, inaccurate in certain respects, hung on the walls, and a stained cot sat in one corner.

'I take it,' she said, 'that this is the unfortunate fellow you told me about.'

'Yes,' Jarla said, 'Dieter, but he isn't what I thought he was. Something happened, and he showed he already knows how to work magic. Even better than Adolph, maybe.' Then, realising what she'd said, she tensed as if she expected her fellow cultist to berate or even strike her. In fact, he glowered, but let it go at that.

The old woman beamed at Dieter. 'I can see we have a great deal to talk about. My name is Solveig Weiss, but everyone calls me Mama Solveig, or just Mama. I'm a midwife, a healer, and something more. I assume you already have some inkling what, or my young friends wouldn't have brought you here. But where are my manners, keeping you all standing? Please, pick up the lights and follow me.'

Dieter took one of the candles and a drip of molten wax stung his finger. Mama Solveig led them out of the clinic and into the area that apparently served as her parlour, where they all settled on one shabby piece of furniture or another.

'Tea?' Mama asked, and looked disappointed when they all declined. 'Well, just let me know if you change your minds. Now let's have the story.'

Jarla started it, but once she reached the part where she went to fetch Adolph, the latter broke in and insisted on continuing it himself. To Dieter's ear, his account of the skirmish with the fiery snake was an ambivalent and somewhat inconsistent affair. It was plain that Dieter's abilities had impressed him, and that he felt it important to convey an accurate sense of them. Yet at the same time, he couldn't bear to admit that his own magic had proved less potent if not entirely useless.

When he finished, Mama Solveig gave Dieter another smile. 'Thank you for helping my friends, and after they drugged and threatened you, too! It's a debt we can never hope to repay. But the question remains, how did you do it? Who are you really? Obviously, not the simple disgruntled peasant you claimed to be.'

Dieter took a deep breath. The moment had come, and now they'd believe the new lies or they wouldn't.

'The story I told Jarla,' he said, 'was partly true. Beastmen did plunder my village, the crops grew strangely afterwards, and then the witch hunters came to finish the task of destroying everything we had. What I lied about was being a farmer. I'm a wyrd. What city folk call a hedge wizard. A knack for a certain kind of magic runs in my family, and my father taught me to use it. To help people, never to harm!'

'We believe you,' Mama said.

'I tried to help when the goat-men came, and I did save a few people. Later, I tried my best to wash the taint from the soil and water. I just wasn't able. Yet when the witch hunters arrived, they came after me immediately.'

Mama Solveig nodded. 'Because you had power you earned for yourself. You didn't go down on your belly and beg it from the colleges, or wear the shackles that would have come with it. No matter how kindly your intentions, people like you, simply by virtue of your existence, pose a threat to the established order. The nobles and priests think they have to exterminate you or you'll one day topple them from their perches.' She leered, providing another momentary glimpse of the fierce spirit lurking behind her mild-looking exterior. 'As you will. As we will.'

He shrugged. 'Maybe.' He'd decided he shouldn't appear too eager, or be too quick and facile when it came to proclaiming sentiments and intentions consonant with their own. As Jarla had recounted it, he'd pushed too hard before, and thus aroused her suspicions. 'Anyway, it was just good luck that I escaped. Afterwards, I hid on the outskirts of the fief to see what would happen next. The witch hunters burned innocent folk and the houses, barns and fields of the survivors, just as I told Jarla. Once it became clear how it was all going to end, I fancied my neighbours might rise up in anger. If they had, I would have joined them. But they didn't. They surely recognised the injustice, but they were too afraid. Afraid of the hunters and the gods they claim to serve.'

'They do,' Adolph said, 'and that's how we know Sigmar and his kind are gods of cruelty and oppression. Fortunately, they aren't the only powers to whom a man can pray.'

Dieter nodded. 'The things you're saying... they're the same kinds of things I started thinking after I had to run away, and the village died. The witch hunters had already condemned me for a servant of the Dark Gods. Maybe it was what I really ought to be. All of a sudden, tearing down the Empire and building something new in its place didn't seem like such a bad idea.

'So I came to Altdorf,' he continued, 'partly just in the hope of losing myself among the crowds, but also imagining that maybe I could find people who felt the way I'd come to feel.' He grinned. 'Looking back, I don't know why I thought I could find them, but you have to understand that out in the country, we rustics like to imagine big cities are rife with all manner of sin and wickedness, forbidden worship included.'

'Our lord led you to us,' said Jarla, her eyes shining. Adolph grunted.

'Maybe so,' Dieter said. 'But where exactly has he led me? Who are you people? A Chaos cult, I understand that much, but what does it really mean?'

'It means,' Mama Solveig said, 'that we renounce the Emperor, the elector counts and the gods who stand behind them. They're all part of one vicious conspiracy to enslave and oppress the multitudes of ordinary people, and we mean to cast them down.'

'With the help of Chaos.'

'Yes. Where Sigmar and his kind forbid, bind and punish, the Great Conspirator permits, liberates and exalts. Chaos is the pure, true essence of magic, and once it drowns the sad, rotten world we know, and we all dwell in the midst of it like fish swimming through the sea, all things will be possible. We'll live forever, and get anything we want just by wishing for it.'

Everyone knew how much death and suffering the hordes of Chaos had inflicted on mankind throughout the centuries, and so Dieter wondered how any sane person could imagine that its triumph would result in the establishment of paradise. Yet, though seemingly rational, Mama Solveig did appear to believe, and so did Adolph and Jarla, hanging on her words even though they'd undoubtedly heard her preach this sermon before.

'Here's what I don't understand,' Dieter said. 'You serve Chaos. Yet a creature of Chaos attacked Jarla, Adolph and me. Why would it do that? How did it even pass from its own world into ours?'

Adolph spat. 'The Cult of the Purple Hand.'

'Perhaps,' Mama Solveig said.

'Who else could it have been? Who else could and would send such a spirit against us?'

'What,' Dieter asked, 'are you talking about?'

'We,' said Mama Solveig, 'belong to the Cult of the Red Crown. Unfortunately, we're not the only Chaos worshippers in Altdorf. The Purple Hand have their own network of covens, and they, no less than the lords and priests, are our foes.'

Dieter felt a crazy impulse to laugh. Or possibly weep. He'd known himself ill equipped to face a single Chaos cult, and apparently Altdorf was swarming with them like an old rotten house full of termites!

'I've heard,' he said, choosing his words carefully, not wanting to appear as if he possessed a suspicious quantity of information, 'that the gods of Chaos can be as hostile to one another as they are to Sigmar, Shallya and the other powers ordinary people worship.'

'That's true,' Mama Solveig said, 'but the Purple Hand purport to serve the Changer of the Ways just as we do.'

'"Purport"? You mean they really don't?'

'No. In their ignorance and vanity, they've strayed from the true path.'

'All right, but even so, why are you so at odds that they would try to kill you?'

'The books,' Adolph said.

'What books?' Dieter asked.

'I haven't heard the whole story.' Mama Solveig sighed. 'As old as I am, I don't suppose I'll ever advance deep enough into the mysteries, and the confidence of the Master of Change, our high priest, to learn the rest. Not in this life, anyway. But some years back, a very great sorcerer and follower of the god lived here in Altdorf. I'm not certain, but I believe he was a magister, who turned to proscribed studies in defiance of the limits his order decreed. In any case, he belonged to neither the Red Crown nor the Purple Hand, but had a relationship with the men who would become the leaders of both sects. Perhaps it's even fair to say they were his apprentices.'

'I take it,' Dieter said, 'that he collected or wrote a number of grimoires.'

Mama Solveig smiled as if she were telling a bedtime story, and he, the grandson had just shown interest by asking a question. 'Yes, dear. Books and papers filled with secrets of what the ignorant call Dark Magic, and naturally both the Master of Change and the chief of the Purple Hand hoped to inherit them someday.

'And in time,' the midwife continued, 'the day arrived. The sorcerer died, fled the city, or grew beyond the need of books. I don't know which. But whatever happened, he bequeathed his library to our leader.'

Or else the Master of Change simply leaped on the opportunity to steal it, Dieter thought. 'And the Purple Hand proved unwilling to accept the disappointment graciously.'

'Yes. Since then, we've tried to destroy one another.' Mama Solveig chortled. 'Although they're hampered by the fact that they don't know many of us, nor do we know many of them. We all guard our secrets well.'

'But we hurt them sometimes!' Adolph said. 'Not long ago, we found out some of them meant to taint the city's water and cause mutations, and we betrayed the plot to the witch hunters and the watch. Anonymously, of course.'

Dieter shook his head. 'I understand there's bad blood between you, but overthrowing the Empire is the hugest, most dangerous undertaking imaginable. If you all worship the same god...'

'Then maybe we should forget our differences and work together?' Mama Solveig asked. 'I'm afraid we can't. Our strategies are incompatible. They want to infiltrate the Imperial hierarchy and subvert it from within. Put their own candidate for Emperor on the throne one day. It's a worthless, cowardly plan. It can't succeed, and even if it did, it would take centuries. Further generations of commoners would live and die in misery.'

'And that's unacceptable,' Adolph said. 'It's why the Red Crown lends its strength to those who strive to topple the Empire by force of arms.'

Like the mutant brigands Krieger told me about, Dieter thought. 'That does sound like the more intelligent strategy. The armies of Chaos have nearly succeeded in conquering us – I mean, the Empire – before.'

Mama Solveig nodded. 'And next time, with help from within, they'll prevail.'

'Right. So: I understand you and the Purple Hand are feuding. Therefore, Adolph assumes they identified him, Jarla or both and sent the fiery snake to kill them?'

Mama Solveig fingered her chin. 'Do you think it odd? I've been thinking the same thing. We don't work magic without good reason, and neither do the Purple Hand. It's inherently risky, and could also attract the attention of the authorities. So I doubt I'd summon a spirit just to murder someone on the street. Not when a ruffian with a dagger could do the job.'

Adolph snorted. 'It's easy enough to explain. They had some notion of the might of my sorcery. Thus, they all feared to confront me face to face, and believed that only a daemon had any chance of overwhelming me.'

'I suppose you may be right, dear. I confess, I can't think of a better explanation. In any case, the important thing is that you and Jarla must promise to be very careful from now on.'

'I promise,' Jarla said, solemn as a child.

Adolph shrugged. 'I'll watch my step, and the Purple Hand had better watch theirs.'

'Good,' Mama said. 'Thank you.' She looked at Dieter. 'And now, young man, it's time for you to make your choice.'

'My choice?' Dieter asked. He understood perfectly well what she meant, but an unexpected jolt of dread made him want to stall for at least a few more heartbeats.

'Of course. We've trusted you with secrets that could send us all to the rack and the stake. After helping Jarla and Adolph, you deserved no less. But now you have to decide whether you want to join us in our struggle or go your own way.'

'Please stay,' Jarla said.

He felt a profound reluctance to say yes, even though it was for that very purpose that Krieger had sent him here. But he knew that, even had he been willing to defy the witch hunter a second time, he had no choice. For all their seeming cordiality, Mama Solveig and her followers would murder him if he declined their invitation. They didn't dare release him to speak of what he'd learned, or, for all they knew, to join a rival Chaos cult.

So he tried to infuse his voice with a bitter fervour. 'Yes. I'll join you. The agents of the Empire destroyed my life. They ruin everyone's life. Somebody needs to cast them down!'

'I'm so glad!' Jarla reached out, squeezed his hand, glanced at Adolph and let it go again.

'We're all glad,' Mama Solveig said. 'So glad that, even though it's late, and a feeble old woman like me needs her rest, we're going to make you one of us right away. Please, take up the lights again and come with me.'

She led them deeper into the cellar, while the shadows slithered away before them. Jarla came to Dieter's side. 'Don't be scared,' she whispered.

'I'm not,' he lied. His pulse ticked in his neck, and his mouth was dry. He peered, looking for anything that might provide some hint of what was to come. He saw only the thick brick columns supporting the weight of the building overhead, junk festooned with cobwebs, and rat droppings.

Then Mama Solveig halted, and twisted her arm and hand through an intricate cabalistic gesture. As when she'd made haste to bar the door, the sure, quick action betrayed no hint of swollen joints or brittle bones, and suggested that her usual slow, unsteady, cautious way of moving was merely a pretence.

Magic sighed through the darkness, and a patch of air rippled as objects wavered into view. Dieter realised a charm had hidden them hitherto, and the old woman had dissolved it.

The items were plainly intended to be tools for working magic, albeit not the specially crafted implements employed by true wizards or even their lowly apprentices. When common folk set out to practise the black arts, they evidently had to make do with the sorts of knives, cups and censers available in any marketplace. Only the wands and staves, meticulously shaped, polished and inscribed with glyphs, looked truly sufficient for their purpose. Most likely one of the cultists earned his living working in wood.

Loose sheets of parchment reposed atop a lectern, but no books or scrolls were in evidence. The cultists had scrubbed a section of the otherwise filthy floor to draw a complicated pentacle in red chalk. They hadn't managed the necessary geometric precision, however. Although Dieter didn't recognise the figure, any true scholar of magic would have perceived instantly that it was either uselessly or dangerously out of balance.

All in all, on first inspection, the cultists' sanctum sanctorum seemed less impressive than Dieter might have anticipated. Or rather, it would have seemed so to an ordinary man. But a mage, particularly a Celestial wizard, sometimes discerned things imperceptible to other folk, and suddenly he glimpsed traces of a sort of oily shadow clinging to even the humblest of the implements assembled in the coven's sanctuary.

It was the taint of Chaos, making his eyes smart, suffusing the air with a carrion stink and twisting queasiness into his guts. But noisome as it was, he thought he could bear it until he discerned the vague shape perched on a plinth at the back of the area, where the flickering light of the candles and oil lamp barely reached. At that point, the foulness overwhelmed him, and he cried out and recoiled.

Jarla grabbed his hand and he jerked it away. Flinging his arms around him from behind, Adolph seized him in a bear hug. Dieter struggled, but couldn't break free of the hold. Mama Solveig whispered under her breath, touched his forehead, and his panic abated.

'Better?' she asked.

He swallowed. 'Yes.' Not only was the instinctive, unreasoning terror fading, the feeling of vileness was bearable once more.

'Now, you mustn't feel embarrassed,' the old woman said. 'The first time is difficult for everyone. How could it not be, when what you feel is the majesty of the god himself?'

Steeling himself to look more closely, Dieter saw that the form on the cheap plaster pedestal was a black carving of a monstrous bird, dragon, or amalgam of the two. Supposedly the Changer of the Ways possessed forms beyond number, but was often depicted in this guise. The sculptor had fashioned it from congealed dark stuff, undoubtedly poisonous not merely to flesh but to the soul and reality itself.

'Don't worry,' Jarla said. 'You'll get used to the way it feels. We all have.'

He supposed they had. Otherwise, they would have dropped dead, or turned into babbling lunatics. But it was difficult to imagine.

'Are you ready?' Mama asked.

Dieter reminded himself that, taint of Chaos or no, icon or no, he still had no choice. Even so, he had to swallow before he could answer. 'Yes.'

'Then kneel and repeat after me.' He assumed the attitude she'd demanded, and she put her left hand atop his head. 'I, Dieter, renounce all earthly ties.'

'I, Dieter, renounce all earthly ties.'

'To family and friend.'

'To family and friend.'

'To land and lord.'

'To land and lord.'

The initiation continued in the same vein for a while, as he swore to renounce every sort of loyalty a sane man might profess. It didn't particularly bother him to do so, which prompted the odd thought that perhaps, in recent years, he hadn't truly felt committed to much beyond his own comfort and advancement of his art. At any rate, except for the noxious psychic pressure of the sculpture, he tolerated the process easily enough.

Next, however, he had to offer prayers and praise to the Changer of the Ways. Fortunately, the litany stopped short of actually requiring him to pledge his soul to the god. He wouldn't have done that no matter what the consequences. But the declarations he was required to make were sufficiently blasphemous that no one could have articulated them without disquiet. He told himself he didn't mean them, that they were only words, but it was scant comfort. As a wizard, he understood the power implicit in language.

At last Mama Solveig said, 'Good. Now, stay on your knees and approach the god.'

'What?'

'It won't hurt you,' Jarla said. 'It hasn't hurt any of us.'

Shivering, soaked in sweat, Dieter knee-walked forwards. With every advance, the malignancy in the sculpture beat at his mind like a hammer.

Somehow he made it to the foot of the plinth. There he had a final invocation to repeat.

Afterwards, Mama chanted in a rasping, hissing language he'd never heard before. The sound of it made his head throb until he thought he couldn't stand it any more.

'And now,' she said, reverting to conventional speech at last, 'for the final consecration. Rise and kiss your new master.'

No! Dieter thought. He'd done everything else, but he wouldn't, couldn't touch the icon. Better to spin around and try to fight his way out of here. The powers of sky and storm would answer his need, even in a basement. Better to run again and hope Krieger couldn't catch him a second time. Better to abandon all hope of ever regaining the life the witch hunter had stolen away from him.

But even as such thoughts howled through his mind, he rose, then bent over the statue. It was as if the prayers he'd recited, Mama Solveig's will, or the poisonous atmosphere in the sanctuary made it impossible to do anything else.

As the statue filled his field of vision, he had the demented feeling it was swelling larger, or else revealing its true size: a thousand times vaster than the tiny, ephemeral world he knew. He touched his lips to its serpentine neck, and icy cold seared them.

'That's long enough,' Mama Solveig called.

Dieter recoiled from the statue. His legs gave way beneath him and he fell.

CHAPTER FIVE

DIETER STUMBLED THROUGH a desert, with masses of granite protruding from the earth and a range of mountains rising in the distance, and moment by moment, everything changed.

Many of the alterations were small but disturbing nonetheless. A dune flattened slightly, a pattern in the sand oozed into a different configuration, or the striations in a pillar of stone darkened. There was nowhere he could rest his gaze to escape the constant, nauseating crawling.

But that wasn't the worst of it. Periodically, change happened on a grander scale. At the edge of the desert, the snow capping three of the peaks exploded into clouds of steam. Then, closer to hand, one of the standing stones melted into a feline-headed giant sunk waist-deep in the earth. The titan glared, hissed and snatched for Dieter, but he scrambled back beyond its reach. The creature struggled to drag itself out of the ground, and he fled. Some time after that, redness ran like streaming blood through the brown terrain. Blades of coarse crimson grass jabbed upwards from what had been sand. The columns of rock became vermilion trees, their branches bedizened with yellow blossoms that smelled like sulphur and trilled to one another.

The universe had gone mad, and was stabbing its madness into Dieter's eyes. Unable to bear it, he lifted his face to the sky, the realm he comprehended and perhaps even loved better than anything on earth. There, change occurred in a stately cyclical dance, according to laws he understood, which meant that in a certain sense, nothing ever changed at all. The heavens would be his refuge.

That was how he needed it to be. But when he looked up, he found the same inconstancy that prevailed below. He couldn't even tell if it was day or night, or if that distinction still possessed any meaning. At first, part of the sky was bright without any sun to shed the light, while the rest was dark and dotted with green luminescences – Dieter couldn't bring himself to think of them as stars – that both churned like eddies and flitted about like flies. Then the whole sky turned mauve, with a white glowing square in the centre. After a time the rectangle crumpled in on itself as if a gigantic invisible hand were crushing it. At the instant it vanished entirely, a robed, hooded colossus appeared where it had been. The immense apparition sat on a golden throne, and legions of daemons, tiny as toy soldiers by comparison, grovelled before it.

Dieter cried out and tore his gaze away, and at that point noticed his shadow. It was changing like everything else, and not just because the light kept shifting.

Shaking, he raised his hands before his eyes. They were pale, then olive-skinned, then mottled with sores. They had four fingers each, and then the left sprouted an extra pair of thumbs. Inconstancy had squirmed its way inside him.

He felt a sudden savage urge to gouge his eyes out so he wouldn't have to see such things any more. But a mild baritone voice said, 'Please, don't be foolish.'

Startled, Dieter jerked around, then screamed and flinched. The speaker wore a simple robe belted with rope, as well as a cowl that shadowed his features. He looked like many a common priest, but also like the transcendent figure the wizard had glimpsed enthroned in the sky.

The newcomer must have realised the source of Dieter's terror, for he pulled back his cowl to reveal a wry, intelligent, human face. 'It's all right! I'm not him. I only want to help you.'

Dieter swallowed. The action felt strange, as if the musculature at the top of his throat had altered. 'Help me how?'

'By pointing you over there.' The priest extended his arm. Dieter followed the gesture and beheld a pool of water amid the writhing scarlet grass.

The pool's surface was still, nor did its silver-grey hue alter even subtly from one second to the next. It was the one steady point in the storm of change, and perhaps that meant it could offer sanctuary.

Dieter dashed to the pool and waded into the cool water. He wondered if he should immerse himself completely.

'That isn't necessary,' said the priest. He must have run, too, to catch up so quickly. 'Just look at the water and nothing else.'

Dieter did as he'd been told, and at first, it helped. The pool didn't change. It didn't even reflect the fluctuations in the sky, or his own face, for that matter, and his fear and queasiness eased a little.

Then, beneath the surface, streaks and blobs of soft colour shimmered into being. He cried out in dismay.

'It's all right,' said the priest. 'This is something different. Just keep looking.'

'Very well.' Why not? Even if the pool altered in some ghastly fashion, how could it be more horrific than the transformations occurring everywhere else?

The colours in the water took on definition until they formed a recognisable image. A man and a woman, both tall, slender and blond, lay on their sides in a canopy bed. The man was facing his companion, but she had her back to him. Though the room was dark, enough light leaked through the curtains to reveal the butterflies and roses in the tapestry on the wall.

Dieter caught his breath in surprise. He was looking at his parents as they'd appeared long before their deaths, when he himself was a child.

'I know you can never forgive me,' his mother said.

'I can and do,' his father replied.

'How?' she spat. 'I betrayed you! I gave birth to an abomination and passed it off as your son!'

He put his hand on her shoulder. 'It was ten years ago, and back then, I was unfaithful, too. So the way I see it, Dieter isn't just the punishment for your sins but for mine as well. The important thing is, the Celestial College will take him. We don't have to live under the same roof with him or even see him again.'

'This never happened,' Dieter said.

'Were you privy to what they whispered to one another in bed?' asked the priest.

'It can't have happened! They didn't fear or despise magic. They sent me to Altdorf because I wanted and needed to go.'

'Just watch,' said the priest.

The scene in the water dissolved into drifting colours, which then flowed together and sharpened to present a new picture. The adolescent Dieter, clad in the blue-trimmed garb of an apprentice of his order, rapped on a familiar door.

'Come in,' Franz Lukas answered.

Dieter entered his mentor's study, cluttered with books, taxonomic charts of birds and clouds, anemometers, astrolabes and other implements of Celestial wizardry. With his brilliant blue eyes shining beneath scraggly white brows, the elderly but still robust and energetic magician was no less emblematic of his particular art.

'Shut it behind you,' Magister Lukas said.

The young Dieter obeyed. 'You sent for me, sir?'

'Yes,' the teacher said. 'You've come a long way in your studies. You're the most promising apprentice I've seen in a while.'

'Thank you, sir.'

'So I think you deserve a reward.' Magister Lukas opened a desk drawer and produced a small book. 'Make sure no one else sees it.'

After a moment's hesitation, the youth took the book and opened the cover. 'The Principles of Alchemy.' He clapped the volume shut. 'Master, this is the Lore of Metal!'

'So it is.'

'Are you testing me?'

'Perhaps, but not in the way you suppose. I know your teachers, myself included, have drummed it into you that you must restrict yourself to the Lore of the Heavens. Any human wizard who seeks to invoke more than one of the eight winds of magic likewise opens himself to the Chaos from which they derive, and must inevitably come to ruin.'

'Yes, sir.'

Magister Lukas snorted. 'No. It's nonsense. The false rationale for a stricture imposed on us to keep us from realising our potential and ordering all things to please ourselves. The best of us, the wisest and boldest, refuse to wear such a shackle. We acquire knowledge and power wherever we can find them. I believe you're one of the best, or at least you could be. Am I right?'

The young Dieter hesitated, then tucked the book inside his shirt.

'No!' his older counterpart exploded. 'I know this couldn't have happened! I was there!'

'Yes,' said the priest, 'you were.'

The scene at the bottom of the pool flowed and became a view of Dieter as a wandering journeyman mage for hire. Crouched behind a stand of brush at the top of a hill, he peered down at the little dirt road than ran along the bottom.

Singly or in groups, afoot or driving carts, laden with bundles or chivvying sheep and cows along, people tramped by below. The older Dieter – the real one, he insisted to himself – inferred they'd all been to market and now were heading home through the deepening twilight.

Eventually a stocky man astride a black mare appeared. The quality of his palfrey and his velvet doublet bespoke prosperity, as did the neatly clad servant or clerk riding a mule behind him.

Dieter the journeyman rose, whispered words of power, and thrust his arm out. Darts of azure light leaped from his fingertips to pierce the horseman, who toppled sideways out of the saddle.

The mare kept walking. The servant reined in his mule and gaped at his fallen master. Apparently he had neither noticed the darts flying nor spotted the assailant on the hill, and thus had no idea how his companion had come to grief. He was still staring when a second such attack stabbed into his torso. He slumped forwards onto the mule's neck.

Dieter looked up and down the road, then ran to the base of the hill. He crouched over the body of the horseman, snatched his victim's purse and rings, and moved on to the clerk. He crooned to the mule to keep it from shying away.

'No!' the actual Dieter cried. 'None of this is true.'

'It wasn't before,' said the priest, his voice now cold and pitiless, 'but it is now. Did you really think a puddle could shield you from Chaos? Chaos is all-powerful. It can transform anything, even the past. Do you perceive your memories changing?'

Dieter felt a churning inside his head.

'Your past made you who you are,' the priest continued, 'so, since Chaos can alter that, it can transform you into whatever it wants. As it has. Go and take your place among your comrades.' He waved his arm.

Dieter turned and saw that somehow the monstrous army he'd seen in the sky had appeared at the edge of the pool. One of the nearest daemons had the body of a huge scorpion and the gurgling, cooing head of an infant. Its drool shrivelled the grass. The entity next to it resembled a seven-legged mastiff pieced together from irregular bits of brass and lead. No two of the creatures were alike, and many, manifesting the same entropy infecting the landscape, oozed and flickered from one shape to another.

'No!' Dieter said. 'I'm not one of them.'

'Of course you are.' The priest scooped up a handful of water and let it go. It fell partway, then froze, hanging in the air in a bright streak that finally reflected Dieter's face with the clarity of a fine glass mirror.

He screamed.

THE DAEMONS GRABBED Dieter by the wrists, to drag him into their ranks by force or tear him apart for his recalcitrance. He thrashed, trying to break free even though he knew it was impossible for one to prevail against so many.

Then suddenly, it wasn't daemons holding onto him any more, and he wasn't standing in the pool. A woman peered anxiously down at him. Disoriented as he was, it took him a moment to recognise Jarla, partly because it was the first time he'd seen her face without its whorish mask of paint. She looked younger, and more shy and tentative without it.

'Are you all right?' she panted.

Far from it. He was still shaking with terror, and his heart thumped as if he'd sprinted for miles. He was also gasping. He laboured to control his breathing, meanwhile insisting to himself that his sojourn in the realm of Chaos had only been a nightmare, a nightmare that was now over, and it blunted the edge of his fear. 'Maybe.' His voice came out as a croak, and he realised his throat was dry and scratchy. 'Is there water?'

'Yes.' She went to fetch it, and as it gurgled from pitcher to cup, he looked about. He was lying on the stained cot in Mama Solveig's infirmary. Up close, the bed smelled of sweat, blood and mildew. Shafts of sunlight fell through the windows, and it appeared that except for Jarla, no one else was about.

She brought him his drink, and, parched though he was, he made himself sip it a little at a time, lest it make him sick. 'Thank you. How long was I unconscious?'

'Hours.' She sat down on a little three-legged stool beside the cot. 'It's afternoon. Mama and Adolph had to leave, but I stayed with you. At the end, when you were yelling and flailing around, I was afraid you were going to hurt yourself, so I took hold of your arms.'

'Thank you,' he repeated. 'You're a good friend.'

She smiled and lowered her eyes. 'It's all right. Mama and Adolph would have stayed, but they had to do their work. My job... well, you know. It's mostly at night. I asked before if you're all right. Do you know yet?'

He took stock of himself. As best he could judge, his memories and character remained as they'd always been. Jarla wasn't reacting to him as if his body had altered in some freakish fashion. Perhaps he'd suffered a frightening dream and nothing more.

Or perhaps not. He felt a strange feverish restlessness and had a throbbing tender spot in the middle of his forehead. He told himself that anyone newly awakened from a delirium would feel unwell, and that he'd likely smacked himself in the face while thrashing about.

'I'll live,' he said, swinging his legs off the cot and sitting up, noticing in the process that someone, most likely Jarla, had removed his shoes. 'I have to say, no thanks to anyone but you, and even you weren't truthful about what was going to happen to me.'

She flinched. 'I didn't know. No one else has ever had such a strong reaction. Mama says it's because you have an extraordinary aptitude for magic.'

'Really?' He hesitated. 'In that case, I'm sorry. I shouldn't have spoken harshly to the person who took care of me.'

In point of fact, he actually did feel a twinge of guilt, and had to remind himself she was a Chaos worshipper who'd turn on him instantly if she learned his true purpose. It would be idiotic to regard her as anything but a threat.

Or a resource.

Because it was plain that she liked him. He didn't know why, except that over the course of their conversations, he'd always tried to appear friendly and never to show disdain for her profession. Perhaps, melancholy, lonely, and dubious of her own worth as she seemed to be, that was all it took to win her affection.

'It's all right,' she said. 'I can understand you being angry. To tell you the truth, I was upset, too. I was afraid the Changer would mark you right away, you'd have to go into the forest with Leopold and his company, and then I wouldn't see you any more. Not until I change.' She sighed. 'If I ever do.'

Dieter peered at her. 'Let me get this straight. You want to transform?'

'Yes. We all do. It's a blessing from the god.'

'Then why do you and the others keep the icon set back from the area where you work your rituals? Why not bring it close and bask in its power as much as you can? I imagine you'd change pretty quickly.'

'Mama says that would be impious. Like trying to force the god's hand. We need to worship as we've been taught.

She says there's a practical side to it, too. Every servant of the Master of Fortune can't acquire his mark and flee to the woods, not all of us at once. He needs human beings here in the city, to smuggle supplies and new recruits to Leopold, and to discover the army's plans and pass those along. I help with that part. Sometimes the soldiers talk when they… spend time with me.'

'Well, maybe it's because I lack understanding, but I'm glad the god hasn't got around to changing you yet. If he had, I never would have met you, and besides that, I like your face the way it is.'

Jarla blushed. Dieter wondered how best to follow up on his flattery, and then the door groaned open. Mama Solveig doddered through, looked at her two acolytes sitting opposite one another, and smiled.

'Dieter,' she said, 'awake at last.'

'Yes.' He pondered how to speak to her and decided that at least a little resentment was in order. Any other reaction might seem unnatural and accordingly suspicious. 'I appreciate Jarla staying with me, but you're the healer. Why weren't you trying to help me?'

'Because you weren't sick,' Mama said, hobbling closer. 'The Changer's touch is a blessing, not an illness. What did you dream?'

He hesitated. 'A world where everything kept changing. Armies of daemons.'

'And it was all wonderful and beautiful, wasn't it?'

'Well… yes.' In a bizarre way, it had been. He'd just been too frightened to realise until now.

'Yet there you sit complaining, just because you had to go to sleep to see it. Don't you realise you're being foolish?'

'Maybe, but I never had a seizure before.'

'And in your place, I'm sure I'd be concerned, too. But I doubt you'll have any more. As I said, it's not that you've fallen sick. You've become one of the elect, and since that was what you wanted, I hope you can forgive me for giving it to you.'

He sighed. 'Well, I suppose. Why not, considering that I came out of it all right.' The tender spot on his forehead gave him a twinge.

Mama Solveig smiled. 'I'm so glad. I'd hate to think we were mistaken about you, and you'd end up regretting it if I did. Do you feel well enough to talk a while longer, or would you like to rest?'

'We can talk.'

'Good.' The old woman turned to Jarla. 'Why don't you go down by the barracks, dear? Earn some money and see what you can learn.'

Jarla pouted as if she found the suggestion uncongenial. But she merely said, 'Yes, Mama,' and took her leave.

'She's a sweet girl,' Mama said as Jarla pulled the door shut behind her, 'but Adolph could make a nasty enemy.'

Dieter hesitated. 'I don't want enemies. I want to fit in and serve the cause.'

'Of course you do, and that's one of the nice things about joining the coven. Perhaps the rest of the world is against you, but you have a family now, brothers and sisters who look after their own. For instance, Jarla told me you've been slaving away for pennies catching vermin, and sleeping in a hostel for beggars and tramps. We can do better than that. For the time being, you can live here and be my helper in the healing trade.'

So she could keep an eye on him and try to make sure he was a genuine convert? Maybe, but conversely, it ought to facilitate the process of spying on her. 'I'd like that. Thank you.'

'You're very welcome. It will be nice to have company in this gloomy old hole. But I'm sure you understand, a family doesn't work if people only take. They need to give back, also.'

'I can see that.'

'I knew you would. So the coven has to consider what
each new recruit can contribute, to his newfound kindred
and the cause we serve, and in your case, the answer is
plain: your magic.'

His forehead throbbed. 'What about it?'

Mama hesitated as though calculating precisely how
much she wanted to share with a new recruit. 'When we
talked before, I mentioned that the Red Crown supports
those who seek to topple the Empire by force of arms.'

'Specifically, someone named Leopold and his comrades
in the forest.'

She stared at him. 'And how do you know that?'

'Jarla mentioned them.'

The old woman sighed. 'She's a good girl, but too chatty.
Apparently I need to remind her that it's for me to decide
what you learn and when. But since she's already blathered
about it: yes, Leopold Mann leads a band of warriors who
all bear the mark of the god. Today, they operate as bandits, but they aspire to become a genuine rebel army. The
Red Crown sends them new recruits and supplies, and
warns them of efforts to locate and destroy them. My hope
is that your skills can help.'

'Well, perhaps.' Perhaps, for the time being, he'd have to
aid the Red Crown in small ways in order to obtain the
information that would ultimately bring them down.

'But even that isn't the main thing,' Mama Solveig said.
'You've seen the sanctuary where we perform our rituals.'
Dieter thought of the grotesque appearance of the icon,
the cold, hard feel of it against his lips, the pulses of psychic force that hammered from it, and his stomach
churned. 'Maybe you noticed a scarcity of books and documents.'

'Now that you mention it.'

'I told you about the great treasure trove of knowledge
our leader possesses. He's entrusted us with a few frag-
mentary texts from that library, and requires us to puzzle

over them until they give up their secrets and so enhance our sorcery. He will then lend us another chapter from a grimoire or something comparable, and the process will start anew.'

Dieter shook his head. 'I don't understand. If the goal is to make you – us – powerful, so we can serve our god as ably as possible, then why not give us all the materials we need to advance quickly? Why not come and instruct us?'

Mama Solveig smiled. 'Many reasons, or so I've been told. The Master of Change can't teach you himself because no one but coven leaders ever sees him. It's a part of the secrecy that keeps us all safe. Besides, learning this way is a sort of test. By passing it, we prove our fitness to enter the deeper mysteries.'

'It still doesn't strike me as an efficient way to approach the task of overthrowing the Empire and changing the fundamental nature of the world.'

'To be honest, I've thought the same. But we have to recognise that the god's designs are both vaster and subtler than mortal minds can comprehend. From time to time, his will, as conveyed by the Master of Change, may impress you as perverse and self-defeating. At such moments, you must simply cling to your faith.'

'All right. If you tell me so, then I accept it. Anyway, we were talking about how I can make myself useful.'

'And isn't it clear? Your father has already trained you in an occult tradition. Your spells were strong enough to destroy a creature of Chaos. You're a powerful, knowledge-able warlock, and I suspect that when you study the texts in our possession, you'll discover things none of us have grasped. So I want you to devote much of your time to doing precisely that, and to teaching the rest of us what you learn.'

He felt a surge of elation, of eagerness, as if he'd found the proper outlet for the restless energy seething inside him. Every wizard lived to learn new spells and secrets, and he was no exception. He'd retired to Halmbrandt for that very purpose, purely for the satisfaction it promised, with no particular intent of ever putting the results of his research to practical use. And here was Mama Solveig offering him the opportunity to pore over lore he could have acquired nowhere else. It was marve–

He realised what he was thinking and felt a jolt of dismay, because the situation wasn't marvellous, it was dangerous. It was only by limiting himself to a single discipline, to the energies derived from only one of the eight winds, that a magician held the Chaos implicit in all sorcery in check. To do otherwise was to court corruption. Had a youthful Dieter dared to dabble in alchemy, he might well have degenerated into the murderous bandit of his nightmare.

Whereas, if the apprentice had immersed himself in Dark Magic, a few years might have sufficed to strip him of his humanity entirely. Manageable if not benign in isolation, the eight lores formed poison when mixed together. Dark lore was virulent in and of itself because it immediately and automatically opened a practitioner to Chaos. It could pollute a wizard as quickly and profoundly as Mama Solveig's icon.

Trapped among the cultists until he completed his task, Dieter had no hope of avoiding all exposure to their arcane secrets. But it was essential that he limit it.

'I'm sorry to disappoint you,' he said, 'but I doubt I can harvest anything from the texts that you haven't already discovered for yourselves. I'm just not as powerful or learned as you think I am.'

Her eyes narrowed in their nests of wrinkles. 'You killed the fiery serpent.'

'I was lucky. Besides, as Adolph said, he and I did it together.'

'Hm. Well, in any case, someone schooled you in magic.'

'My father knew some spells by rote, and taught them to

me that same way. I have no idea what makes them work, and I couldn't create a new one if my life depended on it.'

The old woman sighed. 'What a pity. I had such high hopes of you, and now you almost seem to be trying to make me think you'll be of no use at all. You really wouldn't want me to think that.'

'No, and it isn't what I meant. I certainly have something to contribute.'

'Of course you do, dear. I never doubted it. Now come take your first look at the parchments.'

He felt another irrational thrill of anticipation, and fought to quash it. 'What? I explained–'

'That the rest of us shouldn't expect anything special from you. I understand. But naturally, you'll still study the lore like the rest of us.'

'Naturally.' He couldn't think of any way to refuse. It occurred to him that he should have claimed to be illiterate, but it was too late now. Anyone in his position would have mentioned it sooner had it actually been the case.

Perhaps he could unfocus his eyes and rest them on the documents without actually reading. That might protect him from the venom they contained.

It would be dark at the centre of the cavernous cellar, the shafts of dusty golden light falling through the windows notwithstanding. Mama lit the oil lamp while Dieter found his shoes. The midwife then led him deeper into her domain, and, sketching her arcane sigil on the stale air, revealed the coven's hidden shrine. Pouncing into visibility, the icon of Tzeentch seemed to shift ever so slightly atop its plinth at the far end of the space.

Dieter braced himself to withstand the poisonous atmosphere of the shrine. It made his head throb and his belly squirm, but it wasn't as noxious as it had been the first time. Perhaps a person actually could get used to it. Or maybe his initiation had granted him a measure of resistance.

Mama Solveig set the oil lamp atop the lectern. 'You're still a young man with young eyes. This should be enough light for you to read by. Later on, you won't even need this much. Once you become familiar with the papers – or perhaps I should say, once they come to know you – the words and drawings will shine with their own inner light.'

Trembling, Dieter took his place behind the wooden stand. He felt frightened but exhilarated too, as he had the first time a woman granted him her favours.

Which was crazy. The two situations were nothing alike. He made his vision blur, resolved again to read not a single letter, and lowered his gaze.

Despite his unfocused eyes, meaning surged up at him like a striking snake, and the opening words of an invocation to Tzeentch impressed themselves on his comprehension. He couldn't imagine how, for many of them were unfamiliar, derived, perhaps, from the same unknown language Mama Solveig had spoken at the conclusion of last night's ritual. Yet something of their import conveyed itself nonetheless.

He told himself to wrench his gaze away, even if it compromised his mission. But he couldn't. The writing exerted a fascination stronger than his fear.

Here, contained in a single line, was a crushing rebuttal to the sane, common-sense notion that a thing either existed or did not. A little further along, the author used a term referring to the brittle, flimsy composition of all the mortal world, a word somehow redolent of loathing and contempt even if the reader had never encountered it before.

The word infected Dieter with the sentiments it connoted. He yearned to destroy something.

Then air gusted, and the wavering flame of the oil lamp blew out, plunging him into darkness.

Fortunately, the ink on the parchments didn't glow for Dieter, not yet, and, no longer able to make out the blasphemous words or much of anything else, he finally managed to jerk his gaze away.

When he did, he sensed that Mama Solveig was no longer standing at his side. Nor could any trace be seen of the light falling through the windows set at intervals along the tops of the walls. The murk was all but absolute.

He groped for the oil lamp, took it in his hand, and murmured an incantation. The ceramic body of the vessel began to glow with its own phosphorescence, shedding illumination without the necessity of fuel or flame.

With the light came the urge to return to his reading. Straining against the impulse, making sure he didn't so much as glance at the papers atop the lectern, he raised the lamp and peered about.

He still couldn't see any sign of Mama Solveig, her infirmary or living area, the windows or the walls. The cellar appeared larger than before, too large for his light to reveal all of it.

'Mama Solveig?' he called. His voice echoed. No one answered.

It occurred to him that perhaps he hadn't truly awakened after all. It was possible he was still delirious. Still trapped in the heart of Chaos.

But no. He didn't believe it, refused to believe he might still be incapable of distinguishing between hallucination and reality. This was actually happening, and that meant he'd fallen victim to an enchantment, conceivably an effect he himself had unwittingly evoked from the forbidden text.

The simplest way to cope with the magic and the disorientation it produced might be simply to walk in a straight line. With luck, he'd move out of the illusion that made the cellar seem limitless, and the bounds of the space would come back into view. At worst, he'd bump into a wall, and then could feel his way along it until he found the door.

He took three steps, then froze when he belatedly perceived that he was walking directly towards the icon. Did the sculpture's draconic snarl pull ever so slightly into something more closely resembling a leer?

No, damn it, of course it hadn't. He turned his back on the image and headed in the opposite direction.

Deviating from his course only to avoid one broken, abandoned article or another, he passed a succession of brick columns. Too many. Finally he glanced backwards. The lectern, pentacle and racks of magical implements were all but lost in the gloom. Another pace or two and he wouldn't be able to distinguish them at all any more, and without that point of reference, he'd be completely lost.

No, he wouldn't. Not in a space that surely remained finite however it currently appeared, and not when he had divination to guide him if need be. So why did panic keep welling up inside him?

He decided to seek guidance without further delay, and never mind that it seemed ridiculous to resort to sorcery simply to find his way to the edge of an enclosed space. The magic wasn't likely to speak as clearly here as it would if it could write its message across the sky, but a breeze should kick up to nudge him along in the proper direction.

He cleared his throat, then declaimed words of power. Spiders skittered madly in their webs, and his ears ached as though he'd dived deep underwater.

On the final syllable of the incantation, the air moved, but not as he'd anticipated. It gusted in one direction, then another, then whirled and howled around him, catching his clothing and making it rustle and flap, until it abruptly stopped moving altogether.

Dieter ran his fingers through his sweaty, tousled hair. The divination hadn't pointed the way to the door. In fact, it had seemed to be saying it was impossible to walk out of the enchantment. If so, then maybe he had reason to be frightened after all.

At the periphery of his vision, shadows stirred. He jerked around, but by that time, everything was still again.

'Mama?' he shouted.

Only the dwindling echoes of his own voice replied.

Uncertain if he'd truly seen anything at all, keeping watch from the corner of his eye, he moved, and after a time glimpsed motion. His stalker was slinking from the cover of one support column to the next while gradually creeping closer. It was interesting to observe that once again, the elderly midwife was moving without any hint of unsteadiness or frailty.

Whether she tottered about or prowled like a hunting cat, the knowledge of her proximity had a calming effect on Dieter, because now he at least felt reasonably certain he understood what was happening. The cultist was using her own magic to play tricks on him, and once he got his hands on her, it would likely be easy enough to persuade her to end the game.

So he waited until she was quite near, then wheeled and ran at the column she was hiding behind. 'Got you!'

A creature, possessed of a somewhat manlike shape but utterly inhuman nonetheless, sprang out from behind the support to meet him. It was gaunt and male, with dark hide and a head like a spider's, and, now that it was near enough, gave off a sharp acidic smell. The light of his lamp glinted on the countless bulging, faceted eyes peering not just from its head but its torso as well, its wet, gnashing mandibles, and the blade of its upraised battle-axe. It gave a hideous rasping cry and swung its weapon at Dieter's face.

Somehow he managed to arrest his forward momentum and fling himself back. The axe whizzed by a finger-length in front of his nose, and at the same instant, he lost his balance. When he fell, the ceramic lamp shattered against the floor, spattering his hand with oil.

The spider-thing loomed over him and lifted its axe for a second stroke. He forced himself to remain still – if he moved early, the creature would only compensate – and then, when the weapon hurtled down, rolled to the side. The axe sheared into the floor.

If the gods were kind, it would stick there, too, at least for a heartbeat, but the creature immediately heaved it free and raised it to threaten Dieter anew. With the thing right on top of him and attacking so relentlessly, he couldn't stop dodging long enough to cast a spell.

Nor was it likely he'd evade the axe much longer. So, in desperation, he kicked with both feet at the spider-thing's spindly leg.

Bone cracked. The spider-thing staggered, then vanished as suddenly and completely as a bursting soap bubble.

Panting, Dieter rose and lifted his light. With only a broken piece of lamp left in his oily hand, the enchanted implement shined less brightly than before.

Still, it sufficed to reveal the shadowy forms of other spider-things, all stalking in his direction.

Could the creatures actually hurt him? It seemed likely. The one he'd kicked had felt solid to the touch, and its axe had split the floor.

Yet he was fairly certain they were, if not wholly illusory, at least artificial. For if they were real, they were plainly creatures of Chaos, and it was all but inconceivable that Mama Solveig was powerful enough to summon so many so quickly, or that any other warlock could and would dispatch so many to invade her home.

In other words, as he'd suspected previously, all the alarming things that were happening were manifestations of one elaborate phantasmagoric trick, and, since he'd failed to escape the enchantment by other means, it was time to try to tear it apart. He would have had a better chance under the open sky, or if he felt more himself, but it was pointless to dwell on that.

He took a deep breath, declaimed the opening syllables of a counter spell, and slashed his hands through mystic passes. The spider-things charged.

Points of light, arrayed in patterns like constellations, appeared in the air and revolved around him. Outside the building, thunder boomed as if the heavens were cheering him on.

The creatures vanished, the dissolution wiping them away from the tops of their heads down to their feet. It was as if they were sand paintings spilled and obliterated by a witless attempt to stand them upright.

The cellar seemed to draw in on itself like a fist half-clenching as the walls sprang back into view. Dieter squinted against the reappearance of the light from the windows. After his time in the dark, the diffuse, filtered glow seemed bright.

Hands clapped softly. He pivoted and saw Mama Solveig standing a few paces away. 'Well done,' she said. 'Although it's a pity about the lamp.'

He felt a savage urge to attack her, but managed to resist it. Perhaps, even knowing what he knew, it helped that she was such a persuasive counterfeit of a kindly, feeble old granny. 'I hoped you enjoyed your prank,' he gritted. 'That first spider-thing nearly chopped me to pieces.'

She looked shocked at the suggestion. 'Oh, no, dear, it only seemed that way. I would never have let you come to harm.'

'So you say, but can I believe you? You also said, or at least implied, that your magic isn't especially powerful.'

'It isn't. I'm strongest here at home, where I practise my devotions and my link to Chaos never fails. Where I've laid charms to aid my conjuring and help me escape if the witch hunters ever call for me. Yet even so, when you made up your mind to try, you had no difficulty breaking free of my glamour.'

'Why did you catch me in it in the first place?'

She smiled. 'To test you. To see if your abilities were as modest as you claim. Plainly, they're not, so why did you lie?'

He groped for an acceptable answer and decided something close to the truth might serve. He hoped so, because it was the only thing that came to mind. 'I want to learn as much as I can, for its own sake and to bring the Empire down. I do. It's just that things are happening too fast. After I kissed the icon, my visions were… troubling. I'm still trying to decide what they mean and how to feel about them, and already you want me to immerse myself in dark lore and contend with that as well? I'm not sure I can bear up under the pressure.'

'Don't be a silly goose. Of course you can. Have faith that the Changer brought you here for a reason.'

'I want to believe–'

'Then do. I understand what you're going through. Every new convert has misgivings. All your life, everyone has told you Chaos and evil are the same thing. Then, when you first catch a glimpse of it, it is disturbing, because it's so different and so much bigger than this sickly, drab little world we inhabit.

'But as you persevere in the faith,' she continued, 'you'll come to see how glorious it is. That it's the only ideal worthy of your adoration. But even if it were otherwise, you've already pledged yourself to the god, and he's accepted your troth. It's too late for second thoughts.'

'In other words, stop shirking and study the damn papers.'

'"Shirking" is too severe a judgement, but yes.'

All right, he thought. If she insisted, she could closet him with the documents for hours on end. That didn't mean he had to read them. Now that he knew what he was up against, his will was strong enough to resist the temptation.

Wasn't it?

His forehead gave him a pang, and, in the gloom in the middle of the cellar, something clicked. It was probably a rat's claw tapping on a hard surface. Surely not a carved stone monstrosity changing position.

* * *

JARLA'S HOME, IF one cared to dignify it with that term, was a single cramped box of a room adjacent to the street and handy to the barracks and the marketplace, a place she could bring men willing to pay extra for privacy. Adolph hesitated before pounding on the door. Because the bitch might be with such a customer even now, and if so, he'd rather not know it, even though he understood her whoring aided the cult.

Even though, in a strange, angry, hurtful sort of way, it sometimes excited him to imagine it.

He rapped on the cheap pine panel. For several heartbeats, no one answered. Then Jarla called, 'Yes?'

He scowled. She generally hesitated before answering a knock or doing a good many other things, for that matter. It was one of many annoying habits she had yet to abandon no matter how often he corrected her.

'It's me,' he said. 'Let me in.'

The door was warped, and bent slightly in its frame as she tried to pull it open. After a moment, it jerked loose, and Jarla peered out at him.

She was fully clothed, and, looking over her shoulder, he saw that the room had no other occupants. He wondered what she'd been doing shut away by herself, then noticed the brass pendant she was wearing around her neck. It was a representation of Tzeentch in his draconic guise, but simplified and stylised into an essentially abstract figure. The average person wouldn't recognise it for what it was.

But many a witch hunter would. Adolph hastily entered the room and shoved the door shut behind him to hide the damning display from public view.

'You've been practising your cantrips again,' he said. It was the only reason she'd dare to wear the pendant anywhere but inside Mama's hidden sanctuary.

'Well, yes,' Jarla said.

'I thought you'd given up on ever mastering them.' It had seemed only sensible that she should. As the coven's experimentation had revealed, she possessed a spark of mystical ability, but it seemed too feeble to accomplish anything useful.

'I had. But if the Purple Hand are going to try to kill us, I need some way of defending myself.'

It made a certain amount of sense, but he could tell she was keeping something back. 'Is that all there is to it?'

She hesitated. 'Mama Solveig said that, since Dieter already knows some magic, maybe he'll discover things in the papers that we've missed.'

Adolph sneered. 'I doubt it.'

'Maybe, with his help, I really can learn. Maybe he can teach us all.'

He slapped her, and the crack resounded in the enclosed space. Eyes wide, pressing her hand to her cheek, she shrank back against her rumpled bed.

'Do you think,' he demanded, 'he can do better than me?'

'No! It's just… you figured out a lot, but not everything. Mama and the others teased out some of the secrets before you did. So that just shows, a fresh set of eyes could be useful, especially if Dieter already knows things the rest of us don't.'

Adolph grunted.

In point of fact, he felt torn. He was avid to acquire more learning, more power, and Jarla, for once, was right: Dieter might be the proper guide to lead them all deeper into the mysteries.

Yet it galled him to see a newcomer so favoured and respected. Not long ago, Adolph had been a mere journeyman scribe recording the minutiae of other men's lives. The Cult of the Red Crown had raised him from insignificance as he'd discovered talents for both sorcery and the crimes that aided Leopold Mann. Mama Solveig might be the high priestess of the coven, but her followers had come to regard him as her unofficial lieutenant and heir apparent. He had no intention of relinquishing that status and the good things that came with it.

Good things that included Jarla. She was just a stupid slut, to be discarded as soon as something better came along, but until then, she belonged to him, and he wouldn't let anyone steal her.

He decided he needed to walk a middle course. He'd learn whatever Dieter had to teach, but at the same time, defend his position and prerogatives.

He could start by reminding Jarla whose property she was. 'Take off your clothes,' he said, 'and fetch me the rope.'

DIETER POKED THE corner of his toast into the round yellow yolk, puncturing it. Mama Solveig had prepared his eggs just the way he liked them.

He took a bite, chewed, the morsel crunching, and closed his eyes in pleasure.

'Is it all right?' the old woman asked.

He swallowed. 'Better than all right.' Indeed, the meals Mama Solveig prepared were tastier and more plentiful than any he'd enjoyed since the day Otto Krieger over-turned his life, just as her cellar, squalid though it was, was luxurious compared to a doss house or sleeping outdoors. He still felt restless and irritable, still worried about the twinges in his forehead, but for the moment at least, his new living arrangements, together with his liberation from the noxious toil of rat catching, had brightened his mood.

It almost seemed conceivable that he might survive this lunatic errand after all.

'Should I make more?' Mama Solveig asked.

'No, thank you. You already made more than I can fin-ish.'

Her greasy tin plate and utensils in hand, the healer rose from the rickety, ring-scarred table, a cast-off, by the looks of it, from some tavern or other. 'Then I'll start clearing and washing up.'

'Leave that for me.'

'I most certainly will not. It's women's work, and besides, I like taking care of people. It's why I became a healer.'

And a Chaos worshipper, he wondered, forcing me to wallow in filth and helping mutants waylay innocent travellers? With the thought came a sudden pang of loathing that burst his appreciation of petty comforts and doting care like a soap bubble, and he had to struggle to keep his face from contorting into a scowl.

The mad thing was that he suspected, had he asked out loud how she reconciled her dedication to the healing arts with her service to Chaos, she would have justified it somehow. As he'd observed before, the cultists weren't crazy, it was subtler than that, but their devotions twisted their thinking.

How long would it be before they twisted his? Or had the process begun already?

He finished his breakfast and washed it down with the last gulp of water from his cup. Then Mama Solveig took up her wicker basket of healing implements and led him back into the hidden sanctuary.

His heart thumped and his meal abruptly weighed like a stone in his stomach as they neared the icon. Mama Solveig patted him on the forearm. 'It's all right, dear. You don't have to go near it today. It's too soon, I think. Just stand back and watch.'

Reciting a prayer, she doddered right up to the coiled black sculpture, then opened her basket. She took out a bandage and rubbed it over the image as if to dust and polish it.

Next came a ceramic jar, evidently the repository for some poultice, ointment or medicinal powder. She rubbed her fingertip on the icon, stiffening when a jolt of its power evidently stabbed into the digit, then swished it around inside the container.

She proceeded in the same manner for a while, contaminating a goodly portion of her supplies. Meanwhile, the entire basket was presumably soaking up vileness simply by virtue of its nearness to the statue.

Finally she said, 'That should do it, and about time, too. We have a lot of calls to make, and these old legs can't walk as fast as they used to.' She recited a prayer of thanks as she bobbed her head and backed away.

When they emerged from the cellar, he blinked, and realised it was the first time he'd been outside in the daylight since Jarla had drugged him. The blue sky, breeze and mundane bustle of the streets seemed a bracing relief from dark, enclosed spaces, secrecy, and abominations. But it lasted only until he remembered the Watch, presumably keeping an eye out for a fugitive answering his description, Krieger's agents, spying to make sure he didn't run away, and the Purple Hand, quite possibly lurking about awaiting another chance to strike at their rivals. After that, he felt vulnerable and exposed.

Mama Solveig clung to his arm. Proximity to the taint in her dangling basket made his forehead itch. Her neighbours called out greetings as she passed, and she responded as if she were everyone's doting granny.

At length they reached their first stop, a brick boarding house as smoke- and soot-stained as the one in which she made her home. The old woman looked up the shadowy stairwell and sighed. 'This is the part that's a trial. All the climbing up and down.'

Maybe so, but they tramped all the way to the top floor, and she never called a halt to rest.

She tapped on a door, and a feeble voice called, 'Come in.' Mama Solveig led Dieter into a small room stinking of spoiled food and sweat, and crammed with cots and pallets. A young woman with a small, skinny frame and a distended belly lay on her side on one of the straw mattresses. All the other occupants had presumably gone to work.

'This is Dieter, my new helper,' Mama Solveig said. 'Dieter, this is Sophie.'

'Hello,' Sophie said in the same thin little voice.

'Help me down,' Mama said, and Dieter steadied her and supported her weight as she lowered herself to her knees. 'How are you getting along?' she asked.

'It still hurts,' Sophie said, 'and the baby kicks and squirms and makes it worse. Is he supposed to do it all day and all night? I can't sleep.'

'Poor dear,' Mama said. 'I'm sorry you're having such a hard time.'

Sophie shook her head, spilling a lock of wavy brown hair over her eye. 'I can stand the pain if I have to, but I can't lose this one, too. Is he going to be all right?'

'Let's see.' The midwife began an examination of sorts, first pressing Sophie's abdomen at various points. When she pulled up her patient's skirts, Dieter felt a pang of embarrassment, and wondered if he ought to turn away. But perhaps an assistant healer was expected to observe even the most intimate portions of the process. Sophie must think it appropriate, for she didn't object. Or maybe she was simply too desperate and exhausted for modesty to matter any longer.

Finally Mama Solveig said, 'Well.'

'Tell me,' Sophie pleaded.

'I think both you and the child will be all right.'

Tears welled up in Sophie's eyes, and she blinked to hold them back. 'Thank you!'

'Mind you, you must stay in bed, and you have to keep taking the powder and applying the balm. I brought more of both.' She folded back the lid of the basket and extracted two ceramic jars.

Dieter had understood the point of contaminating the medicines and believed himself ready for this moment. Now he discovered he wasn't. Sophie seemed little more than a child, and the baby in her womb was more helpless and innocent still. He yearned to grab Mama Solveig and fling her away from her victims.

But he couldn't. It would wreck his mission, and it was inconceivable that a relentless brute like Krieger would agree that the good so accomplished outweighed the opportunity lost.

'Thank you!' Sophie repeated. 'I'll drink some right now.' Trembling, she pulled the cork from one of the containers.

Mama Solveig smiled up at Dieter. 'She has a cup right here beside her bed, and I see a pitcher in the corner.'

He fetched the water. The moment felt both horrific and surreal, not unlike his vision of Chaos. He filled the pewter cup. Sophie took it in her dainty hand, spilled a dash of grey powder into it, mixed the contents with her fingertip, and raised it to her lips. Which, he supposed, made him a poisoner. His guts squirmed as if he'd swallowed a toxin himself.

Sophie, however, smiled. Apparently the medicine had eased her soreness, or calmed the agitated life writhing and thrusting about inside her.

As he and Mama Solveig hiked back down the shadowy, creaking stairs, Dieter struggled to hold his tongue. Even though they appeared to be alone, it wasn't safe to talk about the cult and its atrocities in public. Besides, he was afraid that if he said anything, the old woman might discern the depth of his disgust and dismay.

Yet he found he couldn't contain himself. Perhaps the constant gnawing restlessness was to blame.

'I don't understand,' he said.

She turned her head to smile at him. 'Understand what, dear?'

'If you transform a grown man, and he wants to stay alive afterwards, he may well sneak away and join Leopold Mann. But what's the point of altering Sophie or her child?'

'I know, Sophie seems like such a delicate little thing, but if she changes, she may be very different. Even if she's not, the raiders will put her to use in one way or another. As for the infant, it might grow up more quickly than an ordinary child. Some of them do. If not, well, who's to say Leopold and his band won't still be fighting a dozen years hence? We hope to have our victory by then, but we can't be sure. Anyway, altering folk is worthwhile for its own sake. You might even say it's a sacrament.'

'Even when it results in witch hunters throwing a new-born baby on a pyre?'

'Yes, but let's hope it doesn't come to that. You'd be surprised how often it doesn't. Parents are inclined to love their babies no matter what form they take. If the child shows signs of being different, they're often in no hurry to call a priest or witch hunter to carry it away and kill it any more than they'd rush to throw away their own lives. Instead, they ask a trusted healer if anything can be done to reverse the change. Sadly, I have to tell them no, but I do know a way for a sport to survive. Then they give the wee one into my keeping, or perhaps they even accompany it into the forest. Leopold has a few such folk in his band, mothers and fathers who couldn't bear to separate from their children.'

'I guess I see. Well, except for one thing: you betrayed the Purple Hand to the authorities for trying to taint the water supply and change people. Basically, the same thing you're doing yourself.'

'Yes. The Red Crown had to choose the greater good. It's always worthwhile to spread the blessing of the god, but it's vital to suppress the Purple Hand before their doomed strategy places all our goals out of reach.' She chuckled. 'Or before they manage to suppress us.'

'Right.' He held the door for Mama Solveig, then followed her stooped, hobbling form out into the sunlight.

THE PARCHMENTS USUALLY reposed atop the lectern because the cultists read aloud from them during their rituals and observances. But a worshipper seeking to unravel their mysteries in solitude was welcome to do so sitting down, and so Dieter carried both a candle and a rickety chair into the hidden shrine.

Out in the front of the cellar, Mama Solveig hummed while she crushed dried berries with her mortar and pestle.

Heart thumping, Dieter came close enough to pick up the documents with their smell of old dry paper, then froze, paralysed by a sudden acute perception of the filthy power seething inside them. Touching them now would be like thrusting his hand into a tangle of adders, or thrusting a needle into his own eye.

But he had to do it and do it quickly, before Mama Solveig noticed his reluctance. He made himself take them up, shuddered, and sat down. He tried to steel himself for the next and even more difficult phase of his ordeal.

He now knew it wouldn't be possible merely to pretend to study the papers while avoiding comprehension altogether. If he didn't demonstrate at least a minimal understanding, his fellow cultists would realise he'd shirked.

Thus his task was to absorb a certain number of superficialities while evading actual enlightenment. It should be possible, considering that the cultists claimed it was difficult to puzzle out the deeper meaning of the texts even if one studied assiduously.

He shuffled through the parchments. Some of the pages were vellum and some, linen. He noted a variety of inks, hands and scripts. As best he could judge, he was looking at a minimum of six different manuscripts written over the course of the last few centuries.

He decided to skim the document on the bottom. With luck, maybe it wouldn't stab revelation into his head like the one he'd examined the first time.

It didn't, at least not right away. It proved to be something of a metaphysical treatise, devoid of both the fervid exhortations and exotic words that figured in the other work.

Its vileness lay simply in its trenchant argument that Chaos was not merely omnipotent but omnipresent. Order was only an illusion, and thus, in the truest sense, the stable universe of mundane human perception neither existed nor ever could.

Despite himself, Dieter gradually grew intrigued by the elegance of the author's syllogisms even as he was repelled by their conclusions. But more than that, he was curious. As far as he could tell, the essay didn't contain even a hint as to how one might go about actually performing Dark Magic, and come to think of it, the text he'd read previously hadn't, either.

And thank the stars for that! It would protect him. Yet he knew the papers truly must contain such instruction, because Mama Solveig and Adolph had benefited from it, and he couldn't help wondering how such a thing could be. As any true scholar would, he felt a yen to solve the trick of the concealment. Was it possible it would be safe to do so if he stopped with that, and refrained from actually poring over the secret content?

He reread the treatise, more attentively this time, then took up the next document, in its essence a rambling, disjointed paean of praise to Tzeentch.

He read every text, then started over. His eyes smarted, and he tried to blink the discomfort away. The skin on his forehead crawled, and he rubbed it.

So gradually that at first he imagined his eyes were merely playing tricks on him, certain words, syllables and individual letters became more prominent, as if rising slightly from the page while the surrounding text sank into it. Enough, he thought. That's how it works. I understand now, and I should break away. But it seemed only natural to run his eyes over the emphasised characters and decipher the message they'd picked out.

It proved to be a set of instructions for evoking and reading portents, signs that would speak clearly whether a mage stood beneath the open sky or not, because the spell drew its strength not from the Blue Wind but rather a force abundant everywhere. The possibilities would have excited any astromancer, and Dieter was no exception. He murmured the words of power and stretched out his hand.

A clot of shadow writhed into being in his palm. It was cold and soft, and felt like squirming snow. For a heartbeat it resembled a living creature, a knot of coils not unlike Tzeentch's icon, and then it flowed into a firm and static form, arms extending in a circle from a central hub to make a wheel, and glyphs hanging at various points on the radii.

Which was to say, it resembled a horoscope, and though the symbols were unfamiliar to him, as he stared, he began to discern the significance of the pattern: Destruction. Betrayal. Degradation. Damnation.

Alarmed, he cried out and flailed his arm, and his creation vanished.

Something glowed at the bottom edge of his vision. He glanced down to behold the characters on the parchments shining with their own luminescence.

'You see?' asked a baritone voice. Dieter jerked his head around. The hooded priest from his vision stood next to Tzeentch. 'You can't get away from it. The only reasonable course is to wallow in it.'

Dieter screamed, recoiled, and somehow managed to overturn his chair. Crashing down on the floor knocked some of the panic out of him. As he scrambled to his knees, he still felt frightened, but he also drew breath and raised his hands to cast darts of light.

But he didn't need to. The priest had disappeared, and the ink on the parchments had stopped shining.

He drew a ragged breath, and told himself the priest hadn't really been there. His imagination had played a trick on him.

It might have been more reassuring if he'd ever hallucinated before. Or if he hadn't just been filling his head with the outlandish but strangely persuasive proposition that the distinction between reality and nightmare was fundamentally a false one.

It occurred to him that Mama Solveig must have heard his shout and the bang he'd made falling over in his chair. She must be hobbling over to see if he was all right. He turned in the direction of her shabby little infirmary.

She wasn't there. At some point, she'd gone out without him noticing, and that wasn't the most disquieting part. It was dark outside the windows. Several hours had slipped by while the parchments held him entranced.

It was more evidence of just how insidious their influence was. Not that he needed it, considering that he'd just performed a work of Dark Magic.

He had to extricate himself from this situation as soon as possible, which meant he needed to avail himself of opportunities like the one Mama Solveig had now provided. He rose, took up the candle, and proceeded to search the old woman's work and living spaces.

Making sure to leave everything as he found it, he opened drawers, boxes and chests, and rummaged through their meagre contents, looking for anything that hinted at the Master of Change's true identity or the location where he met with his lieutenants. Unfortunately, if such an item existed, Mama Solveig had hidden it well. In the end, unwise as it seemed to attempt any more magic so soon after performing the Chaotic spell, he cast a divination. To his relief, it didn't have any adverse consequences, but it didn't point to anything helpful, either.

He should have known, he thought glumly, that it wouldn't be that easy. Nothing else had been. He wondered what he ought to do next and felt a fierce, sudden craving to return to the parchments.

No! He'd already learned more than enough to satisfy the Red Crown for the time being. But then again, why not? The texts were inescapable in any case. He'd have to expose himself to their influence over and over for as long as he remained here. So why not learn as much as he could as quickly as possible? It was conceivable that he'd acquire some bit of knowledge or a spell that could solve all his problems.

He looked into the shrine, and Tzeentch leered back at him. The writing on the papers began to gleam. Then someone tapped softly on the door.

He scurried to the source of the noise and peered out the peephole. Jarla's pretty, painted face was on the other side. He threw open the door.

'I should be working,' she said, 'but I wanted to say hello.'

He grabbed her by the shoulders. 'I'm so glad to see you!' He realised his voice was too shrill, too agitated, and tried to bring it under control. 'Mama gave me a little money. Will you take supper with me?'

Jarla smiled. 'Yes, I'd love to.'

'Then come on.' He seized her hand, and, struggling not to stride along so quickly that he'd end up dragging her, conducted her up the stairs and along the street.

CHAPTER SIX

SINCE JARLA KNEW the eastern part of the city far better than he did, Dieter suggested she pick the restaurant. Promising that the food was better than anyone would guess, she took him to a ramshackle place lit by a paucity of candles. The gloom failed to conceal a general air of shabbiness and grime.

Still, at this moment, any setting free of the taint of Chaos seemed pleasant to Dieter, and he smiled at the waiter. 'My friend says venison stew is your speciality.'

The server, a fat man with coppery side-whiskers, a freckled face, and the stink of sweat wafting from his stained armpits, scowled. 'It is, but we don't have any. The hunters are scared to go into the woods and get it. Damn bandits!'

Jarla looked crestfallen.

'In that case,' Dieter said, 'bring us a couple of bratwursts and whatever usually comes with them.' The waiter grunted and tramped off to pass the order to the kitchen.

'I'm sorry,' Jarla said.

'It isn't your fault.' Dieter glanced around and decided their corner of the establishment was far enough removed from the other diners that no one was likely to overhear them if they whispered. 'Or maybe it is. The army might already have caught the raiders if not for you.'

'I really am sorry.'

He shook his head. 'Relax, will you? That was a joke, or a compliment if you like. I don't care about the stew. I like sausage, and I like the company.'

She smiled and lowered her eyes.

'Do you know,' he said, 'you're about the last person I would have expected to take part in this enterprise of ours. You're brave and resourceful, I found that out the night you tampered with my drink, but you also seem gentle. Sweet. How did you become involved?'

She sighed. 'Adolph.'

'I should have guessed.'

'Not that I regret it!'

'Well, no. Why would you?' Aside from the risks of arrest, torture, execution, mutation and eternal damnation.

'Things were hard when I was little. My father and brothers all… mistreated me. Other people knew, but no one helped me. When I finally got away from my family, I resolved to make a good life for myself, but somehow things just never worked out the way I hoped. The cause is my chance to finally be happy, or at least to help make a world where others like me will be.'

They stopped talking while the waiter fetched the bratwursts, blackened and still sizzling on the plates.

'I understand,' Dieter said when the fat man had gone away again. He sliced off a bite of sausage. 'Still, I'm surprised you'd join after hearing all your life that such efforts are unholy and depraved.'

She hesitated. 'You came to Altdorf knowing exactly what you wanted, so when the rest of us offered it to you, we did it in a straightforward sort of way. Some recruits don't realise what they're seeking, and to them, the faith reveals itself in stages. When I joined, I was told the group exists to help people and fix things that are wrong, but at first I didn't realise how ambitious and dangerous its plans really were. But now that I do, I'm proud to be a part of it all.'

Or else you just assume you're in too deep to get out, Dieter thought. 'Did Adolph know what the cult truly was when he brought you in?'

'No. I asked him once, and he got angry that I would even wonder. Because he wouldn't trick me.' Her voice lacked conviction.

'That's good. You certainly deserve a better man than any who'd betray your trust.'

She coloured. He could see it even beneath the layers of rouge. Perhaps because she didn't know how to answer, she took another bite of the spicy, chewy meat. Reminding himself it was better not to push too hard, Dieter did the same, and they ate in silence for a while.

But it wasn't long before anxiety and impatience compelled him to go to work on her again, although this time he took a different tack. 'So, is it really true you've never seen our leader, or is that just something you old hands tell to new recruits like me?'

She glanced about, likely making sure no one had wandered close enough to eavesdrop. 'It's true.'

'And you've never met a single member of one of the other covens, either?'

'No.'

'It would be funny if there weren't any others, and no Master of Change, either.' Actually, it wouldn't be, not for him, because even if he discovered it was so, his instincts told him Krieger would never believe it.

'You mean, if being part of something big is just a lie Mama tells to make us feel brave and important? I can't believe she'd do that. Anyway, the sacred pages have to come from somewhere.'

'I see your point. Does she meet the Master at a regular time every week or every month? Or does she tell you when a meeting's coming up?'

Jarla cocked her head. 'That's an odd question.'

He shrugged. 'I'm just curious about the way things work. Remember, this is all new to me.'

'I understand. When I joined, I felt the same. Anyway, I have no idea when she goes to see him.'

Then what good are you, Dieter thought? He imagined himself reaching across the table and slapping her face back and forth, leaving handprints in the cosmetics.

Then the spasm of anger subsided, and he felt sick at the urge that had momentarily possessed him. By the comet, what was happening inside his brain?

Three labourers, sweaty and dirty from their work, tramped in and sat at a nearby table. Jarla indicated them with a shift of her head, warning him it was no longer safe to discuss clandestine matters.

They drifted into talking about his imaginary village as it had supposedly been before disaster overtook it. He invented friends and a lass he'd fancied, all lost to him now, and felt a certain sneering superiority when his fraudulent reminiscences prompted her to pat his hand in sympathy. It was a spiteful, mean-spirited reaction, but he couldn't entirely suppress it.

In time they finished their meals, rose, and headed for the door. As they passed the labourers' table, the biggest of the three said, 'Hey, darling. When you finish with skinny there, come back. I'll feed you a sausage.' His companions laughed.

Dieter pivoted, snatched up a ceramic tankard from the table, and backhanded the largest labourer across the face with it. The mug shattered, spattering foam and pungent ale.

The big man lurched back in his chair and clapped his hands to his face. His friends started to rise, and Dieter brandished the remains of the tankard at them. The jagged edges, or perhaps something they saw in his glare or posture, froze them in place.

Jarla pulled on his forearm. 'Come on!' she said, and he allowed her to haul him outside. The cool evening air felt good on his flushed, sweaty face.

Now that his rage was subsiding, he was appalled at himself. He'd fought during his time with the army, but only with sorcery and only when necessary. He hadn't used his hand to strike a blow since he was a child, and he'd never in his life lashed out so viciously in response to such minimal provocation.

'Why did you do that?' Jarla asked.

He sucked in a deep, steadying breath. 'I didn't like the way that bastard spoke to you.'

She lowered her eyes. 'He spoke to me the way a man speaks to a whore. Which is all I am.'

'Not true. That's simply the mask you wear. In reality, you're a fighter risking her life to help the whole world. Nothing could be worthier than that.'

'Do you really think so?'

'Absolutely.' He took hold of her chin, lifted her head, and kissed her. She pressed and ground against him. He pulled her into the dark, narrow space between two buildings.

He remembered his resolve to take things slowly, and Mama Solveig's warning that Adolph could prove a dangerous enemy. He told himself he didn't need to manipulate and exploit a woman he had, despite himself, come to like, not to this extent, particularly if she knew as little as she claimed.

Meanwhile, he kept pawing at her.

* * *

His BEHAVIOUR STILL troubled him hours after he'd separated from Jarla and returned to the cellar. Yet at the same time, he felt a thrill whenever he remembered smashing the labourer across the face, or the frenzied coupling in the dark.

He prayed that a good night's rest would make him feel more in control, more like his old self. He rose and turned towards the grubby cot in the infirmary.

Mama Solveig said, 'I thought we might work on your magic for a while.'

Her statement kindled the now-familiar urge to plunge back into his study of the parchments no matter what the consequences. Struggling to quash the impulse, he said, 'I can't spend all my time reading in the dark, even if I have good eyes and the writing glows. I'll go blind.'

'That's all right. I didn't mean you should return to the papers, not this time. Instead, I'll teach you some of what I've already managed to learn.'

His mind seemed to lock up. He wondered if he couldn't think of a viable way to refuse because he didn't really want to. 'I thought…'

She smiled. 'That you were required to learn every trick without any help from anyone? That truly would be inefficient. I wanted you to familiarise yourself with the holy texts as soon as possible. I believe it prepares the mind for everything that follows. But now that you have, you might as well benefit from everyone else's discoveries.'

He felt a crazy impulse to laugh. Of course. Might as well, especially when he craved it anyway.

Can't get away. The only reasonable course is to wallow.

'That would be wonderful,' he said. 'During the battle with the spirit, Adolph stole Jarla's shadow and made it fight for him.'

Mama smiled and nodded. 'That is a good one. But you'll have to detach your own shadow. You wouldn't want to put a strain on this worn-out old heart of mine.'

They repaired to the hidden shrine and set to work under Tzeentch's watchful eye. As it turned out, Mama Solveig couldn't articulate the underlying principles, the whys and wherefores, of the spell with anything approaching the lucidity of Magister Lukas and Dieter's other instructors at the Celestial College. But she did an adequate job of imparting the proper words and gestures, and after a few repetitions, he felt Chaos beginning to rouse.

It dismayed him just how much he liked it. Working Celestial wizardry could be as bracing as a drink of frigid mountain spring water. In contrast, Dark Magic was like guzzling raw spirits. He felt a fierce, heedless elation welling up inside him, and tried his best to hold it in check.

Once Mama Solveig was satisfied with his timing and articulation, it was time to try the spell in earnest. He spoke the words of power, and the darkness around him seethed. Someone laughed. Perhaps it was the icon, the priest, or the stranger he seemed in danger of becoming. Maybe they were all the same thing.

He looked at his shadow, vague in the wavering candle-light, and sensed just how much it would hurt to rip it from its moorings. But it didn't matter. He was as eager to suffer the shock as he'd been to ravish Jarla.

He snagged his fingertips in the cold flatness of it, gathered in a handful as if he were wadding up a piece of cloth, and yanked. The shadow tore free, and he cried out and staggered at the jolt.

Afterwards, he gasped for breath and clutched at the lectern lest his legs give way. Yet despite the weakness, he felt wonderful. It was always exciting to master a spell, whatever the circumstances, and this time had seemed more exhilarating than ever before. He hadn't just channelled the attenuated power of the Blue Wind. Rather, he'd reached into the pure heart of magic.

No. No. That was a stupid, suicidal way to look at it, and he tried to shove the notion out of his head.

'Make it do something,' Mama Solveig said.

I should make it rip your head off, Dieter thought, but instead, he decided the shadow should walk back and forth, and, obedient to his unspoken will, it did.

'This is grand,' Mama Solveig said. 'I'm so proud of you! When Adolph taught me, it took me days to catch the trick of it. The others still haven't mastered it. Shall we try something else?'

His immediate impulse was to say yes, but then the cellar seemed to spin as vertigo overwhelmed him. He grabbed for the lectern again, but this time failed to seize hold of it. He fell to one knee, banging it painfully against the floor. His stomach churned, bile burned in his throat, and for a moment, he was sure he'd throw up.

He realised that casting the dark spell had made him sick, and he was glad. Now Mama Solveig wouldn't insist that he continue his studies immediately, and even more importantly, he had, for the moment, lost the self-destructive desire to do so. All he wanted was to lie down.

Mama Solveig patted him on the shoulder. 'Poor lamb,' she said. 'It happens this way sometimes, but the sickness will pass, and the next time you cast the spell, it won't bother you as much.'

DIETER WOKE CLENCHED, almost flinching, as though, even before his waking mind resumed his labours, he dreaded the new day on some deep instinctual level.

The cellar was still almost as dark as it had been when he closed his eyes, with only a hint of morning turning the windows into grey rectangles floating in blackness. He wondered what had roused him, then heard Mama Solveig moving about.

Most likely she'd got up to use the chamber pot. He pulled the covers up over his head in the forlorn hope it would stifle the sound, and then the bar securing the door groaned in its brackets. The panel creaked open and bumped shut.

If she was sneaking off without telling him, did that mean she was going to see the Master of Change? He'd imagined the coven of coven leaders meeting in the dead of night, but he supposed that actually, they could assemble at any time, including the hours immediately before dawn.

He threw off his blankets, sat up, and groped around on the floor for his shoes. It seemed to take forever to find them. He jammed them on his feet, then hurried out the door and up the steps.

Mist hung in the street, blurring and softening the square masses of the buildings. Despite the haze and the feeble predawn light, he could just make out Mama Solveig rounding a corner some yards ahead.

He stalked after her, wondering how close he ought to follow. He didn't want to lose her, but mustn't let her spot him, either.

Other early risers trudged past him, and he hoped he didn't look as much like a creeping malefactor as he felt. The clammy mist chilled him. His cloak would have warded off the cold, but in his haste he'd neglected to put it on.

Mama Solveig turned into what he knew to be a warren of twisting, branching alleyways. Even if she continued to hobble, it would be easy to lose her in that circumscribed but treacherous maze. He quickened his pace to make up some of the distance between them.

As though to hinder him, the mist thickened. The old woman was heading in the general direction of the river that had given birth to it, and the sun hadn't yet risen to start burning it off. All but forsaking caution, Dieter strode faster still.

Even so, another minute brought him to a point where the alley he was following crossed another, and no matter how he peered and listened, he simply couldn't determine which way Mama Solveig had gone.

He was reluctant to use magic to pick up her trail. His assault on the labourer, brutish copulation with Jarla, and helpless thirst for dark lore all combined to make him feel contaminated and vulnerable. He feared that, until he recovered some stability, even the tamed Chaos bound in Celestial wizardry might further pollute him, or that the magic might escape his control and twist into something ghastly. But unless he was prepared to abandon his current enterprise, it seemed he had no choice.

He glanced about, making sure no one was currently in eyeshot, then started whispering a spell. He was four words into it before he realised just how well founded his misgivings actually were. He wasn't performing Celestial wizardry but rather the divination from the forbidden texts.

Even then, it was hard to stop. The syllables seemed to articulate themselves like water gushing from a spring. But he clamped down on them and cut them off.

Now more concerned with reasserting his identity as a practitioner of Celestial magic than with acting surreptitiously, he declaimed the spell he'd originally meant to cast in a louder voice and with sweeping passes. When he finished, he looked up, and for one terrifying moment could discern no transformation in the sky. The few stars still visible despite the imminence of morning simply continued to fade as though spurning and forsaking him.

But finally one throbbed to point him in the right direction. He closed his eyes, and for a moment, his body felt slack and heavy with relief. Then he tramped onwards.

The stars led him to a narrow strip of earth too steep for anyone to bother building anything on it, even in teeming Altdorf. The descent ran down to the Reik with its warehouses, boatyards and jetties. The fog lay atop the water like a mass of cotton. He could only just barely make out the shapes of the boats and barges moored along the bank, or the arch of a nearby bridge, which appeared to float unconnected to either shore.

He peered about in perplexity, because it was difficult to see how Mama Solveig could have continued on from here. She would have needed to backtrack to make for the bridge, and it didn't seem likely she would have clambered down the hillside, which lacked stairs or even a path, to rendezvous with a boat and embark on the river. Had she entered one of the buildings rising close at hand? Hoping for further guidance, he looked up at the heavens. Something plopped onto his cheek.

Dead flies were falling from the empty air. Jagged red lines snaked across the world like cracks ruining a fresco.

The fleeting phenomena indicated someone was working magic. Dieter cast about for the potential threat, but the mist obscured it. A spiral of shadow swirled up around his body, then snapped tight to bind his limbs. Its embrace stung like a row of ant bites, even through his clothes.

It was the same spell Adolph had attempted to use to bind the fiery serpent. Dieter rattled off a spell of protection, and the coil of shadow frayed and vanished. He pivoted, seeking his adversary once more.

That brought him face to face with Mama Solveig, who was just climbing up the rise onto level ground. Perhaps she'd hidden behind a tree, or maybe it was simply the mist that had prevented him from spotting her hitherto. She clutched a lancet in an overhand grip. It wasn't much of a fighting knife, but quite capable of killing a man who couldn't move.

Her eyes widened, and she clapped her empty hand to her bosom. 'Dieter! Oh, my goodness!'

'Mama Solveig, are you all right?' It was all he could think of to say.

'I'm fine, but I could have killed you. What are you doing here?'

'I... I woke just as you were going out, and at first I thought, well, if you hadn't asked me to go with you, then I didn't need to. But then I thought of the Purple Hand lurking about, waiting for the chance to pick us off, and I had the feeling you were in danger. So I tried to catch up with you, but you were too far ahead, and I lost you in the mist. I finally used a charm to track you.'

Mama Solveig sighed. 'I sensed someone following me, assumed the worst, and hid. When you turned up, these short-sighted old eyes couldn't make out your face. The fog's too thick, and I had a bad angle peering up from below. So I sought to defend myself.'

He grinned. 'I'd say you were succeeding pretty well.'

She waved a tremulous hand in dismissal. 'That's a kind thing to say, but you didn't have any trouble breaking free of my enchantment. You know, dear, I don't think the Purple Hand have figured out who I am, and even if they have, I doubt they'll bother us this morning. The only person I felt coming after me was you.'

Was she saying she knew he was lying? 'Well, I hope you're right.'

'Dieter, I want you to listen to me very carefully. This life we live is holy and full of wonders, but it wears on the nerves. The secrecy, the danger, opening yourself to the god... it's all a strain, and from time to time, you may find yourself imagining things.'

'I can understand that.'

'But whatever you're thinking or feeling, you mustn't follow when I go off alone. Trust me to look after myself. Because if you follow me to the wrong place, I'll know it, and if I don't, others will. And then we'll kill you. It's just as simple as that.'

'All right. But I was only trying to help you.'

'I know, dear. I'm very grateful, and the fact of the matter is, you can.' She nodded towards the slope. 'See the mushrooms?'

He did now, though he hadn't noticed them before. The pale, spotted caps poked up through the grass. 'Yes.'

'They're what I came for. I use them in my medicines, and they're best if gathered just before sunrise. Come help me pick them.'

MAMA SOLVEIG TOTTERED about the cellar setting out cakes and cheese, just as if she were preparing for an ordinary party. Dieter attempted to help, and as usual, she shooed him away.

She did allow him to play doorman, and he admitted the coven members one by one. It was the first time he'd met any of them except for her, Jarla and Adolph, and it struck him just how ordinary the others appeared. The rage, misery, or fundamental perversity that had drawn each to the Changer of the Ways lay buried beneath a quotidian facade.

Of course, the obvious mutants all ran away to join Leopold Mann.

Someone else knocked. Dieter opened the peephole, and Jarla, her wistful face scrubbed clean of paint and her hair pulled back, peered in at him. His forehead gave him a pang, and, fumbling with the sliding bar, he admitted her.

She offered a tentative smile, and then, after a moment, squeezed his forearm. 'Should we talk?' she asked.

'Probably.' He waved her towards Mama Solveig's workspace. Since the others had congregated around the food and drink in the kitchen, the infirmary offered a modicum of privacy. She sat on the cot, and he took the stool.

'What happened in the alley,' she murmured. 'It was nice.'

'It was.'

'I didn't tell Adolph.'

He supposed that, considering her trade, it was ironic that she thought it mattered whether she had or hadn't. Yet he understood the difference between what she did for her own fulfilment and what she did for coin, and he suspected Adolph was sensitive to the same distinction. 'Do you intend to?'

'I don't know. We've been together for a while. He takes care of me.'

'From what I've seen, he bullies you.'

She shrugged as if the two things were the same. 'I'd never want to hurt him, and I need someone in my life.'

'Are you telling me what happened between us shouldn't happen again?'

'I don't know! I guess I'm asking, if I did decide to leave Adolph, would you want to be with me?'

He had no idea how to answer.

He was a wizard of the Celestial Order and she was a common streetwalker, and yet, he did like her. He just didn't know if the emotion ran deep and true, or merely sprang from the fact that, lonely and frightened, he overvalued any comfort that came his way. Or perhaps it was a symptom of the mental sickness he'd contracted from Dark Magic.

Not that it actually mattered what he felt or why. She was a cultist, his enemy and the enemy of everything healthy and sane, and if he hoped to go on breathing, all he could afford to care about was how best to deal with her to safeguard himself and further his mission.

But how was that, exactly? He could strengthen the bond that had sprung up between them, but was there a point if she had no way of helping him find the Master of Change? Was it worth antagonising Adolph?

He suddenly felt a spasm of impatience with his ambivalent, torturous calculations. He wanted the bitch, he might still find a way to exploit her to accomplish his purpose, so why not take her? He could handle Adolph. If need be, he could squash him like an insect.

He smiled at Jarla. 'Of course I want to be with you.'

'Then I have a choice to make.'

It wasn't the response he'd expected, and it irked him. It made him feel she was teasing and toying with him. He felt an urge to grab her, kiss her, master her, and then something seethed at the periphery of his vision.

He turned to see shadow squirming into being by the door. The clot of darkness sprouted hands which slid the bar aside, then withered into non-existence.

Adolph swaggered through the doorway. Mama Solveig gave him a look that mixed affection and exasperation in equal measure. 'Dear, we've talked about this before: don't cast spells for trivial reasons, don't do it out in the open, and particularly, don't do it outside my home.'

Adolph grinned. 'No one was looking.' Dieter assumed the idiot had chosen to make an impressive entrance to remind everyone who was accounted the ablest sorcerer and Mama's de facto lieutenant.

The scribe looked about. When his gaze fell on Jarla and Dieter sitting together, his mouth tightened, and he tramped in their direction. Jarla hastily rose and moved to greet him. Dieter didn't want the other man towering over him, so he stood up as well.

Adolph barely acknowledged Jarla. He gave Dieter a glower. 'So. I hear you'll try to teach us something tonight.'

'Yes,' Dieter replied. Mama Solveig had insisted on it.

'Something you found in the holy writings?'

'No.' The only new spell he'd discovered therein was the charm of divination, and he didn't dare share that one. Somebody could use it to discover his true identity and intentions. 'Something my father taught me.'

Adolph snorted. 'Hedge magic.'

'All magic derives from Chaos and is accordingly sacred in the eyes of the Changer of the Ways. But if you haven't absorbed even that basic truth, I suppose you can stay out here and drink cider.'

'Is that what you'd like me to do? Then I'm sorry to disappoint you. I never neglect a chance to worship, and I won't mind picking up your little cantrip. It's just that I'm disappointed. Mama told us to expect miracles of you.'

Dieter was still trying to decide how to respond to the sarcasm when Mama Solveig clapped her hands to attract everyone's attention. The drone of conversation died away.

'We're all nine of us here,' she said, 'so let's begin.' She opened a chest sitting atop a table. 'Come put on your regalia.'

Said regalia proved to be tabards sewn from irregular scraps of cloth, pink, puce and purple, primarily, garish as a jester's motley. Only Adolph's costume deviated from the common mould. He reached into the box, removed a black velvet cloak with a purple satin lining, shook it out, and swirled it around his shoulders. The costly garment was an extravagance for a fellow earning a journeyman's wages, but apparently he imagined it made him look like an adept.

When Mama Solveig revealed the shrine, the icon seemed to pounce out of the dark. The writing on the parchments started to glow.

Prayer followed, and then the sacrifice of two young goats. Adolph slit the throats of the bound, bleating kids and laid the bodies at the foot of Tzeentch's pedestal. Dieter felt a sudden elation and struggled to deny it, to clear his mind, to be himself, and not the newborn other who continually tainted his feelings and skewed his judgement.

'Now,' Mama Solveig said, 'Dieter will teach us a spell.'

He'd pondered exactly what to impart. It shouldn't be anything the Red Crown could use to hurt others, or anything overtly evocative of the powers of storm and sky. Adolph, Jarla and Mama Solveig had already seen him use such abilities, but even so, he preferred not to provide any more reason for people to suspect that he wasn't a humble wyrd but rather a Celestial wizard.

In the end, he'd decided on the simplest of spells, the charm to make a handheld object shine with its own inner

light. He started instructing Mama Solveig, Jarla, Adolph
and a boatman named Nevin as he'd once taught apprentices of his own order. The remaining cultists supposedly
lacked any trace of mystical aptitude, and so they simply
stood and watched.

To Dieter's surprise, despite their lack of any clear, com-
prehensive grounding in the theory of magic, his current
pupils seemed to catch on quickly. They'd plainly derived
some benefit from their study of the blasphemous texts,
and learning a basic charm with the help of a competent
teacher was considerably easier than uncovering, compre-
hending and mastering the complex hidden spells.

Finally the little pewter vial in Jarla's hand radiated sil-
very light. She stared at it in what seemed a combination of
delight and disbelief. 'I did it! I did it the first of anybody.'

Dieter smiled. 'Good for you.'

Adolph scowled and continued to scowl when the quill
in his own grasp and the objects in the hands of Mama
Solveig and Nevin began to shine white, yellow or blue.
Oblivious to his displeasure, the boatman and Jarla
grinned and congratulated one another. Dieter gathered
that their attempts to learn magic generally ended in frustration, but tonight each felt like a genuine magus.

When the lesson concluded, Mama Solveig beamed at
her flock. 'This is splendid. As I've told you, nine is a sacred
number, and the ideal number for a coven. Now that we've
completed our circle, it's plain that we'll do great things.
But it's time to finish up for tonight, lest those who wait
for you at home wonder where you tarried so late. Dieter,
will you read a benediction from the holy texts? Whatever
you choose will be fine.'

'I deliver the benedictions!' Adolph said.

'More often than not,' the old woman replied, 'because
my bleary old eyes have trouble making out the characters,
and you read well. But so does Dieter, and the god loves
change, so let's give him a turn.'

Actually, Dieter, or at least the still-sensible part of him, would have been happy to let Adolph do the reading. He didn't want to subject himself to the influence of the luminous words so soon after working sorcery, even of the most benign and trivial sort. But he couldn't think of a plausible excuse to refuse.

He chose a rambling screed on the ultimate invincibility and inevitable triumph of Chaos. So far, it had never fascinated him to the extent that some of the other passages had. If he steeled himself against its enticements and stopped after a few lines, maybe it wouldn't be able to chip away at him.

He began to read, and it was all right. The blasphemous words sought to entrance him, but by now he and the texts were like fencers who duelled one another every day. He'd learned their tricks, and the knowledge aided his defence.

He reached the final syllables with his head still clear, or as clear as it ever was any more. Then Adolph cried out, startling him. He faltered.

'Keep going!' Adolph snapped. He was all eagerness now. Dieter realised that something hidden in the screed had begun to reveal itself to him, and he was as avid as any magician on the verge of discovering a new enchantment.

Dieter looked to Mama Solveig. 'Yes,' she said, 'keep reading. We mustn't waste the opportunity.'

That left him no choice but to continue. It was now more difficult to hold himself aloof from the spiritual pollution implicit in the text, because he was just as curious as Adolph to discover what secret lurked encoded in the surface message. It would be even more poisonous, but what true wizard could turn away from it?

He reached the end of the document. Adolph told him to start over and he did.

The second time though, certain syllables started emphasising themselves. He didn't articulate them any louder, but they somehow resounded in the mind.

Stringing them together, knowing instinctively where the breaks ought to occur, he constructed words of power. Other cultists cried out or laughed crazily as they too glimpsed the hidden pattern.

'I've got it!' Adolph shouted. He snatched one of the staves and brandished it over his head, an action that spread his handsome cloak like a pair of wings. Evidently he meant to try the spell.

'Wait!' Dieter said. 'We aren't ready. We don't understand it yet.'

Adolph sneered. 'Maybe you don't, you and your stupid little lights. I'll show you some real magic.' He slashed the gleaming oak rod through a mystic pass and uttered the first word of command.

Dieter hoped Mama Solveig would intervene, but she didn't. She and the other cultists simply watched, plainly apprehensive but eager for a marvel as well, apparently trusting in Tzeentch to protect them. The icon's snarling grin seemed to stretch a little wider.

Adolph shouted the final word of the spell and thumped the butt of the staff on the floor for emphasis. Power whined in a crescendo that died abruptly.

For a moment it seemed that apart from the shrill noise, nothing had happened. Then a sort of oval-shaped distortion, seething and running with sickly colour, opened in empty air.

Hanno, the squat, grizzled cabinetmaker who fashioned the cult's wands and staves, stepped closer to peer at the writhing, floating abnormality. 'It's a marvel,' he said in a bullfrog voice, 'but I don't understand the use of it.'

Likewise rippling and oozing with colour, hands and forearms shot up out of the oval as if it had become a hole into another world, as, perhaps, it had. They grabbed Hanno and jerked him forwards. He screamed but fell silent when his head disappeared into the opening.

CHAPTER SEVEN

No one else made a move as the woodworker's kicking feet disappeared through the wound in the fabric of reality. It had all happened too quickly.

But then Dieter shook off his paralysis. He circled around the lectern to a point from which he could look straight into the opening. He thought he saw a human figure in the multicoloured churning, but it was small, as if he was seeing it from far away. It floundered as though drowning, and other shapes flitted around it like sharks closing in on an injured fish.

At least Hanno was still alive, for the moment, anyway. Dieter wanted to rescue him, but didn't know if he was up to the challenge. Had he understood the enchantment Adolph had cast, it might have been easier, but the imbecile had precluded that by acting so precipitously. Dieter drew a deep, steadying breath, preparing himself to cast a counter spell, and then hands seized him from behind. Arms wrapped around him and dragged him backwards.

He fought back, managing to grab the little finger of his attacker's left hand, bend it back, and snap it. That loosened the bear hug sufficiently for him to twist and see who was grappling him.

A second tear had opened in midair, and another Chaos creature had reached through, torso and limbs elongating to cover the distance to its intended victim. Its head was vaguely lupine, and its six eyes flashed like mirrors catching the sun. It snarled and struggled to squeeze Dieter into immobility.

Fortunately, it didn't seem to be any stronger than he was. Perhaps the pain of its broken finger even hindered it a little. He wrenched his right hand free and gouged one of its eyes with his thumb. That made it falter. He hammered its snout with the heel of his palm, then tore free of its embrace.

It reached for him again, but he sprang back beyond its reach. Evidently something constrained it from leaving the tear altogether; perhaps the opening would close behind it if it did. It snatched for him again, still falling short, and then he heard everyone else screaming.

He looked about. The scene was so frenzied it was difficult to take it all in, but more rips had split the air, and it looked to him as if a couple of other cultists had already been dragged into them. The rest struggled against their attackers, using punches, kicks, knives and blunt instruments for the most part, too panicked to think of attempting magic even if they were capable of it.

Mama Solveig was an exception. She conjured coils of shadow to bind one spirit, but a second burst from another hole, seized her by the hair, and yanked her towards it.

A cultist bolted for the door, but new holes opened in front of him to bar the way. New apparitions reached for him.

Hands grabbed Dieter's throat and dragged him upwards like a hangman's rope. Strangling, he peered up to see that, its orientation more horizontal than vertical, a rent had opened near the ceiling, and its inhabitant had reached down to seize him. So far, though, it couldn't quite muster the strength to lift him into its domain. One moment, he was entirely off the floor, but then the creature let him slip, and the toes of his flailing feet brushed and bumped it once again.

He pounded, scrabbled, and tore at the apparition's hands and arms until it lost its grip. He dropped, then staggered out from underneath it. Another creature lunged like a striking serpent, and he forced himself to scramble on beyond its reach before pausing to gasp for air.

He saw that he couldn't stay still for long. There were too many tears, and more ripping open every moment. At least half the cultists were gone, Mama Solveig included. Those who remained were threatened from every side.

A few paces away, Jarla and Adolph stood together. She flailed at their attackers with one of the ritual staves. He cast splinters of shadow from his fingertips. Then a gap opened right beside him, and a spirit surged out of it. He hastily stepped behind Jarla. The creature grabbed her by the shoulders and pulled her forwards.

Dieter rattled off an incantation and hurled darts of blue light into the apparition. It vanished. Jarla staggered a step, then caught her balance.

Dodging the hands that snatched for him, Dieter scrambled to her and Adolph. 'You conjured the enchantment,' he panted to the scribe. 'Do you have any notion at all how to dissolve or control it?'

Despite the dire circumstances, it took Adolph a moment to admit he didn't.

'Then the two of you keep the creatures off me,' Dieter said, 'while I see what I can do.'

He then visualised the sky, or projected a portion of his consciousness there. For mystical purposes, it was the same thing. The stars blazed, kindling flares of strength within his spirit, and the cold wind whispered secret counsel. When he felt focused, calm, yet full to bursting with power, he spoke the opening words of his incantation.

Meanwhile, Adolph and Jarla battled frantically.

Dieter reached the last syllable and swept his hands through a final flourish. For a moment, the apparitions flickered, and he grinned – prematurely. The entities reasserted their hold on reality and came back on the attack.

'It didn't work!' Adolph cried.

He was right. Though it was one of the most powerful counter spells the Lore of the Heavens had to offer, it hadn't broken this particular enchantment. Which meant only dark knowledge could save them now.

Dieter cast his thoughts over all the sickening, fascinating, half-comprehended information he'd gleaned from the blasphemous texts, hideous truths that, yielding to curiosity, he'd lapped up avidly and secrets that forced themselves on his consciousness despite his attempts to resist. His forehead throbbed in time with his pounding heart, and he shuddered as though he'd imbibed some stimulant drug.

Until he saw a possibility.

'Keep fighting!' he said, then attempted the counter spell once again but this time in altered form, weaving a skein of Dark Magic into the pure wizardry of the sky. If it worked, it would enable the spell to strike more accurately, to cleave to the very heart of the enchantment Adolph had wrought. It would quell a manifestation of Chaos, but even so, it was a perversion of the Celestial Order's teachings and felt like the vilest thing Dieter had ever done, worse even than poisoning Sophie and her unborn child.

And at the same time, he revelled in it, glorying in new magic, new power, as any sorcerer would.

He slashed his hands through the ultimate pass and shouted the final word. The cellar blazed white as though contained in a lightning bolt, and he had to close his eyes against the glare.

When, blinking, he opened them again, both the Chaos creatures and the gaps in the air were gone, and the latter had evidently disgorged their prisoners as they closed.

He felt a surge of joy at his victory, but the feeling died when he realised it had come too late to save everyone from genuine harm. Nevin and another man lay torn and motionless on the floor, and even folk who were still conscious bore bloody wounds and blisters too, as if they'd swum in acid. One sobbed, another ran his fingers through his hair over and over again, and in general, they looked as if their reason hung by a thread.

The floor tilted abruptly, and Dieter pitched forwards into blackness.

JARLA SQUEALED AND started towards the fallen Dieter. Adolph lifted his hand to grab her and hold her back, but then thought better of it. Under the circumstances, it might make a bad impression on the others.

Meanwhile, Mama Solveig, tough old hag that she was, ignored her own burns and the gash in her shoulder to scurry to Nevin, squat down, and examine him. After a moment, she shook her head, then moved on to Maik. He proved to be dead as well.

Adolph realised the situation had the potential to become even more unpleasant than it was already. He considered making a break for the exit, but didn't. The cult meant everything to him, and he wouldn't forsake it no matter what the risk.

Mama Solveig strode to the door and peered out the peephole. From the calm manner in which she turned away again, it seemed she hadn't observed anything alarming. The coven's struggle for survival, frenzied though it had been, hadn't made enough noise to attract the notice of neighbours or passers-by. Maybe she had a ward in place to muffle any commotion.

'How is Dieter?' she asked.

Kneeling beside the miserable whoreson in question, Jarla rolled him onto his back, then poised her hand in front of his mouth and nostrils. 'He's breathing. I think he just fainted. But you should look at him.'

'I will,' the healer said, 'but first I need to tend the folk who are actually wounded, and you need to help me. Fetch my basket.'

Adolph noticed that, though he was still essentially unharmed, Mama hadn't asked for his assistance. Perhaps it was because she was angry with him, or maybe she felt his proximity would agitate the people who'd been pulled into the holes.

In any event, he was left to stand and watch as she ministered to both the flesh and spirits of the injured. Along with catgut sutures, bandages and ointments, she dispensed soothing words, and perhaps she infused them with a subtle magic, because they seemed to exert more influence than Adolph might have expected. People stopped weeping, gasping and shaking. Their eyes no longer shifted wildly to and fro. Unfortunately, once they regained their composure, they glared and glowered at Adolph, and he felt another pang of uneasiness.

Finally, as Mama lowered herself to examine Dieter, Hanno snarled what everyone was evidently thinking: 'You stupid, arrogant bastard! You killed Nevin and Maik and nearly the rest of us too!' Others growled in agreement.

Adolph felt anger, alarm, and a pang of guilt as well, but the latter emotion only heightened the others. 'I did what we're all supposed to do! What we've vowed to the god to do: try our best to master whatever spells we uncover. And what an enchantment this one is! You could use it to destroy the Emperor and his entire court.'

'Perhaps so,' Mama Solveig said, pressing her fingertips against the side of Dieter's neck, 'but we're not obliged to work recklessly. We have a method for studying a new spell, a patient, careful way that lessens the risk. You know it. I taught it to you. But you forgot all about it tonight.'

Obviously, she was right. It had irked him to see them all so delighted with Dieter's paltry little trick of luminescence, and so he'd jumped on what had seemed an opportunity to remind them of his own abilities. 'Maybe I did act rashly, and obviously, I mourn the loss of our friends. But we all know that being one of the Red Crown is dangerous, and because I took a chance, we're weeks, maybe months, ahead of where we'd be if we'd tackled the spell in the usual plodding way.'

'Only because of Dieter,' Hanno said.

'Because of him and me!' Adolph snapped. 'Maybe, stuck inside your hole, you couldn't see, but we both used our magic to fight the enchantment. Tell them, Jarla!'

Refusing to meet his eyes, Jarla shrugged her shoulders and mumbled something inaudible.

Her betrayal outraged and astonished him. Was it because he'd used her for a shield? Hadn't she understood the necessity? He was a genuine sorcerer, she wasn't, and magic had been the only hope of extricating everyone, including her, from danger. So it had been vital that he protect himself at any cost.

Or maybe, fickle, ungrateful trollop that she was, it was her manifest letch for Dieter that kept her from speaking up in his defence.

Either way, she'd pay for it. They both would.

'Dieter and I, working together, saved you all,' he insisted. 'He couldn't have accomplished anything without me protecting him.'

'I don't see it that way,' Hanno said. He reached for the knife at his belt. Adolph lifted his hands to cast an attack spell.

'Stop!' Mama Solveig said. Hanno faltered with his blade half-drawn, so Adolph hesitated as well. 'I won't have you fighting with one another when the cause needs you both.'

'Didn't it need Nevin and Maik?' Hanno demanded.

'I suppose it did,' she replied, 'but killing Adolph won't bring them back. Better to let him atone for their deaths by serving with zeal and obedience from now on. That is what you intend to do, isn't it, dear?'

'Yes,' Adolph gritted. Apparently they weren't all going to try to tear him apart, and he supposed he should be grateful for that, but he still resented the old woman's attitude. He hadn't meant to hurt Nevin and Maik – and in fact, he hadn't, the spirits had – so what was the point of upbraiding him over an accident? Hell, with his magic, he was far more useful than the two of them had ever been.

'Good,' Mama Solveig said. 'You can start by lifting Dieter onto the cot.'

AT PRESENT, THE sky was an inverted rippling green ocean, and the three suns, luminous blurs shining in its depths. On the yellow plain underneath it rose a white marble palace capped with minarets, and on one of its terraces sat Dieter and the priest. Below them, a giant with the head of a cat lay staked spread-eagled on the ground while inhuman torturers vivisected it. It tried to scream but could only manage a sort of hiss. Perhaps its tormentors had begun by cutting its vocal cords.

The priest gestured towards the raw, bloody morsels on Dieter's plate, meat freshly extracted from the giant's body. 'Try the liver.'

A part of Dieter wanted to sample it, so why not do it, or indulge any other urge he happened to feel? He suspected this was only a dream, so what was the harm? Still, the portion of him that clung to a measure of caution, or that, perhaps, simply found the repast repulsive, compelled him to refrain. 'I don't want it.'

'Are you sure? Cook went to quite a lot of trouble. The giant actually only existed for a little while before it changed into something else entirely. It had to be recalled from the void.'

'Why bother?'

The priest raised his eyebrows. 'Why, to punish it for trying to hurt you. No one and nothing is permitted to do that, unless, of course, the attempt succeeds.'

'Why would the lords who rule here seek to protect me?'

'Now you're being wilfully obtuse. It's a good thing you don't play these foolish, stubborn little games when your life is in danger.'

'What do you mean?'

'You turned to dark lore for salvation.'

Dieter shook his head. 'I used a spell I learned at the Celestial College.'

'Infused with the power of Chaos.'

'I... modified it slightly to make it more effective, but it was still fundamentally the same magic, and I'm still the same man. Whatever you imagine, your poisons haven't changed me.'

'Then why are you eating giant meat?'

He looked and saw the gory slice of flesh in his redstained hand. He tasted the gamy, salty aftertaste in his mouth. He retched and screamed at the same time, choking himself, and the palace, plain and ocean-sky dissolved into something altogether different.

IN THE FINAL nightmare, a creature resembling a colossal hornet stung Dieter in the centre of his forehead. When his eyes snapped open, the agony of that wound turned to a sensation that fell just short of pain but throbbed with every heartbeat.

He lay on Mama Solveig's lumpy cot with Jarla sitting close at hand. He studied her and the cellar, looking for anomalies, trying to verify that he was truly awake at last. The delirium had fooled him before.

Everything looked all right, and he felt weak, feverish and queasy, as was frequently the case when he'd studied or sought to use the dark lore. 'This is getting to be a habit,' he said. struggling to sit up. 'Me passing out. You keeping watch over me. Damn it, I thought Mama told me I wouldn't throw any more fits.'

'It wasn't like the first time. You didn't thrash and roll about, and you didn't stay unconscious nearly as long. Mama said you just strained yourself. Or something like that.'

He tried to figure out if that was good or bad and decided he lacked the knowledge to make a judgement.

'Are you thirsty?' Jarla asked. 'Or hungry?'

He remembered the smell and taste of raw giant meat, and his stomach churned. 'Not yet.'

'While I sat here, I practised the light spell. I think I'm getting good at it. I never understood much of the magic before, but you made it plain what I needed to do.'

Curse her, why did she keep babbling when he felt so jittery and strange? He drew breath to bark at her to shut up, and then his perspective shifted. He remembered he was fond of her and recognised that she was trying to take care of him. 'You were a good pupil. You have a knack for that particular charm. It must be because of your sunny disposition.'

She blushed and lowered her eyes. 'Do you remember what we talked about before Adolph arrived?'

'Of course.'

'Well, I want for us to be together, if you still do. If not, I understand. I mean, I'm just a–'

He reached out and laid a finger across her lips. 'Hush.' Wondering if he knew what he was doing or even what he truly felt, he leaned forwards and kissed her.

THE DAYS AND nights slipped past, and some Dieter spent afraid of everything. At such times, he longed for his safe, pleasant life in Halmbrandt with an intensity that twisted his guts and made him want to cry. It was generally then, too, that he made another attempt to locate the Master of Change, each such effort merely repeating a ploy that had already failed. But he'd already tried shadowing Mama Solveig, ransacking her possessions, quizzing the other members of the coven and casting divinations, all to no avail. What was left?

But on some days, or at least for certain hours, the grinding fear abated. During those times, awareness of his old life faded, and he spoke of his fraudulent past as a hedge wizard glibly, as though it were the reality. Except for Adolph, the cultists seemed friends and kindred, their treasons and blasphemies simply a routine albeit covert part of life. Even when Mama Solveig poisoned a patient with the taint from Tzeentch's icon, he sometimes had to remind himself what a foul, despicable crime it actually was. Dark lore was just an engrossing study, and his spasms of anger, seething restlessness and aching brow, merely familiar, unremarkable aspects of who he was.

The moments following such interludes, when he felt he had nearly warped into an entirely different person, were the most alarming of all. Then he yearned to run but didn't, for fear of Krieger, or because he still clung to the hope of recovering what he'd lost. Or maybe the forbidden texts held him, tempting him back for just one more perusal and one more whispered secret, seducing him again and again and again.

The coven gathered anew, and Mama Solveig quavered, 'It's time for another trip into the forest. There's a fellow who needs to get away from the city, and Leopold could use some fresh supplies.'

'I'll go,' Adolph declared. Dieter wasn't surprised. Ever since the debacle with the spell that jabbed holes in reality, the scribe had worked hard to regain his status among his peers.

Mama Solveig smiled. 'You're a good, brave boy. You always volunteer.'

Adolph smiled back. The expression looked out of place on his surly face. 'Well, I'm not so brave that I wouldn't like some help. The raiders have been almost too successful lately. They've got everybody stirred up, and I believe the army suspects Leopold has allies here in town. Will you lend me a hand, Dieter? You're a good magician, and you need to meet our allies sooner or later.'

Dieter could think of few things he was less inclined to do then venture into the wilderness with Adolph. The latter plainly still harboured a grudge against him even though, in recent weeks, he'd struggled to hide it. But it wouldn't look well to the other cultists if he refused.

'I'll go,' he said. Jarla stared at him as if he'd lost his mind.

Shrewd as she was, Mama Solveig must have harboured the same suspicion that Adolph meant him ill, but it didn't show in her demeanour. She beamed as if they were two quarrelsome grandchildren who'd finally learned to play together nicely.

CHAPTER EIGHT

It was well after sunset, but the benighted street was still busy. Filthy and stinking, many labourers were only now shuffling home after a long day of toil, even as the night people, painted whores, slinking cutpurses, and their ilk, began to emerge from their lairs.

Which meant Dieter had to wait for a break in the traffic. When it came, he glanced about. As far as he could tell, no one was paying any attention to him. He stooped, picked up a pebble, and used it to scratch a triangle divided by a diagonal slash on a grimy brick wall.

It had been easy enough to slip off on his own to inscribe the sign. Mama Solveig had come to trust him. But as he trudged back the way he'd come, he wondered if leaving the mark would actually do any good. If Krieger's agents hadn't actually been observing him a moment ago, would they find that one bit of graffiti amid all the enormous bustle that was Altdorf?

What if no one made contact? Dare he take it as proof the witch hunters had lost track of him, and if he did, would he then see fit to run?

Behind him, a male voice said, 'It's about time.'

Startled, Dieter whirled to behold Krieger. The big man had exchanged his black garb for nondescript clothing and now, with his sword and pistol, looked like a bravo or mercenary.

'Is something wrong?' Krieger asked.

In fact, the moment had the jarring, disjointed quality that too many situations possessed of late, but Dieter saw no reason to go into that. 'You just surprised me. I wasn't expecting someone to pop out at me almost as soon as I drew the sign.'

Krieger grinned. 'I told you, somebody's always keeping track of you. It happened to be my turn. Come on, I know a good place to talk. I'll even stand you a mug of ale.'

Krieger led him to a tavern, its four-panelled door crudely painted with bottles and overflowing flagons. Excited voices jabbered on the other side. When the witch hunter opened the door, a stench composed of stale beer and sweaty, unwashed bodies wafted out, and Dieter spied a number of soldiers among the crowd in the candlelit common room.

He froze. 'Are you out of your mind?'

The witch hunter chuckled. 'Those fellows may have been told to keep an eye out for you, but I promise you, none of them is likely to recognise you at the moment. Not when they're all at least half-drunk, and intent on their sport.' He pushed Dieter over the threshold.

Once inside, immersed in a stink compounded of beer, sweat, and blood, Dieter saw that a fighting pit yawned in the centre of the floor. Two bare-chested dagger-men, their muscular bodies gleaming with oil, stood glaring at one another at opposite ends of the sunken arena. Most of the patrons were indeed preoccupied with the contest to come, either arguing over who was likely to win or placing bets with a fat man behind the bar, who employed a chalkboard to keep the tally.

Krieger insisted on placing a wager of his own, and in the process bought two mugs of ale and hired what in this seedy establishment passed for a private room: a cramped alcove with a curtain to isolate it.

The witch hunter sampled his drink and made a sour face. 'Tastes like they emptied the latrine back into the barrel to stretch the supply. Still, foul drink is better than none, especially when there's cause to celebrate.'

'You mean, because I've found the Master of Change? I haven't.'

Krieger gave him a stare. 'I told you not to draw the mark until you did. It's too risky.'

'You don't understand. The man has hidden himself too well. We'll never find him using the approach you dictated.'

'Do you have a better idea?'

'Yes, two–'

The spectators beyond the curtain roared as, presumably, the fight began. The sudden bellow drowned out Dieter's voice. He waited for the clamour to partially subside, then began again.

'Two of them. The first is, arrest Mama Solveig, the old midwife–'

'Who leads your coven. I know who she is, and I explained to you why it won't work.'

'It will if we manage it correctly. I'll be with her when you come for her, and I'll use my magic to make sure she doesn't escape or kill herself.'

The crowd howled, possibly because one of the fighters had landed the first slash or stab.

'We had a wizard working with us when we tried to arrest one of the others,' Krieger said. 'It didn't help.'

'But she trusts me, and I'll be standing right beside her.'

Krieger shook his head. 'You said you had another idea?'

'Yes. The cultists are sending me into the forest to carry supplies and a new recruit to the mutants.'

Krieger cocked his head. 'And so?'

'And so you have some scouts or skirmishers or some such shadow me, and a company of soldiers follow them. They can find and exterminate the raiders, and isn't that the main thing? Every day, I hear people grumbling about how the mutants butcher innocent people, hamper trade, and affect the price and availability of goods. Every day, folk lose more of their faith in an Emperor, who, despite all his knights and men-at-arms, can't seem to deal with a threat lurking just outside the walls of his capital city.'

Krieger leered. 'I didn't realise you were such a keen student of politics.'

'Damn it, you know I'm right!'

'Maybe you are, wizard, maybe you are. But when mutants stop concealing their deformities, run away to the wilderness, and turn brigand, I don't have to worry about them any more. At that point, they become the army's problem. My job is to ferret out the corruption hiding in our midst, and at the moment, my target is the Master of Change.'

'It's possible Leopold Mann – the leader of the bandits – knows the Master's identity. If you take him alive, maybe you can get it out of him.'

'Not the worst notion I ever heard, but I'm inclined to stick with the original plan.'

Dieter had to clamp down hard on an urge to jump up and strike the big man in the face. 'That isn't sensible or fair! I've brought you more than you had any right to expect, and I've explained how it can be used to deal with the Master of Change and the marauders as well. I deserve to be set free and cleared of the charges against me.'

'That's one point of view, but for better or worse, I'm the one who decides when your work is done.'

'Do you want me to die? Because that's what's likely to happen if I go into the forest, and then you'll derive no benefit at all from all my spying.'

'You tell me your sorcery's potent enough to manage this Mama Solveig. Then it ought to be strong enough to protect you out in the woods as well.'

'Even if it is, I can't stay where I am, doing what I'm doing. I–' Dieter abruptly realised what he was babbling, and stopped short. He didn't dare tell Krieger that he'd come to find dark lore fascinating if not addictive, or about the incipient changes in his mind and body. Bargain or not, the witch hunter might well deem such an admission ample justification to send him to the fire when his task was done.

Krieger studied him. 'Go on, finish your thought.'

'Never mind. What's the point? You aren't going to change your mind no matter what I say.'

The big man grinned. 'Now there's the discernment a good spy needs.'

The crowd beyond the curtain roared, most likely in appreciation of the death stroke. Then they started chanting, 'Tzeentch! Tzeentch! Tzeentch!'

Dieter cried out and jerked in his chair. His flailing hand knocked over his tankard, spilling beer across the tabletop.

Quick as a cat despite his heavy frame, Krieger jumped up and put his hand on his pistol. 'What's wrong?'

'Nothing,' Dieter said, 'just my ears playing tricks on me.' The spectators were actually shouting, 'Zeyd,' no doubt the name of the victorious pit fighter.

The tender spot on his forehead throbbed to the beat.

THE ARMOURY WAS a massive, ugly limestone building, a small fortress in its own right. Standing beside the wagon with Adolph and Lampertus, Dieter stared at the recessed double doors in the centre of the wall and tried to avoid picturing what was happening on the other side.

Adolph chuckled. 'It galls you, doesn't it?'

'What?'

'Knowing that right now, behind those doors, Jarla's lifting her skirts for another man. Better get used to it. It's what whores do. It's the reason I cast her off.'

Dieter sneered. 'You cast her off.'

'Did she tell you it was the other way around? Well, she would, wouldn't she?'

Dieter thought how satisfying it would be to blast Adolph with his magic, or simply to hit him. Perceiving the barely restrained hostility between his companions, Lampertus looked from one to the other with perplexity and trepidation manifest in his expression. Dieter could scarcely blame him for his reaction, considering that he was entrusting his life to them.

Lampertus was a smallish, middle-aged coppersmith with a round, jowly face. Troubled by aches in his hips and knees, he'd submitted himself to Mama Solveig's poisonous ministrations. Now some new extremity grew from his chest and periodically squirmed of its own accord, the motion perceptible even beneath his layers of baggy clothing.

Dieter tried to produce a reassuring smile. 'Don't worry. We like to mock and taunt one another, but it's all in fun.'

'If you say so,' Lampertus replied.

The right-hand leaf of the double door cracked open. Jarla beckoned from the shadows. Adolph climbed back up onto the wagon, flicked the reins, and the two mules started forwards. Dieter and Lampertus jogged alongside, swung the doors open wide enough to admit the conveyance, and closed them behind it.

The interior of the armoury was a square, high-ceilinged box of a place, with barrel upon barrel, rack upon rack and shelf upon shelf of swords, poleaxes, shields and helmets that looked like severed heads in the gloom. Enticed by Jarla's charms, a bargain price, and the offer of a swig or two of wine to sweeten the transaction, the sentry had fallen victim to the same sleeping powder that had once rendered Dieter insensible. He now lay snoring on the floor with his breeches undone and his manhood peeking out. Jarla noticed Dieter looking at the fellow, and winced and lowered her eyes.

Dieter reminded himself that she'd done only what he and Adolph had asked of her, and dredged up the resolve to react as was her due. He smiled and squeezed her shoulder. 'Well done. Did you take his purse?'

Jarla nodded. 'I remembered.'

With luck, when the guard found his money missing, he'd believe the whole point of the incident had been to rob him, and would fail to notice someone had stolen from the arsenal as well. If so, it was unlikely he'd report the crime, considering that he'd forsaken his responsibilities to consort with a streetwalker.

The cultists scurried about the store, taking swords here, shot and arquebuses here, never too many of any one item or too much of anything from any one place, and stowing them in the hidden compartment beneath the wagon's cargo bay. Throughout the process, Dieter's nerves jangled with the fear that someone would walk in and discover what was happening. But nobody did, and in less than half an hour they were ready to claim the final prize: two casks of gunpowder. The item Leopold Mann supposedly needed most of all.

The barrels were too bulky to fit in the concealed compartment. The robbers lashed them down in the wagon bed and draped a tarpaulin over them to conceal the marks of the Imperial forces and the Blackpowder Men. Then they made their exit.

If there's another sentry, Dieter thought, peering down from the ramparts, or if anybody else is looking and decides it's strange for four civilians, one of them a whore, to be driving out of the armoury at such an early hour, we're as good as dead. But their luck held, and, the team's hooves clopping and the wagon wheels rumbling on the cobbles, they rolled on while the first grey hint of dawn appeared in the eastern sky.

They stopped in the miniature lumberyard behind Hanno's shop, where the stacks of wood concealed the beer barrels stolen two weeks previously. They loaded and secured the kegs on top of the gunpowder, and then Jarla kissed Dieter goodbye. 'Be careful,' she whispered.

Dieter, Adolph and Lampertus donned caps sewn with the badge of the Brewers' Guild. Thus disguised, if one could call it that, they climbed back onto the wagon and drove on towards the northern gate.

As planned, they reached the immense arch, portcullis and iron-bound valves shortly before the soldiers who'd stood watch through the night were due to be relieved. Tired, the guards had little inclination to question any of the merchants and other travellers lined up in hopes of an early start. They simply waved Dieter and his companions through with the rest.

Lampertus twisted around and stared back at the metropolis slowly dwindling behind them. He'd probably spent his entire life in Altdorf, and was now trying to come to terms with the truth that he was unlikely ever to walk its streets again. Rather, he must now struggle to survive in a wilderness infested with bears, wolves, beastmen and countless other perils.

Dieter squeezed the coppersmith's shoulder. 'It will be all right,' he said. 'Mann and his people will take care of you. You'll be safe with them as you could never be in Altdorf. There, it was only a matter of time until the witch hunters came for you. Here, you're going to live.'

Lampertus took a deep breath. 'You're right,' he said. 'You got me out, I'm going to live, and I'm grateful. Thank you both.'

Adolph responded with a smile. 'You're welcome,' he said.

For his part, Dieter felt irrationally touched by the mutant's jubilation, and envious of it too. What a wonderful thing it must be to escape! He certainly hadn't. Even out here in the countryside, he was still enmeshed in a web of danger, deception and puzzles without answers, of fear, hope, ambivalence and unhealthy fascination. He drew what solace he could from contemplating the sky as it ought to look, with no tangle of spires eclipsing it and without smoke or smog besmirching it.

People spoke of raiders lurking just outside the city walls, but, of course, the situation wasn't quite that bad. The capital rose amid a circle of farmland. It took all morning to cross the fields and reach the forest beyond. Uncomfortable as it looked, Lampertus eventually managed to stretch out atop the barrels and doze. The growth beneath his shirt switched back and forth like a cat's tail, more active when he was asleep.

Adolph forsook the highway for a secondary road, and when it forked, took the narrower of the two branches. After every such choice, there was less traffic than before.

Late afternoon found them jolting along a track scarcely better than a game trail. Brush swished and rattled on the underside of the wagon, and walls of mossy tree trunks pressed so close on either side that the vehicle only barely had room to pass. Resentful of the hard going, the mules baulked repeatedly, and Adolph, no expert teamster, snarled obscenities and lashed them with the reins to goad them into motion once again.

'If the track gets any worse,' Dieter said, 'we won't be able to continue.'

'I know what I'm doing!' Adolph snapped.

Dieter resisted the impulse to take a similar tone. 'I wasn't suggesting that you don't. After all, you're the one who's visited the raiders before. I'm just saying, I hope we didn't overload the wagon.'

Adolph grunted. Then, after a pause, he drew back on the reins, halted the team, and said, 'I admit, I thought someone would make contact with us before now.'

'Could the raiders have moved their camp?' Lampertus asked. The constant bumping and swaying had long since put an end to his napping. 'Mama Solveig told me they sneak around a lot to stay ahead of the soldiers.'

'The Master has ways of keeping track of them,' Adolph replied, 'and he told Mama this is the right area. Still, if something's happened within the last day or so...' He turned to Dieter. 'Is there any chance you can locate them with your magic?'

Dieter hesitated. 'Perhaps.'

'Then give it a try. I'd rather sunset found us in Leopold's camp, not alone and bewildered on the trail. The god's children aren't the only things living in these woods.'

'All right.' The branches arched and tangled so densely overhead as to virtually hide the sky, but Dieter recalled a better view a turn or two back down the track. The trick would be to take advantage of it without providing further evidence that all his magic derived from the heavens. 'But I think I'll focus better if I don't have the two of you looking over my shoulder. Do you mind if I walk a little way back down the trail?'

He actually expected Adolph, ever avid to observe and master all the sorcery he could, to insist on accompanying him, but the scribe surprised him. 'Fine. Lampertus and I will guard the wagon. Just don't go too far.'

'I won't.' Dieter hopped down from the bench and hiked back the way they'd come. Even with the undergrowth clogging the path and making walking strenuous, it felt good to stretch his legs after hours of perching on a hard, unsteady seat.

When he sighted the patch of open sky, the tender spot in his forehead squirmed. No, he told it, I'm going to cast a spell, but not your kind – the kind I was born to cast. He took a deep breath, then declaimed the words of power and swept his hand through the proper passes.

The wind whispered to him and ran its cool fingers across his face. Grey and silver ripples streamed through streaks of wispy cloud to point the way. It appeared Adolph had been heading in the right direction after all. Dieter felt both relieved and disappointed, the latter because it would have gratified the spiteful part of him to inform the scribe he'd blundered.

Then, for just an instant, the streaming bands of dull and bright took on a crimson tinge, and though the resemblance was tenuous at best, Dieter instantly thought of blood flowing from an open wound. He stared, trying to read the significance of the additional and unexpected portent, but the manifestation ended before he could interpret it.

It indicated danger, that much seemed clear. He hesitated, wondering if a second casting would provide additional insight. But if the peril was imminent, it might be better to rejoin his companions as quickly as possible. He turned and ran back up the trail.

The wagon was still where he'd left it, with the mules standing stolidly in their traces. But at first he could see no sign of Adolph or Lampertus. He had to run closer before he spotted the motionless form all but buried in the brush.

It was Lampertus, unblinking eyes staring at the sky, mouth twisted. His deformity, a thick, warty tentacle terminating in a round, fanged mouth like that of a lamprey, had burst through his clothing but now lay flaccid and inert. Though disgusted by the unnatural growth, Dieter forced himself to kneel down to determine if the fugitive was still breathing.

He wasn't. Something had killed him, although the cause of death wasn't immediately apparent.

Dieter rose and turned, peering, seeing only rank upon rank of trees, wondering who or what was watching him. Wondering what had become of Adolph.

ADOLPH STRODE THROUGH the forest, trying to hurry but move quietly as well. He didn't want Dieter to track him by the noise.

He still felt rattled from the close call he'd just experienced, and wished he'd had the prudence to open a wider distance between Lampertus and himself before hurling his shadow knives. But he'd expected the other man to go down instantly. Most people did.

Lampertus, however, hadn't. Perhaps his transformation had made him inhumanly tough. He'd pivoted and rushed his attacker, and the eel-like growth on his chest had punched through his clothing to strike at Adolph like a snake. Adolph hadn't expected such an assault, and it was pure luck that the tentacle hadn't snagged him with that nasty ring of fangs.

He was lucky, too, that the deformity only had time for one bite. Then, at last, Lampertus's legs buckled, and he swayed and toppled over backwards.

It was actually too bad about Lampertus. Adolph had had nothing against him. He'd even felt vaguely moved by the coppersmith's gratitude. But a man had to do what was necessary to look after himself. It was simply the way of the world.

He resolved to put Lampertus out of his mind and concentrate on the next phase of his scheme. Everything was going even better than anticipated, for he hadn't expected that Dieter would be obliging enough to wander off on his own and so facilitate matters, and in fact, the rest should be easy enough. The raiders knew and trusted him. Still, a ready tongue and an earnest manner would serve him well.

Suddenly a green and brown mass surged up in front of him like mud and liquefied grass and dead leaves flowing in defiance of gravity. It rapidly took on a degree of definition, sprouting limbs and a hairless bump of a head, but remained a sexless and unfinished-looking thing. It stuck a three-fingered hand inside its own semi-solid torso, extracted a javelin, and hefted it to throw.

'No!' Adolph said. 'I belong to the Red Crown! I've seen you before. Don't you recognise me?'

The sentry hesitated. 'Red Crown?' it asked in a mushy voice.

'Yes.' He prayed the bandit understood. Sometimes the god's mark diminished a person's intelligence, and the guard appeared a case in point.

'Sweetmeats?' asked the sentry, peering past him. 'Treats?'

'I brought supplies,' Adolph said, 'but something's wrong. I need to speak with the others immediately.'

The sentry simply stood, seemingly struggling to comprehend, until he wanted to scream at it. At last it said, 'Come,' floundered around, and led him onwards, its boneless gait somehow awkward and flowing at the same time. With each step, it looked on the verge of collapsing and melting back into shapelessness again.

The raiders had pitched their tents, built their lean-tos, and dug their fire pits and latrines in what passed for a clearing in the dense and ancient wood. Many of the band were simply lazing about, and, curious, came scurrying when the sentry conducted Adolph into view. In moments he found himself surrounded by faces with beaks, scales, doglike muzzles, or set upside down so the mouth split the top, the nose was inverted, and the eyes blinked and shifted at the bottom. Voices, many barely intelligible, croaked, growled, and hissed greetings and questions. As Adolph had learned from past experience, not all such creatures stank, but enough of them did that when they clustered around him, the eye-watering funk was like the reek of a dirty kennel mixed with the foetor of a plague pit.

In other words, the bandits provided a glimpse of the glory that would reign everywhere once Chaos obliterated the conventional human world, and on previous visits, Adolph had always tried to rejoice in the promise they embodied – and to quash the weak, unregenerate part of himself that persisted in finding them hideous and dreaded the day when he too would change and join their company.

Today, however, both adoration and repulsion were beside the point. He needed to enlist the marauders' help as expeditiously as possible. 'Is Leopold here?' he asked.

'I am,' a shrill voice answered from overhead.

Adolph looked up just in time to see a grey-black bundle hanging upside down from a tree limb unfurl the furry wings wrapped around its body. Then the claws on its toes released their hold and it dropped, not to take flight as a true bat might, but to bound from one branch to another like a squirrel. Some of the boughs snapped beneath the considerable weight, but still provided momentary support sufficient to prevent a bone-shattering plummet all the way to the ground.

Leopold Mann landed with a thud. Despite his stunted legs and forward cant – leaning his weight on his knuckles, he generally used his arm-wings like crutches when he walked – he was so huge that his eyeless head with its enormous pointed ears showed above the heads of his followers even before they parted to make way for him. He swung himself forwards, the golden, wire-wrapped hilt of his greatsword gleaming above his shoulder and folds of alar membrane dragging on the ground like an overlong cloak.

'You look upset,' Leopold said, although how Adolph could 'look' any way to a being without eyes, he couldn't imagine.

'I had trouble,' he answered. 'I was bringing you supplies and a recruit. A new member of the coven rode along with me. Mama Solveig thought it was time for him to meet you.'

'Go on,' Leopold said, still in the soprano voice that was so incongruous squealing from his barrel chest.

'He's a magician, too,' Adolph said, 'and he used a spell to murder Lampertus, the recruit. Then he tried to do the same to me. It all caught me by surprise, and I only just managed to escape.'

'Why would he do that?' Leopold asked.

'I don't know.' Adolph hesitated, making a show of pondering. He didn't want to seem too facile producing an explanation. 'Unless... suppose he's a spy, who infiltrated the Red Crown in the hope we'd lead him to you. As, to my regret, I did. But as we approached, his nerve failed at the prospect of actually meeting you. Perhaps he imagined that, what with all the amazing gifts the Changer of the Ways has given you, one of you would see through his disguise. At any rate, he decided that he'd discovered the general vicinity of your camp, and that was good enough. He'd kill his companions, flee, and lead the army back here to wipe you out.'

Leopold snorted. 'We'd be far away by the time the soldiers came.'

'But only if you knew they were coming. If Dieter – the spy – had succeeded in killing me, too, you wouldn't realise anything was amiss.'

'I suppose that's true.' Leopold's mouth was no longer shaped much like that of an ordinary human, but it managed something approximating a fang-baring leer. 'Anyway, I don't feel like moving camp just yet.' He turned to his followers. 'Find the spy and kill him.'

And that's that, Adolph thought.

Much as he would have liked to learn every secret Dieter might conceivably have taught, it had become clear to him that if he was ever to regain his privileged position within the coven, his woman, and, if he was to be honest with himself, his pride, the wyrd had to go. Yet he'd hesitated to attempt the deed with his own hands, partly because he'd acquired a healthy respect for Dieter's powers and partly because he worried that Mama, Jarla and the others would suspect him if the hedge wizard turned up dead inside the city.

Fortunately, it was inconceivable that Dieter's sorcery, formidable though it was, would suffice to fend off a small army of brigands, and afterwards, if anyone asked questions, the outlaws would support Adolph in his claim that his companion had been a spy. Having slaughtered Dieter, they could only assume the act was warranted. It was human nature to justify oneself, and Adolph was confident that even the most extreme transformations hadn't cured his dupes of the habit.

As he watched them lope, hobble and even slither on their bellies in search of their prey, he had to clamp down hard to stifle a laugh.

CHAPTER NINE

DIETER STOOD BESIDE the wagon watching twilight overtake the forest and wondering what to do. One of the mules tossed its head as though to convey scorn for his paralysis.

He felt the same way about it, or at least he had a rest-less sense that he ought to be pursuing some plan of action, that he was in danger, and it deepened with every moment he failed to put himself into motion. But since he didn't understand what had happened, it was difficult to formulate an appropriate response.

Though he'd feared that once they entered the forest, Adolph might try to do him harm, what reason could the scribe have had to kill Lampertus? But if his companion hadn't done it, who had, and either way, where was Adolph now?

Should Dieter search for the cultist, who might be wait-ing in ambush? Try to find the bandits, who didn't know him and might not believe he was a Chaos worshipper? Flee back down the trail, forsaking the errand on which

Mama Solveig had sent him and jeopardising his standing within the coven? Stand guard over the wagon and its contraband, and hope either Adolph or some friendly outlaw would happen along eventually?

Perhaps divination held the answer, and perhaps it ought to be a different spell than before. That would maximise the chances of it yielding insights his previous effort hadn't produced, and in any case, with anxiety and restlessness gnawing at him, the delay involved in going back down the trail seemed insupportable. He swept his hand through a pass and whispered the first line of the oracular spell he'd acquired from the dark lore. His forehead throbbed. One of the mules brayed, and, straining against the wagon's brake mechanism, the team attempted to distance itself from him.

A javelin arced out of the trees and plunged into the ground mere inches from his right foot.

Even so, for a moment, he kept conjuring. He wanted to finish the spell, or perhaps, like a frantic lover unwilling to stop short of consummation, it wanted to be finished. But then the rational part of him screamed that more missiles were surely coming, that he was utterly vulnerable standing out in the open chanting and flapping his arms, and somehow he mustered the will to break off the incantation.

He dived to the ground, scrambled under the wagon, and crouched behind one of the wheels. Guns banged and flashed, smearing the air with their smoke. The barrage battered the wagon, cracking and splintering wood. Beer gushed from punctured kegs. An arrow hit one of the mules, and the animal stumbled and screamed.

The wagon provided insufficient cover, which soon would become even less adequate: Dieter could make out darting shadows spreading out to flank his position. He needed magical protection, and as soon as he conceived the thought, Chaos whispered, urging him to invoke its power as he stupidly, unthinkingly had before. Denying the impulse, he spoke to the heavens, and they cloaked him in the halo that had shielded him from the serpent of fire.

Thus armoured, he shouted to his attackers, who, though he had yet to see them clearly, he assumed to be the brigands. 'Stop this! I'm an ally! A follower of the Red Crown! I've brought you supplies!'

'Liar!' they screamed in answer, as well as 'traitor,' 'witch hunter,' and 'spy.' Then, as if their own clamour had excited their bloodlust beyond bearing, they charged.

Dieter sprinted in the opposite direction. He hoped his flight wouldn't stop them from running close to the wagon, and, glancing back, he saw that it hadn't. As far as they knew, they had no reason to swing wide and avoid it.

He halted, pivoted, rattled off words of power, and thrust out his arm. A tongue of flame leaped up in the wagon bed.

The kegs of gunpowder exploded, and the fiery blast tore the wagon and mules apart. Chunks of blazing wood and fragments of equine flew through the air. Burning like a torch, a mutant with the head of a bird shrieked and reeled. Squinting against the glare, Dieter couldn't tell how many other bandits the blast had killed or injured. Not all of them, obviously. Possibly only a couple. But he hoped the blinding flash, deafening boom and sheer shock would make the others falter and so enable him to increase his lead. Willing himself not to flag – he was casting too many spells in quick succession, and it was already testing his stamina – he turned and ran on.

He veered off the trail into the trees. He hated to do it. It would be harder going, and the forest was his pursuers' domain, not his. But his only chance was to elude the mutants, and that would be impossible if he stayed in the open.

Wishing full night would hurry and engulf the wood, he ran down one slope and clambered up another. Behind him and to the right, the raiders called to one another, some in voices so garbled or bestial he couldn't understand them. One outlaw fired a gun, and a companion cursed him for a fool and told him to wait until he was certain he saw a target.

Crouching behind an oak, Dieter hoped that none of the brigands could see him. He whispered another spell. A pang of discomfort twisted his guts, as if he were feeling the effort tear another measure of his strength away. But when he scurried onwards, he strode twice as fast as before. Fast enough, he prayed, to outdistance his pursuers and shake them off his trail.

In fact, the ploy kept him alive and uncaught for a while longer, until darkness shrouded the land, and stars gleamed through the few gaps in the branches overhead. But eventually the enchantment ran its course, and in its aftermath, he crouched exhausted, fighting to control his breathing lest someone hear the tortured rasp. For, as the rustling brush and crunching dead leaves on every side attested, even with his augmented speed, he hadn't succeeded in eluding his pursuers. Their superior numbers and knowledge of the terrain had made it impossible, and now they were all around him.

He smiled a bitter smile. He'd struggled as hard as he could and attempted every trick that came to mind. Now, he supposed, it was time to admit his life was over.

'It doesn't have to be,' said a baritone voice.

Dieter jerked around to find the priest standing beside him, robe belt dangling, cowl pushed back to reveal the shrewd, sardonic face and tonsured pate.

'Don't worry,' the man in the robe continued, 'the brigands can't hear me.'

'Because you aren't real,' Dieter whispered.

'That assertion implies you aren't, either.'

Dieter closed his eyes in the hope that when he opened them, the priest would be gone. He didn't want to spend the last moments of his life mired in a hallucination. 'Leave me alone.'

'To die? You wouldn't want that. Over the past several weeks, you've fought hard to survive. As you can survive again, if you employ all the resources at your command.'

'Use Dark Magic, you mean. No. The spells I've learned wouldn't be any more effective than my darts of light and blasts of wind, and I won't end my life with that filth in my thoughts and on my tongue.'

'How perverse that even when your survival depends on it, you refuse to recognise the bounty laid before you. The Master of Fortune offers gifts far more precious than the small boons you've accepted so far. Even now, it's not too late to accept them. All you need do is extend your hand.'

'I told you to go away!' It took him a moment to realise he'd shouted.

His eyes snapped open. The priest was gone, not that it mattered. His outcry had revealed his position, and now he could hear the bandits closing in on him.

It was frightening, but even more than fear, he felt outrage at the utter unfairness of his situation, for by every star that shined in the heavens, he was an innocent man! He hadn't hurt anyone back in Halmbrandt, yet Krieger had been able to control him just as if he had. Nor had he murdered Lampertus, but the brigands were about to punish him for it anyway.

And surely the innocent had the right to resist unjust treatment by any means that came to hand. Straining to focus despite his exhaustion, he contemplated the spells and bizarre, paradoxical dogma he'd absorbed from the forbidden texts, seeking some deeper truth that had yet to reveal itself. A part of him clamoured that he was courting a fate worse than being shot or hacked apart, but now, with death mere heartbeats away, the raw animal urge to survive rendered the caution meaningless.

Words articulated themselves in his mind. He didn't know how, for they didn't occur in any of the coven's parchments, nor did he understand their meaning, but he jabbered them as eagerly as a drowning man would clutch at a lifeline.

Sudden as a lightning strike, power burned into the tender spot on his forehead and on through every portion of his body. The sensation was ecstatic and excruciating at the same time. Above all, it was so overwhelming as to render thought or purposeful action impossible, and he jerked and stumbled mindlessly in its grip.

Then the paroxysm ended as abruptly as it began, leaving weakness in its stead. He pitched forwards onto his knees, and just barely managed to catch himself with his hands to avoid ending up with his face in the dirt.

He realised the blades of grass and dead leaves beneath his dangling head looked different, although he couldn't say precisely how. They just did.

An exchange of excited voices and the tramp of footsteps put an end to his dazed contemplation of such minutiae. The brigands had found him.

To be exact, they'd caught up with him at a moment when he was too feeble to attempt any more magic or do anything else to defend himself. The priest had promised Chaotic lore would save him, but evidently not.

Dieter wished he could die on his feet, but he lacked the strength to rise. Still, he could at least demonstrate that he had the courage to look at his killers, and so he laboriously lifted his head.

To behold three brigands. The one on the right, a woman, appeared to have no skin, as if a torturer had flayed her. The man in the middle seemed to have leeches attached all over his body, although Dieter assumed the dark, pendulous masses were actually blemishes. The remaining fellow looked normal, and maybe he was. Perhaps he was one of the folk who, according to Mama

Solveig, joined the outlaws because they couldn't bear separation from someone they loved.

Like the ground, the three bandits looked different than they ought to look. At first, Dieter saw a dim phosphorescence crawling on their bodies. Then, for a moment, the figures multiplied, and he beheld more than one of each. It was as if, moving, they left phantasmal after images hanging in the air.

The normal-looking brigand shouldered his crossbow and squinted as he aimed. The leech man turned and shoved the weapon out of line. 'Don't!' said the mutant. 'Look at him!'

Look at him? Dieter realised the sensitive spot in the middle of his brow felt different than it ever had before. Hand trembling, he reached to examine it by touch.

'Does it matter?' the crossbowman asked. 'He killed the recruit. He blew up the wagon and killed and hurt some of us.'

'Still,' the leech man said.

The spot was moist and soft. A flap of skin flinched down to cover and protect it when Dieter fingered it with any force at all. Now he understood why things looked different. How could they not, when he'd grown a new eye?

In other words, he'd transformed. His exposure to the icon had started the process, his studies of Dark Magic had advanced it, and that final invocation, which had opened his body and spirit to Chaos, had enabled it to produce overt deformity. The realisation was so appalling that for the moment it even blunted his fear that the outlaws were about to kill him.

'Well, what do you want to do with him?' the crossbowman asked, a hint of petulance in his voice.

'Take him to Leopold,' the skinless woman said, the raw wetness of her face glistening even in the gloom. 'If we end up killing one of our own kind, let it be because our leader ordered it.'

'He's dangerous,' the man with the crossbow said.

'Maybe not any more,' she said. 'He looks worn out. Anyway, you two can hold onto his arms and I'll walk behind him with my spear, ready to stick him if he tries anything. You hear that, warlock? I will kill you if I even suspect you're starting a spell.'

Dieter managed a nod, and the men hauled him to his feet.

Calling to their comrades that the hunt was over, his captors half-marched, half-carried Dieter through the forest. On the way, a portion of his strength seeped back, shock and horror loosened their grip on him, and he realised that, even altered as he was, he still wanted to go on living. So he strove to fix his thoughts on that goal only. There'd be time to grapple with the full implications of his transformation if he survived the night.

By the time he and his captors reached the clearing, most of the other brigands had gathered there as well. Even in the dark, the sight of so many malformed bodies, no two alike, was too complicated and sickening to take in all at once. It made his head spin, made him feel as if he were dreaming once again of Tzeentch's legions.

But this was no vision, and he couldn't afford to stand dazed and passive as if it were. He bit his tongue, and the stab of pain dispelled that insidious feeling of unreality.

'Kill him!' urged a familiar voice. 'He's dangerous!'

Dieter cast about and spotted Adolph standing alive and well among the bandits. He realised the latter took him for an enemy because the scribe had murdered Lampertus and then laid the blame on him. Stupid of him not to have guessed before, but then, he had been busy running and fighting for his life.

When he peered at Adolph, he perforce gave the cultist a clear look at his altered face. Adolph's eyes widened in surprise and, perhaps, dismay. That's right, you bastard, Dieter thought. You haven't won yet.

His captors marched him up to a mutant as grotesquely deformed as any he'd seen, whom he assumed to be their chieftain. Despite his hugeness, his stunted legs, lack of eyes, and the way he appeared to use his elongated forelimbs as crutches might have led one to infer he'd be helpless in a fight, but the two-handed sword strapped to his back suggested otherwise.

'Good evening, Herr Mann,' Dieter said.

The raiders in general seemed surprised at the display of civility. Leopold Mann cocked his bat-like head.

'I've hurt some of your people,' Dieter continued. 'I regret that more than I can say. But your band attacked me. I had no choice but to defend myself.'

'We attacked you,' Mann answered in a startlingly shrill voice, 'because you murdered another who bore the Changer's mark.' He shifted the weight resting on his knuckles, and as he eased himself, his single form split into four, each slightly different from the rest.

Dieter wondered again precisely what he was seeing. The phenomenon tugged at him as if it was important he comprehend it. But it could scarcely be as important as arguing his innocence.

'I didn't murder Lampertus,' he said. 'I had no reason to, and even if I did, I'm not stupid enough to do it out here in the forest, where I don't know my way around and scores of the god's faithful servants were camped close at hand to avenge the treachery. Adolph killed him so he could falsely accuse me and convince you to slay me in my turn. Or, failing that, so he'd have justification to dispose of me himself.'

'Liar!' Adolph snarled. 'You killed Lampertus and tried to murder me too because your nerve failed, and you were afraid to meet Leopold and his people.'

Dieter looked up at the outlaw leader. 'Does that gibberish ring true to you? Isn't it plain that even if I were a spy and afraid, the safer, more sensible course of action would

be to continue my masquerade, not reveal myself and provoke your anger? Only a man lost to panic would do
otherwise. Do you think the witch hunters recruit agents
who are prone to panic? Did I seem like a coward or idiot
as I struggled to keep your band from killing me?'

One of Mann's several images spat, then the next, and
then a third. The gob of saliva seemed to take its time
splatting on the ground. 'It would have been stupid for you
to kill your companion,' the bandit said. 'But it would have
been almost as risky for Adolph to try it. Why would he
want you dead badly enough to take the chance?'

'No reason!' Adolph cried. Tendrils of mauve and crimson shimmer oozed on his body.

'Every reason,' Dieter said. 'Your lover forsook you for
me. On top of that, I'm the better magician, and as a result,
neither Mama Solveig nor the other cultists think you're
anything special any more. Essentially, I've taken away
everything that made you feel like a man.'

Perhaps trying to control the fury welling up inside him,
Adolph took a long breath. 'Leopold, you and your comrades have known me for a while now, and I've never done
you anything but good. This wretch is a stranger to you,
and you know for a fact that he's killed a couple of you,
wounded others, and destroyed the black powder and
other supplies I smuggled out of Altdorf. So I ask you:
which of us ought you to believe?'

'The one who carries the Changer's mark,' Dieter said. 'If
he and his friends are wise, they'll put their trust in one of
their own kind.'

'You didn't carry the mark at the start of the day,' Adolph
said.

'But I do now.' Dieter shifted his regard back to Mann.
'Think about it: you have known Adolph for a long time.
He's worshipped before our lord's icon for almost two
years. Yet the god has never seen fit to mark him. Now me,
I've only belonged to the Red Crown for a few weeks, and

I've already transformed. If the Changer of the Ways so favours me, how can his children do otherwise?'

The mutants clustered about growled and muttered to one another. From what Dieter was able to overhear, he'd persuaded some, but not all.

Just as his followers found themselves unable to agree, Mann appeared divided and uncertain in his mind. He stood and pondered, his image split into three selves, which shifted their weight in quick succession. It seemed to take a heartbeat too long for the whisper of alar membrane dragging on the ground to reach Dieter's ears. He wondered if that was merely his overstressed nerves playing tricks on him.

Finally Mann thumped a fist on his massive chest. The other brigands fell silent.

'No member of this clan,' the bat-thing said, 'saw Lampertus die. We only know what Adolph and Dieter have told us, accounts that clash with one another. Of course, we know Adolph. He's our trusted ally. Yet Dieter's claims sound convincing, and he's one of our own kind.'

With that, Mann paused, as if he'd said all that need be said. After a moment, Adolph exploded, 'And so? I don't understand! What is your judgement?'

Mann snorted, the nostrils in his blunt snout flaring. 'My judgement is, I don't know what to believe. Fortunately, the band has a way of deciding such questions: the two of you will fight. The Changer will reward his true son with victory and punish betrayal with death.'

Adolph gave a nod. 'Let's do it.'

'Adolph's fresh,' Dieter said. 'I'm worn out. Surely you'll give me a chance to rest. Otherwise, it won't be a fair fight.'

Adolph sneered. 'I have to return to Altdorf as soon as possible. If I stay away too long, and my employer becomes suspicious, it jeopardises everybody's safety. And besides, murderer, I thought you claimed to be the better warlock. Isn't that why I'm supposed to be jealous? Well, your mystical gifts should compensate for the fact that you've been running around and I haven't.'

Dieter peered up at Leopold. 'Physical exhaustion hinders spell casting as much as it would hamper a swordsman's ability to cut and parry.'

The raider grunted. 'If the god favours you, your weariness won't matter, and if he doesn't, you could rest for a year and it wouldn't help.' He raised his squeal of a voice: 'Clear a space!'

The other marauders vacated an oval-shaped area twenty paces long. Leopold gestured, and Dieter trudged towards the far end of it. He imagined himself whispering to the sky, asking for lightning, blasting a hole through the ranks of outlaws and sprinting through the gap, but recognised that even if there had been a storm brewing overhead, it probably wouldn't have worked. His captors would butcher him in a heartbeat if he attempted any such escape.

He turned. Adolph had taken his place at the other end of the oval. The scribe glared, and Dieter, trying to look just as resolute and confident of his prowess, responded with a glower of his own.

'Begin!' Mann shrilled.

Adolph charged. Perhaps he meant to close the distance to punch, grapple, and bring his superior strength and mass to bear, to turn the duel into a purely physical confrontation.

Dieter rattled off words of power and slashed his hands through mystic passes. He thought he was performing the spell correctly, but with the final syllable, abruptly sensed that he hadn't. No wind rose to slam into Adolph and hold him back. Rather, several spectators cried out in surprise as the patch of earth beneath them liquefied and their feet sank into muck, a useless, random consequence of magic gone awry.

Dieter immediately resumed chanting. Adolph kept charging. No doubt, at this point, he was confident he could reach his adversary before Dieter could complete another incantation. Dieter was all but certain of it, too, but he hoped that if he pretended to attempt another spell, it would encourage Adolph to come at him as fast and therefore recklessly as possible.

The scribe lunged, and Dieter stopped reciting, twisted aside, and threw a punch. His skills as a brawler were rudimentary at best, but he managed to avoid Adolph's headlong rush and drive his knuckles into his temple. Adolph lost his balance and dropped to one knee.

Dieter kicked the other man in the spine. Adolph lurched forwards. Teetering on one foot, Dieter struggled to re-establish his equilibrium so he could kick again.

Adolph spun around with a knife in his outstretched hand. The slash streaked at Dieter's belly. He flung himself backwards, narrowly avoiding the stroke, but the frantic effort robbed him of his precarious balance and sent him staggering. Begrudging the moment it would take to rise, Adolph snarled the opening words of the spell that hurled shadow blades, and his single self splintered into several.

Dieter could almost have laughed. Apparently it wasn't a severe enough handicap that he had to fight when he was tired. His eyes needed to resume playing tricks on him as well.

Dark missiles leaped from the hand of the Adolph acting in advance of all the others. Dieter attempted to dodge but knew he wouldn't manage it. He was still off balance, and the attack flew too fast.

The first set of darts blinked out of existence partway to the target. As did the next, launched from the fingertips of another Adolph's whipping arm. So did the third. It was only the last flight of missiles that travelled far enough to reach Dieter. He had in fact sidestepped quickly enough to evade those, and they hurtled harmlessly by. His multiple selves collapsing into a single image once again, Adolph goggled in manifest surprise that the attack had missed.

Dieter was just as surprised, but at least he thought he suddenly understood how it had happened. He'd surmised that his third eye sometimes saw a trail of after images a person or object in motion left behind, but he'd been mistaken. In actuality, it was peering into the future, providing glimpses of what was about to happen an instant before it did.

It was an ability he might conceivably have turned to good advantage – except that, now that he finally understood it, his altered vision reverted to normality.

He scrambled back, opening up the distance once again. Adolph clambered to his feet. Judging from his grimace, it cost him a twinge of pain. Maybe Dieter's punch and kick had done some damage.

But not enough to keep Adolph from edging forwards, knife extended, or beginning another incantation.

Dieter shouted, and his voice was thunder. The deafening bellow jolted the ground and knocked twigs and leaves out of the trees. The spectators staggered.

At the very least, Adolph should have done the same. The blast of sound should have rocked him back, spoiling his conjuring, possibly stunned him or broken bones. But none of that happened. Evidently buttressed by some protective charm or his innate mystical strength, he stood steady despite the roar. Indeed, it was Dieter, taxed by the extreme effort the thunder spell required, who swayed and tottered.

Adolph's form fractured anew. The image moving ahead of the others spun darkness from its fist, a continuous length of shade that whirled at Dieter like a whip.

Even forewarned, Dieter could tell he wouldn't be able to get out of the way. The true attack would arc at him too quickly, even as it would reach farther than he could retreat. But as he contemplated the curling shadow, he glimpsed the intricate pattern of deeper and lesser darkness comprising it, and that in turn enabled him to understand the binding more profoundly than he ever had before.

He made no effort to avoid the shadow whip, and it cut him and coiled tight around him. Adolph jerked on the other end of the lash and dumped him on the ground. The cultist then rushed forwards, knife gripped overhand. He realised that, given a few moments, Dieter could likely dissolve the binding with a counter spell, and he meant to finish him before he could recite the words.

But thanks to his heightened understanding, Dieter only needed a single word. Enduring the stinging embrace of the binding as best he could, he waited until Adolph was standing over him ready to stab, then gasped it out.

Instantly obedient as a loyal and well-trained hound, the black coils released him, leaped at Adolph, and whirled themselves around the scribe. Immobilised, Adolph toppled and fell across the body of his foe.

Dieter squirmed out from underneath, then straddled Adolph's back. He reached to grip the cultist's neck and strangle the life out of him, then realised that even that wouldn't provide an adequate outlet for the hate and fury burning in his guts. It would be more satisfying to kill the other man by beating him to death. It would likely take a lot more effort, too, but Dieter didn't feel exhausted any more. He grabbed a rock.

Every time he smashed the stone into the back of Adolph's head, he bellowed. Blood splattered, and bone crunched. In time, the dark coils dissolved, but by then, the scribe had long since lost the ability to resist.

Indeed, a part of Dieter comprehended that he was now simply battering a corpse. Still, he couldn't bring himself to stop until agony stabbed through his skull, eclipsing his rage and robbing him of his hysterical strength in an instant. It was the onset of a headache the like of which he'd never known, and as he started to weep with the pain, he inferred it was the price for using the exotic capabilities of his new eye.

even if he did, he'd likely mistake it for a comr-
ish or meaningless little bump

CHAPTER TEN

DIETER STUDIED HIS face in the dainty hand-held looking glass, plunder from one of the caravans the brigands had despoiled. An ordinary person might have thought it strange that any mutant would want to possess such an item, but some if not all of them plainly gloried in their deformities.

But Dieter most emphatically did not, and now tried to find reason for hope in the fact that his own alteration wasn't as conspicuous as it might have been. When last night's headache began, his third eye had closed and remained so until he deliberately opened it again. Further experimentation had revealed that, at least under normal circumstances, he should be able to keep it shut when he needed to.

With the lid down, an observer probably wouldn't notice there was anything peculiar about his forehead, and even if he did, he'd likely mistake it for a common blemish or meaningless little bump.

Dieter swiped his hair down over his brow, and that was better still. Cosmetics might help too, when he could lay his hands on the right shade.

Finally he murmured a charm. Illusion and disguise were the province of the Grey wizards, but the minor lore available to all magicians included petty charms of diversion and obfuscation, and it was his good fortune that he'd learned a couple.

With the enchantment in place, the third eye was virtually invisible, or at least he thought so. But perhaps he was so desperate he was deluding himself. He turned towards Leopold Mann, who, despite his lack of any eyes at all, seemed to perceive as much as any sighted person. 'Tell me the truth. Is it hidden?'

'I can't tell it's there,' shrilled the outlaw chieftain, sitting on the ground with his back against an elm, and a strip of bacon, the last of his breakfast, in his clawed and furry hand. 'That doesn't mean a witch hunter wouldn't.'

Dieter shrugged. 'I'll just have to take my chances.'

'No,' said Mann, 'you don't. You're one of us now, so why not stay with us? Why go back to Altdorf where you'll be in danger every moment?'

'I already was, just by virtue of serving the Red Crown.'

'Not like you will be henceforth. You think you can hold the eye shut, but what if you can't? What if the god marks you a second time, with a change you can't conceal? The authorities will burn you for certain.'

Yes, they would, and perhaps if Dieter had any sense, he would remain with the brigands. Like Jarla, Mama Solveig, and all the cultists except for Adolph, they'd been friendly and hospitable to him, and Krieger wouldn't be able to get at him if he joined their fellowship.

Yet he still wanted his old life back. He could live it while concealing a deformity if he had to, and maybe he wouldn't, not permanently, anyway. He was a magician, and it was a kind of magic that had altered him. Given time, perhaps he could find a way to change himself back.

The alternative was to abandon not merely his possessions and station but his very self, to become completely and irredeemably the creature that had revelled in smashing Adolph's skull and craved the filthy lore of Chaos the way a sot craved drink. What was the difference between such a surrender and death?

'Thank you for the offer,' he said. 'It's more than generous, considering how we began.'

Mann waved the bacon in a dismissive gesture. 'The bloodshed was Adolph's fault, not yours.'

'Be that as it may, I can't stay. Maybe someday, but not now. I need to go back to tell the coven what happened. That the supplies were lost, and we need to get more to you as soon as possible. Besides, as I mentioned when Adolph and I were arguing back and forth, I have a woman waiting for me.'

Mann snorted. 'That last is the true reason, isn't it? Amazing how stupid a man can be when he thinks with the wrong organ. All right, go, but return before your luck runs out, and bring her with you.'

'Thank you.' Dieter hesitated. 'Will you satisfy my curiosity about something?'

Mann shrugged. 'If I can. What is it?'

'The Master of Change. For us of the Red Crown, he's the centre of everything, but Mama Solveig hardly tells me anything about him. She says her reticence makes us all safer, and maybe it does, but I can't help wondering about him. It's my nature. Now you, you're in communication with him. You must know things I don't.'

Mann smiled, baring his rows of fangs. 'Not so much as you hope. Not nearly enough to satisfy my own curiosity. Not long after I started to change, escaped to the forest, and met up with a few others like me, a voice spoke to me from the empty air. It told me I could make myself an outlaw chieftain and take revenge on those who'd condemned me, that conspirators in Altdorf would help me, and it all turned out to be true. The Red Crown started sending supplies and information not long after.'

'And that's all the Master's ever been to you? A voice coming out of nowhere?'

'I'm afraid so.'

Dieter sighed. He'd turned into a mutant and nearly lost his life venturing here, and it hadn't brought him a step closer to completing his mission. He realised he'd been stymied for so long that it would have surprised him if things had worked out any differently.

DIETER REACHED ALTDORF at sunset, when both the sky behind the city's countless spires and the river cutting through it burned red as fire. The sight of the towering torch-lit gate froze him in place.

He'd begged a hooded cloak from the mutants to help conceal his third eye. Yet despite that and all his other precautions, he suddenly felt an irrational pang of near-certainty that the guards would spot his mutation. Everybody on the street would notice. The only rational course of action was to turn and flee back the way he'd come.

Instead, he drew a deep breath, squared his shoulders, and hiked on towards the entry, where the sentries permitted him to pass through without so much as a question.

On the avenues and in the plazas, it was the same. His heart hammered and his muscles clenched whenever people chanced to glance in his direction, but their gaze always drifted incuriously on.

Gradually his fear abated to a degree, making space for a sort of crazy exhilaration. It was exciting to fool everyone. It woke his sense of mocking superiority. He knew that malicious arrogance was a manifestation of his ongoing psychic transformation and had often tried to suppress it, but not now. It was better than being terrified.

He found Jarla on the corner where she often plied her trade. When she noticed him, she ran to him and threw herself into his arms. The embrace both warmed him and quickened a different sort of fear. He didn't want to lose her – for one thing, her companionship kept him from feeling quite so utterly alone – and it was possible he might.

'Mama said not to worry,' she murmured, 'but when you were late coming back, I couldn't help it. I was afraid soldiers searched the wagon or followed you or something.'

'Nothing like that,' he replied, 'but I did run into trouble. I need to tell you about it, but not standing on the street. Can we go to your room?'

Jarla said yes, of course, conducted him to her shabby little stall, and shut the door behind them. The cramped space smelled as stale as usual. She lit a candle, and then they sat down side by side on the bed. 'What happened?' she asked.

'Adolph tried to get rid of me. He killed Lampertus and told the outlaws I did it, so they'd murder me in turn.'

She winced. 'I was so afraid he meant to hurt you.'

'In the end, he wasn't able to make the lie stick. Leopold ordered a trial by combat to decide who was telling the truth, and I won. To do it, I had to kill Adolph.'

He held his breath as he watched to see how she'd react. For after all, she'd known and loved Adolph long before she ever met Dieter, and he suspected the scribe still held a place in her heart. She wasn't the sort of person to turn her back entirely on anyone who'd given her affection, however selfish or abusive.

Such being the case, could she forgive the man who'd slain Adolph? Would she even believe the reason why? If not, it seemed unlikely that any of the other cultists would credit it.

Tears flowed from her eyes, cutting channels in the paint on her face. 'Thank our lord you're safe.' She pressed her lips to his, and, relieved, touched by her devotion, he returned the kiss just as fiercely and fumbled with the fastenings of her dress.

Afterwards, he lay blissfully spent on his back, and, propping herself on one elbow, she smiled and studied his face from mere inches away. It was then that she gently caressed the lid of his third eye with her fingertip. 'What's this?' she asked.

He meant to tell her he'd simply suffered a blow to the head while fighting Adolph. Unfortunately, the eye chose that moment to open of its own accord. Jarla gasped and jerked backwards.

Appalled that she'd seen the deformity, Dieter wanted to cringe, but then shame gave way to a surge of anger. How dare she find him monstrous when she professed that she wanted to change, also? When she herself had led him to the cult, the icon, and so bore responsibility for all that followed?

He sat up and closed his fist to strike her, and then she started to sob. 'Now you'll have to go away, and how am I supposed to stand it?'

Was it possible she wasn't repulsed? He put her hand on her shoulder, and she didn't pull away. 'This… change. It doesn't sicken you?'

Eyes squinched shut in a futile attempt to stanch the stream of tears, she shook her head. 'It startled me. Maybe I'd need to get used to it. But I would, except that I won't get the chance. You'll go back to the raiders and I'll never see you again.'

'I promise that won't happen.'

She blinked. 'Everyone who changes goes to the forest.'

'They don't need to if they can hide what they are. I can, and if a time ever comes when I can't, I already have Leopold Mann's permission to bring you with me when I join his band.'

'Truly? The two of you already talked about it?'

'Truly. I wouldn't leave you behind.'

'Thank you!' She kissed him, and he tasted the salty tang of her tears. For a moment, he felt he adored her with all his heart, and then the notion seemed ridiculous.

How could genuine love exist between them when she didn't even know who he really was? When he lied to her every hour they spent together? When he intended to destroy the cause to which she'd pledged her life even though it might well entail destroying her along with it?

Yet he felt what he felt. It was true and false, real and unreal, just as Tzeentch's teachings would have predicted. Just as all the world supposedly was when a person saw it clearly.

IN TIME, DIETER came to find the situation comical, albeit in a grotesque sort of way. He'd returned from the wilderness with a ghastly deformity right in the middle of his face and the blood of a fellow cultist on his hands, and yet nothing changed.

Glimpsed and dismissed by the blind, indifferent gazes of countless labourers, beggars, merchants, and even soldiers and priests, he walked the teeming streets of Altdorf as unremarked as ever. Jarla still loved him, and as far as he could tell, neither Mama Solveig nor any of the other cultists held Adolph's death against him. They'd all been aware of the scribe's jealousy and rancour, and they remembered how his reckless experimentation with magic had nearly killed them. Perhaps, though no one said it outright, they believed they were well rid of him.

Dieter supposed that, generally speaking, he was lucky that things continued just as before, but in one respect, it was as unfortunate as could be. He still had no idea how to discover the Master of Change's whereabouts.

He worried about the problem as he accompanied Mama Solveig on her rounds, taught his pupils in the coven petty magic that he hoped would prove useless for committing treason, and pored over the forbidden parchments. He knew his studies were self-destructive, perhaps the gravest of all the perils facing him. Yet he returned to blasphemous texts again and again, and feared he always would so long as they were available. His only hope was to complete his mission, then hand the documents over to Krieger or throw them in a fire.

Late one night, he sat and read with Mama Solveig's soft snore buzzing from the darkness enshrouding the cellar. The wavering light of a single taper illuminated Tzeentch's ebony leer and the pentacle chalked on the floor. He'd used the candle to light his way to the shrine, but no longer needed any such implement to peruse the parchments. The characters glowed like hot coals as soon as he touched the pages.

It was strange how he could read the same words over and over again, and yet his fascination never abated. Perhaps it was a symptom of incipient insanity. He smirked at the thought, then wondered why, for a moment, he'd found it so amusing.

The writing on the page began to flicker as ripples of brightness ran through it. Certain characters shined more brightly, while others dimmed.

Excitement swept all of Dieter's worries and discouragement away. A new truth, maybe a new enchantment, was about to reveal itself.

It was a spell, and unlike the magic Adolph had unleashed to imperil the entire coven, in no way ambiguous or enigmatic. Its purpose and the proper way of performing it were immediately apparent. Indeed, they almost seemed to brand themselves on his understanding.

With comprehension came a spasm of nausea so powerful that, for the moment at least, it even loosened the grip of his obsession. He'd appeased his helpless hunger, gorged on the magic even though it sickened him, and now perhaps he could rest. He put the parchments back on the lectern, picked up the candle, and made his way towards his cot.

Mama Solveig snorted and groaned in her sleep. The noise snagged Dieter's attention, and, fatigue and revulsion both forgotten, he began to reflect on her and the problem she represented. That in itself wasn't unusual. He did it every day. But now his thoughts ran in a new direction, as if the lore of Chaos had stimulated his mind.

The midwife was the coven's sole link to the Master of Change. He'd understood that from the first time he met her, but had found himself unable to turn the knowledge to his advantage. Now, perhaps, he was starting to grasp how, but it took several hours of sleepless rumination before he realised how the new spell could figure in his plans. Maybe that was because he hadn't wanted to see.

FIRST, HE HAD to find a place to work. He couldn't perform the ritual in the cellar for fear Mama Solveig would return home unexpectedly and catch him. Nor could he cast the spell out in the open. Someone else might see, quite possibly a wizard, sensitive to the play of unnatural forces, or one of the ubiquitous witch hunters, and even if that weren't the case, he couldn't bear the thought of engaging in such obscenity beneath the sacred living sky.

In the teeming capital city, privacy proved elusive, but eventually he noticed a small, dilapidated brick warehouse above the Reik. From the look of it, it was deserted. Most likely, it had served some failed mercantile venture, and the owner hadn't yet managed to sell it or find a renter. In any event, it would do for Dieter's purposes.

He bought a lamb and left it inside the building with feed and water. Mama Solveig wandered off on her own three nights later. He hurried back to the warehouse, wrapped the struggling animal in a cast net he'd pilfered from the docks nearby, then tied its mouth shut.

Once that was accomplished, the ritual could commence. He chanted the first invocation. Other voices seemed to whisper the words along with him, and a choking carrion stench filled the air. The lamb writhed and bucked, fighting to break free of the mesh.

It struggled even harder when he drew his knife and starting cutting it. Its flailing and the obstruction of the net made it difficult to carve the glyphs with the proper precision, but with patience and care, he managed.

It came to him as he strained to hold the lamb still, stabbed and sliced, that perhaps the exactness of the symbols was less crucial than a college-trained wizard might have assumed. It was more important that the animal suffer intensely and that it be thoroughly mutilated, stripped of any ability to walk or breed or see, that its tormentor transform it into a squirming, bleeding rebuttal of the very concepts of health and happiness as the general run of men understood them.

It was likewise important that the magician enjoy the animal's terror and pain. Only thus could he properly attune his spirit. Dieter had questioned his ability even to perform such cruel acts, let alone take pleasure in them, and in fact, a moment arrived when he found himself unable to make the next cut. His old self shrank from the act in nausea and self-loathing. But the new Dieter, born of exposure to Tzeentch's icon and blasphemous lore, full of anger and the will to dominate, to be the hammer and not the anvil, stepped from the darkness to assume control of his wet red hands. Afterwards, he sneered as he worked, and even laughed from time to time.

Eventually, the lamb bled out. He carved one last glyph, then brandished the knife in ritual passes and commenced a final incantation. His third eye throbbed to the rhythm.

As he drew breath to recite the concluding couplet, agony stabbed through the centre of his forehead as if something had smashed open his skull to expose the brain inside. He screamed, then seemed to hurtle upwards through the breach in his head, sudden, fast and helpless as a ball shot from a gun.

CHAPTER ELEVEN

DIETER FLOATED SO high above the world that he could see it curve. His vicious elation had vanished and so had his pain, both supplanted by fear and confusion.

It seemed obvious that his ritual was responsible for his current situation. But this was scarcely the effect he'd intended, and the magic had exploded into existence before he completed his conjuring.

Did that mean he'd botched the casting? If so, what was the consequence? What was it that had actually happened to him?

He had hands he could see when he held them in front of his face, and that felt solid to one another when he clasped them together. Still, a normal human body could scarcely have drifted on the wind this way. He must be pure spirit now, plucked from its shell of flesh and bone. But was it a temporary separation, or was it possible magic had literally shattered his head? If so, his body was a corpse, and he, a ghost.

The thought was distressing but, to his surprise, sparked a perverse sort of hope as well. For if he was dead, mightn't that mean he was done with struggle and desperation? Beyond the reach of doubt and fear?

The face of the land altered, or rather, his perception of it did. Though he hadn't dropped any lower, he could suddenly see the heights and valleys seething with life like a busy anthill. It defied common sense that anyone could observe individual men and women or even the grandest works of humanity from such an altitude, yet he was doing it nonetheless. Somehow, he even knew their thoughts.

A farmer planted and tended his crops with the utmost diligence. Drought seared them, and he and his family starved.

A ruffian knifed a friend in a drunken brawl, and a magistrate sentenced him to hang for it. Then, however, the count announced his betrothal, and in celebration emptied out the jails. The murderer continued to kill, for profit now, and was never caught again. He lived a long, happy life on the proceeds.

The lake always froze solid as stone in winter. No one could remember a time when it hadn't. Yet the little girl skated over a thin spot and crashed through. The villagers found her body after the thaw.

A mother lavished care and affection on her children until a lump flowered in her brain. Then voices whispered, exhorting her to deliver them from sin. To that end, she whipped them every day.

A man digging in his garden unearthed a chest of old gold coins. Miserly by nature, he reburied them, told no one of their existence, and lived meanly all the days of his life. Even as he lay dying, he kept the secret, condemning his neighbours, kindly folk all, to poverty.

It was all unjust and ultimately cruel, for even those few people who attained some measure of happiness came to loss and infirmity by and by. Worse, it was senseless and uncontrollable. No matter how wisely a man laid his plans and how hard he laboured, it was happenstance that determined his fate in the end.

But though the tale of human existence lacked any point or semblance of moral order, it did display a progression. As the generations passed, Chaos crept through the world and all that man had built like an infestation of rats taking possession of a house. Monstrous armies swept down from the north to sack cities and lay waste to principalities. Mutants were born in increasing numbers. Converts flocked to hidden altars to offer to Tzeentch and his ilk.

Emperors and other lords of mankind did everything in their power to drive back devastation and decay. Indeed, they fought so savagely they became horrors in their own right. Yet it was all to no avail, and as defeat followed defeat, the world itself transformed. Trees grew shaggy pelts instead of bark. Horses chased and devoured prey like wolves. Rivers dried up one hour and ran deep with blood the next. New stars flared into being as if someone were stabbing wounds in the sky. Until finally, Dieter could see no difference between the actual world and the landscape of his nightmares, nor between Tzeentch's warriors and the gibbering, shambling beasts mankind had become.

He screamed, and at last the spectacle ended.

Or at least it shrank to a scale the human mind might apprehend without breaking. Everything whirled and broke apart, and then he stood on a strip of bone-white sand beside a crimson sea. As the waves broke, images formed and dissolved in the foam, providing glimpses of the tortures he'd inflicted on the lamb.

Before him stood a familiar figure in a cowled brown robe.

Dieter swallowed. 'All this time, I thought you were a figment of my imagination.'

The priest cocked his head. For a moment, his eyes caught the crimson colour of the waves. 'Have we met before?'

'Don't play games. You're the creature who's been working to corrupt me.'

The older man smiled. 'Time has little meaning here. That's why you were able to watch the future of your world unfold. It also allows me to see you in the past as well as the present, and it looks to me as if you worked to corrupt yourself. You worshipped the Changer's icon and conjured Dark Magic. Perhaps you even invented a phantom tempter you could blame to ease your conscience.'

'If my "tempter" wasn't you, then why do you look exactly like the figure I saw before?'

The priest smiled. 'I can look like a great many things' – his shape seemed to flicker as if he'd become something else, then turned back again, too quickly for Dieter's eyes to quite follow the double change – 'but most of them would strain what's left of your sanity. This guise seemed more conducive to conversation.'

Dieter took a deep breath. It was frustrating that the priest wouldn't admit he'd been haunting him all along, but did it truly matter? Perhaps he'd do better to focus on the business at hand. 'I was trying to summon a daemon.'

'And maybe you have.'

'You were supposed to appear before me in the warehouse.'

'It takes a great exertion of power for a daemon to fully manifest in the human realm. One day, it will be otherwise, but for now, it was less trouble for me to bring you here.'

Less trouble, Dieter thought glumly. It also made a mockery of the idea that he was truly in control of the proceedings.

'Don't worry,' the priest continued, 'you aren't dead. Assuming we reach an accord, you can return to your flesh. Which I suppose is bad news for the race of sheep.' He grinned – for just an instant, the leer made his face look like a naked skull, but then it was the same as ever – and waved his hand at the visions in the breaking waves. Shooting stars arced across the sky as if the heavens too were pointing at the sea.

'I conjured you,' Dieter said, trying to assert some semblance of the dominance that by rights should belong to the summoner, not the spirit, 'because I require a service.'

'Then you'd better tell me what it is.'

'I need you to kill Mama Solveig.'

'The doting old woman who took you in and cooked you all those wonderful meals? Won't you feel even more guilty when the treachery is done?'

Dieter scowled. 'My emotions are no concern of yours.'

The priest shrugged. 'Perhaps that's true. But I do have a legitimate concern. Solveig Weiss is a faithful servant of the Architect of Fate. Why, then, would I want to harm her?'

'What you want is irrelevant. You're going to kill her because I command it.'

'And if I resist, you'll chastise me. But are you certain you can master me on my home ground? Perhaps I can call a thousand maimed lambs bleating and floundering out of the surf to take their vengeance on you.'

Dieter raised his hands as if to conjure. 'If so, you'd better start them crawling.'

The priest laughed and lifted his own hands in a pacifistic gesture. His voluminous sleeves slid down his forearms. 'Easy! There's no need for unpleasantness, at least not yet. I was only teasing you. In truth, the god doesn't care about the old woman's welfare. He cares about you.'

'What do you mean?'

'Isn't it obvious? No matter how you try to run away from our lord, every stride carries you closer. You now wear his mark. Your knowledge of Chaos and its powers grows by the day. That's because the god has chosen you to be his sword, and is leading you down the path you walk to forge and temper you.'

'Nonsense.'

'Deep down, you know it isn't. But as it's your fate and accordingly inevitable, it isn't anything we need to quarrel about. Let's concentrate on the business that brought you here. I take it you hope that if Solveig Weiss dies, the Master of Change will choose you to succeed her as coven leader.'

'Yes.' At which point, the sorcerer would summon him to his lair, and he would at last discover where the damn place was.

'It's a reasonable hope,' said the priest. 'You're the ablest magician in your circle, and on top of that, the god has altered you, so who else would the Master pick? But do you really need a daemon to murder the crone? Just take her by the throat and choke her.'

'I have to make sure suspicion doesn't fall on me, so I can't kill her in the cellar, and it would be chancy doing it elsewhere. She has magic that alerts her when she's being followed, and any passer-by could observe me doing the deed. In addition to which, I'm still not certain just how formidable her sorcery is. All things considered, it just seems wiser to act through a powerful proxy like a daemon. Afterwards, my comrades of the Red Crown will assume the Purple Hand summoned the entity just as they conjured the fiery serpent.'

'I follow your reasoning, and I'm glad it isn't simply squeamishness that makes you baulk at butchering the old woman yourself. Nevertheless, that's what you'll have to do.'

'No, I'm commanding you to do it.'

'Command all you like. Neither you nor I have the power to keep me hovering about in your world until an opportune moment to strike arises. What I can do is teach you an enchantment to alter your form sufficiently to conceal your true identity. The spell may also help you get closer to your prey before she spots you, and aid you in actually making the kill. Are you interested?'

'Perhaps.'

'Then what will you give me in exchange?'

'Nothing. You're constrained to help me.'

'I wonder if we really will have to put that to the test.'

'You said the Changer of the Ways wants me to walk the path I'm on. If so, why should I have to barter? You should be eager to help me.'

'Maybe I should, but daemons tend to dislike helping humans. We certainly detest taking orders from them. And perhaps paying the price is the next step on the path. So: I'll help you kill Solveig Weiss and so further your schemes. But you will reward me for my trouble, or else suffer the consequences of your intransigence.'

Dieter hesitated. According to the principles of wizardry, he should be able to control an entity he'd summoned no matter how it sought to deceive and intimidate him. But in point of fact, he hadn't completed the ritual, it hadn't functioned as anticipated, and he had little confidence in his ability to return to his body without assistance. All in all, it made fighting a daemon in its own world about as unappealing a prospect as he could imagine.

Yet sealing any sort of covenant with the entity could prove equally disastrous. Daemons were infamous for the cunning malice with which they often perverted such compacts. Bargainers discovered too late that the treasures they'd acquired were actually curses, or that the seemingly token prices they'd agreed to pay entailed the forfeiture of their lives, their souls, or the slaughter of their loved ones.

Still, if Tzeentch really did mean for Dieter to survive this encounter relatively unscathed, and if he was careful, bargaining might be at least a little safer than battle, and the bleak truth was, now that he'd recklessly landed himself in this terrible place, he had to try something. 'What do you want?' he asked.

'Oh, how about a memory or two? I promise not to take anything you need. In fact, I'll only extract material that hinders you, that burdens you and slows you as you travel the Changer's road.'

'In other words, memories that buttress my sense of the man I truly am.'

The priest smiled. 'If your identity is so fragile that the loss of a few moments will annihilate it, then you might as well give it up now.'

'Promise me I'll still remember my identity and my mission. That I'll still possess all my magic, skills and faculties. That I'll remain just as capable as I am now.'

'Didn't I just guarantee as much? But very well. I agree to all your conditions. I swear by the Changer of the Ways. Now do we have a bargain?'

Dieter noticed he was breathing hard and struggled to control it. He flinched from the thought of trading away even a tiny portion of himself. But he feared it was necessary, and besides, a part of him, the part that grew stronger every day, wanted to learn the spell the priest had promised. He craved it as he'd come to hunger for every new piece of dark lore, no matter what it cost him.

'All right,' he said, 'I agree. But no tricks!'

The priest chuckled. 'I believe we already stipulated that. The way you keep harping on it, a person might almost imagine you're afraid.' He advanced to within arm's reach. 'If you'll allow me?' He raised his hand and touched his fingertips to Dieter's temple.

Pain ripped through Dieter's head. He cried out and stumbled.

'I'm sorry it's uncomfortable,' said the priest, 'but at least it's quick. Certainly quicker than squinting and puzzling over a musty old grimoire for days on end. Now go home and make me proud.'

He shifted his hand to the crown of Dieter's head and pushed downwards. Dieter's body plunged into the sand as if he were a tent peg, and a hammer stroke were sinking him deep into soft earth.

Then the blinding, smothering grit vanished, and he plummeted through a lightless, frigid void until that space disappeared just as abruptly. He landed in his own world and physical body with what felt like a considerable jolt, although, since pure spirit had no mass, he knew the shock was only in his mind.

Mouth dry and heart pounding, he cast about. The lamb's carcass looked no different. The candle he'd lit didn't appear to have burned any lower, nor did the blood on his hands feel any dryer. Apparently his sojourn in the realm of Chaos had only lasted a few moments.

He could feel the new knowledge in his head waiting to be savoured and explored, but for once, something else took precedence. He had an anguished sense of loss and violation, and with them came a stab of fear that the priest had broken his promise and taken something vital.

He thought of his parents and his childhood. His training at the Celestial College. Halmbrandt. His name. His mission. Jarla.

As promised, the contents of his memory seemed essentially intact. The priest certainly hadn't crippled him. Yet he couldn't shake the feeling that something precious was gone forever, and somehow, the fact that he had no way of even guessing what the recollection had been made the loss seem even more unbearable. He looked at the lamb again, remembered how he'd relished hurting it, and puked.

IN TIME, THE sense of loss faded. Though it continued to gnaw at Dieter, it loomed no larger than the rest of his countless worries.

He waited impatiently for Mama Solveig to give him the chance to strike at her, and tried to believe his eagerness stemmed from his desire to satisfy Krieger and go home. In large measure, it was even true. But he couldn't deny that he also yearned to cast the new enchantment simply for its own sake. He'd spent hours contemplating the incantation the priest had planted in his mind, but that was scarcely the same as actually experiencing the magic.

Finally, one night an hour after sunset, as he sat rereading the forbidden parchments, Mama Solveig hobbled up behind him and put her hand on his shoulder. 'I have calls to make,' she said, 'and then I thought I might stop at the Four Dancers. I like the minstrel who's singing there. Do you want to come along?'

Pulse ticking faster, he turned his head to smile at her. 'Unless you need me, I believe I'll stay here. I think I may finally be on the verge of figuring out how to cast the spell that Adolph found without the power turning against us.'

'It will be wonderful if you can. Well, there's cheese and baked apples left over from supper, and half a jug of ale. Go read by the hearth if you feel chilly. I think this old hole is getting danker and more draughty by the day!'

'Yes, Mama.'

She patted him on the shoulder, collected her basket and shawl, and eventually hobbled out the door.

He forced himself to count to fifty, just to make sure she didn't turn right around and come back in, either because she'd forgotten an item or thought of something else she wished to say. Then he sprang up from his seat, put the pages back on the lectern, drew a deep breath, and declaimed the first words of the incantation. A sickly-sweet smell suffused the air. The ceremonial wands and staves clinked and rattled in their storage rack.

As he started the final rhyming lines, he braced himself. Everything else he'd experienced as a result of his communication with the priest had been painful in one way or another. It seemed unlikely that this would be any different.

Yet it was. When the change took him, melting and reshaping him from the bones outward, the feeling was so pleasurable he laughed helplessly, as though putting aside humanity was the greatest ecstasy to which a person could aspire.

Once that wild elation faded, he inspected his hands. They were bigger and covered in black scales. His nails had lengthened and thickened into talons. The icon leered at the transformation.

Because his hands were so different in and of themselves, it took Dieter a moment to realise that vision itself had altered in some subtle fashion. His third eye was open, and for once, it probably didn't matter. Not if the enchantment had altered his face as thoroughly as it had his extremities.

He felt his features to see if that was in fact the case. Scales had sprouted there as well, and the lower half of his face had extended slightly into serpentine jaws. His teeth were fangs.

No, it wasn't likely anyone would recognise him. The trick would be to keep people from noticing his deformities as he pursued his victim, and the petty tricks that generally served to conceal his third eye were inadequate to the purpose. He cast about for the hooded cloak the mutants had given him, spotted it, and reached it in a single bound. That was wrong, and so, he abruptly realised, was the half-crouch which seemed to be his new body's natural posture. He needed to walk like a man, and stand up straight.

He should also get moving before he lost Mama Solveig's trail. He donned the mantle, pulled up the cowl to shadow his face, and headed out the door.

Head bowed as if by woe or weariness, trying not to shrink from the gaze of passers-by, he caught up with the hobbling old woman easily enough. Now that he was viewing her with his new eye, a purple shimmer crawled on her body. If she didn't sense his presence, he could attack as soon as she was alone.

Unfortunately, he suspected she wouldn't be alone any time soon. In fact, the streets were growing more crowded as she doddered towards a square notorious for its taverns, fighting pits and brothels.

Perhaps he could trust his cape and hood to protect him from the casual scrutiny of one or two folk at a time, but it was unlikely to do so if he ventured into close quarters with dozens at once. He wondered how he could continue following Mama Solveig, and instinct nudged him to look upwards.

For a moment, he imagined he was simply feeling the familiar lure of the sky, the Celestial wizard's fascination with the heavens that, thank the gods, had yet to fade no matter how he polluted himself with Chaotic lore. But that wasn't it. It was the rooflines that tugged at him, not the stars and clouds. He surmised that was because the form he'd adopted could clamber over the tops of the buildings as easily as it could traverse the streets that sliced and snaked between them.

He scuttled into an alley, glanced about to make sure no one was watching, then pulled off his shoes. They were cramping his feet anyway, because his lower extremities had enlarged, also. The toes were longer, and their nails were claws.

It turned out that scaling a wall was easy. He was stronger than he'd ever been before, and his talons dug deep into soot-stained, decaying brick and mortar. He reached the sloping, shingled roof in a matter of moments, then peered down until he spotted his quarry.

Mama Solveig doddered on and he trailed her, springing from one rooftop to the next when necessary. That, too, was generally easy. In the poorer precincts, the builders of Altdorf jammed in their structures close together.

Suddenly, the midwife froze. She peered about as if she'd lost her way.

Dieter surmised that in reality, she'd sensed someone was stalking her and was trying to identify her shadow. He crouched low and held himself still.

But he needn't have bothered. She didn't think to look above street level, and Dieter sneered at her foolishness.

She stopped twice more to cast about, and still it didn't occur to her to glance upwards. Meanwhile, her course carried her into darker, narrower streets, where fewer folk were walking. Dieter worried that she'd realise she was safer in a crowd, turn, and retrace her steps, but she didn't. Instead she hobbled into the enclosed passage, in effect a sort of tunnel, that ran between two buildings.

Dieter dashed along the roof of the walkway. No one was in the courtyard at the far end, which made it a perfect place to close with his quarry at last. He poised himself to leap down on her the instant she stepped out into the open.

Unfortunately, she didn't, and eventually, he realised he wasn't going to. She was hiding in the corridor to waylay her stalker just as she'd surprised Dieter beside the river.

Which was to say, she could have chosen a safer course of action, but had instead decided to discover and confront whatever danger threatened her and, by extension, the coven she led. It occurred to Dieter that it was a courageous choice. It inspired respect, and with respect came uncertainty.

He didn't want to kill an old woman who'd been kind to him. Who could say that it would actually force the Master of Change to reveal himself? Dieter's mind was sick and at least half-addled with desperation and forbidden knowledge, so it seemed entirely possible that his plan was crazy as well.

But no. Curse it, no. He wouldn't fall prey to qualms and misgivings now. Mama Solveig was a monster. She turned innocent people into monsters. She'd turned Dieter himself into a mutant, or started the process, anyway. She deserved to die, and even had it been otherwise, this scheme was the only one he had, his last chance of regaining the life Krieger had stolen from him.

Besides, it wasn't really true that Dieter didn't want to kill her. A part of him did. It would revel in her destruction as it had the lamb's.

She was presumably peering out at the end of the passage that opened on the street. He could take her from behind if he attacked from the courtyard side.

As he crawled down the wall headfirst, he wondered whether to assault her with a spell or brute force. In almost any circumstance, he would have opted for the former. But if he ripped her with his claws, the manner of her death would lend credence to the notion that some inhuman agent of the Purple Hand had slain her.

In addition to which, he was curious to see how it would feel. That, too, was a part of experiencing this new magic for the first time.

Planning to creep down the passage, he flipped to the ground. Mama Solveig was at the other end of the walkway just as he'd expected. What he hadn't anticipated was that she was looking right at him. Somehow she'd finally discerned or simply guessed where he was.

Dieter charged her, and she recited words of power. Though she spoke softly, her high, quavering voice echoed in the enclosed space, with each repetition louder than the last. She lashed her arm through the air, and splinters of darkness hurtled from her hand.

Dieter leaped high and to the side, but the darts diverged as they flew, and despite his attempt to dodge, one pierced his leg. He hissed at the pain, and stumbled when his foot thumped back down on the ground.

He realised he could no longer run or spring with the same nimbleness and speed as before. Mama Solveig evidently recognised it, too, because she judged she'd have time for a second spell before he closed with her. Backing away, but slowly, so as not to hamper her conjuring, she recited and swirled her hands through mystic passes.

Dieter almost laughed. She was casting the shadow binding, the spell that he now knew how to turn against the caster. Thanks to her previous attack, he was limping already, and now he exaggerated it, slowing down and making sure she had time to finish.

She whirled a twisting length of darkness from her hand. He spoke to it as he'd spoken when Adolph sought to snare him with the same effect.

Or rather, he tried. It was the first time he'd attempted to talk since his transformation, and now he discovered that reshaping his jaws and tongue had cost him the ability to articulate without care or effort. The word came out too sibilant and slurred.

So, naturally, the binding didn't heed it. It whirled around him and snapped tight, stinging him and tying his legs together. He toppled to the ground amid the shards of a broken wine bottle.

Doing his best to ignore the hot, stabbing pain of his bonds, he tried twice more to speak the word of command, and still couldn't manage it correctly. Meanwhile, Mama Solveig chanted. Luminous cracks zigzagged and forked through the stone walls and ceiling as the repeated evocations of Chaotic forces hammered at the structure of reality.

The old woman cast another barrage of darts. Dieter rolled, jabbing and grinding pieces of broken glass into his body. He dodged some of the missiles, but two more pierced him, and he bucked in agony.

Such attacks weren't like spear thrusts. They didn't leave open, bleeding, tangible wounds. But they could kill nonetheless, and surely would, if he had to endure many more of them.

In desperation, he began the counter spell his masters at the Celestial College had taught him. It was comprised of a number of words, any of which his deformed mouth might conceivably mispronounce. But he'd cast it successfully hundreds of times, during his apprenticeship and after. Perhaps all that practice would offset his handicap.

At the same time, Mama Solveig rummaged in her basket. He wondered if, deeming him helpless, she thought it safe to come close and employ a blade or some toxic agent to finish him off.

He whispered the final word of his incantation. His bonds frayed into nothingness. He scrambled to his feet and lunged at Mama Solveig.

Her eyes opened as wide as they could go, but surprise didn't paralyse her. Magenta glow oozing on her hunched, skinny form, she slashed her hand through the air and screamed a single word.

Already cracked and weakened, a portion of the ceiling shattered, and chunks of stone dropped. Dieter leaped to get out from under them, but some of them caught him anyway, bashing him back down onto the ground.

Mama Solveig had never taught him that spell. Maybe it was a secret weapon she'd kept from everyone, or maybe she hadn't known it herself until now. Perhaps it was knowledge that had insinuated itself into her unconscious mind as she studied dark lore, to reveal itself at the moment she needed it most.

Dieter struggled to shrug off the weight of the rubble. Maybe this show of resilience made Mama Solveig fear he was unstoppable, because, whirling and running like a woman forty years younger, she fled back out into the night. In a moment, she was lost to sight.

Dieter floundered up from the broken stone, and, his whole body throbbing and aching, staggered out of the passage. He cast about and spotted a smear of purplish glimmer vanishing around a corner. Thanks to his new eye, he hadn't lost the trail.

He dashed after Mama Solveig as fast as his abused and battered body could go. Maybe he should try to hammer her with a blast of wind or a shout infused with thunder as soon as she came back into view. He'd thought to rend her with his claws and avoid using magic that anyone might associate with Celestial wizards in general or himself in particular. But now, after all the punishment he'd absorbed, he just wanted to make the kill as expeditiously as possible.

He rounded the corner and was pleased to see she wasn't as far ahead as he'd expected. Even if her usual appearance of feebleness was only a mask, her exertions were apparently taking a toll. He halted, drew a deep breath, and raised his hands.

It was then that half a dozen soldiers, a watch patrol, judging from the lantern on a pole the first one carried, emerged from a side street several paces ahead of Mama Solveig. At once she resumed her hobble and became a perfect picture of fragile senescence once again.

'Help!' she gasped. 'Mutant! Chasing me!' She peered back down the street, then pointed. 'There it is!'

The soldier with the lantern peered, cursed, set the light on the ground, and drew his sword. His comrades readied their own weapons, and they all trotted forwards.

Dieter had no desire to hurt them, nor did he want to give them a chance to hurt him. But, limping as he was, he doubted he could escape them even if he tried, which meant he had to fight. It was either that or be cut down from behind.

Enunciating carefully, he spoke to the sky, and knives of light flashed from his outstretched hand. The missiles pierced two of the soldiers, and they dropped.

Their comrades baulked. Backing away, Dieter whispered another charm. Hoping that he'd begun to master the trick of pronouncing his words properly even with a reptilian mouth and tongue, he risked speaking more quickly.

One word came out slightly garbled, but the heavens saw fit to help him anyway. Blue light outlined his limbs. Layered on top of his scales, the mystical protection might suffice to protect him from the soldiers' blades.

He gave them a level stare. 'You see how it is,' he said. 'I'm a sorcerer. If you make it necessary, I can strike every one of you dead. So don't. I have nothing against you, and the old woman isn't what she seems. Just walk away–'

One soldier howled a battle cry, and then they all charged.

Dieter struggled to stave off panic and think. It seemed obvious that they'd try to surround him, and that he needed to prevent it if he could. He faked a step backwards, then sprang at them instead.

The sudden pounce took them by surprise. Even so, the soldier directly in front of him did a fair job of swinging his sword into line, but the armour of light deflected it, and the point glanced off Dieter's shoulder.

The soldier managed to block with his round steel shield as well. Dieter crashed into it, and his momentum slammed the obstruction back into the soldier's body and knocked him staggering. A backhand swipe of Dieter's claws slashed horizontal cuts across his face.

Dieter felt both savage satisfaction and revulsion, and knew he had no time for either. He whirled to find out what the other soldiers were doing.

They'd already turned to threaten him anew. Fortunately, stumbling about, helpless with shock, pain, or, conceivably, the loss of his eyes, the soldier Dieter had clawed was in their way. Dieter grabbed him and shoved him into one of his fellows, and the pair fell to the ground together.

For the moment, that left two soldiers to menace Dieter. Hoping that simple tricks and fierce aggression would continue to serve him well, he faked a grab at one man, then pivoted and lunged at the other.

His target warded himself with a deft shift of his shield that was virtually an attack in its own right. Dieter slammed into the rock-solid barrier with bruising, stunning force, rebounded and reeled off-balance.

His momentary loss of equilibrium gave the soldiers time to flank him. He retreated, bounded this way and that, trying to get out from in between them, but they matched him step for step.

Meanwhile, their swords leaped at him. He dodged some strokes, and so far, the others were only slicing shallow cuts. He knew that luck couldn't hold. His defences notwithstanding, it wouldn't be long before one of his adversaries struck hard and true enough to kill him.

He, of course, struck back at those infrequent moments when the pressure of their onslaught abated sufficiently to allow it. His new body was strong and quick – or at least it had been before enduring so much abuse – and seemed equipped with a feral instinct for physical combat that the human Dieter could never have matched. Unfortunately, that wasn't enough to offset the soldiers' advantages of training, teamwork, and the longer reach their swords afforded them. Nor could he cast a spell with the blades flashing at him so relentlessly.

The soldier he'd merely knocked down clambered to his feet and came running to assist his comrades, and that surely meant the end of the fight was at hand. Dieter was about to die.

Or so he assumed until he glimpsed motion from the corner of his eye. He glanced and spied Mama Solveig lashing her hands through the passes required for the binding spell. It had held him once, for a few heartbeats anyway, and she evidently assumed it would do so long enough for the soldiers to dispatch him.

It was a considerable miscalculation from someone who was generally so shrewd. Even though they weren't looking at her, she was running a risk using magic in the soldiers' presence, and they certainly didn't need her aid to kill him. She should have been able to tell that, but evidently his monstrous appearance and dogged pursuit had so rattled her that she couldn't.

Or perhaps Tzeentch had clouded her judgement because he had plans for Dieter, just as the priest had claimed.

Dieter thrust that ghastly notion out of his mind. He couldn't afford to think about that or anything but dodging, blocking and keeping the soldiers' blades out of his vitals for a few more tortured breaths.

A coil of darkness spun from Mama Solveig's hand. He spoke to it, and this time pronounced the word of usurpation clearly. Two of the soldiers were standing close enough together for the length of shadow to entangle them both, and it spun around their upper bodies and smashed them together. They lurched off-balance and fell with a clash of shields and armour.

Dieter pivoted towards his remaining opponent to find the soldier's sword streaking in a horizontal arc at his neck. He barely managed to duck beneath the cut, then grabbed the other man's fighting arm before he could recover. He gave it a vicious yank and twist, his claws shearing muscle and his strength popping it out of the socket. The soldier's face turned white, and the hilt of his weapon slipped from his fingers.

Now that his foe was helpless, Dieter wanted to kill him, wanted to butcher all the soldiers who were still alive. Why not? They'd done their utmost to slaughter him. But the ashen, wide-eyed face beneath the helmet looked very young, a boy's visage, not a man's, and perhaps that was what made him hesitate. He reminded himself Mama Solveig was the real enemy, and these wretches, merely her dupes, and it gave him the strength to throw the lad to the ground and pivot in her direction.

She fled, and he sprinted after her. His wounded leg throbbed every time his foot impacted the street, but he was too furious for the pain to baulk him.

At the last moment, she tried to turn and face him, but she was too slow. He leaped onto her shoulders and carried her down beneath him.

He hooked his claws in the sides of her neck and pulled, shearing flesh. Blood spurted from severed arteries. He knew that was sufficient, she'd be dead in a moment or two if she wasn't already, but he was too excited to let it end so quickly. He flipped her over onto her back and ripped at her face and torso.

It wasn't until he'd obliterated every trace of her features that he started to calm down, and then he noticed the shreds of raw, gory meat caught on his talons. It occurred to him that the old woman could give him one last meal, and the notion made him smirk. He raised his right hand to his mouth.

LIKE A GOOD many of the dolts who patronised the Axe and Fingers, Niklas the pawnbroker erroneously fancied himself a wit. Leering, he served up the same lewd plays on words Jarla heard at least once a night, that she had, in fact, heard a dozen times from him. She giggled and replied in kind, leaned over as she served him his beer so he could see down her bodice, and eventually breathed an invitation in his ear.

Eager as she'd expected, he stood up so quickly he nearly overturned his chair, and inwardly, she winced. It was strange. Dieter never sneered at her for being a whore, and yet, now that he was her lover, selling her favours seemed more difficult and unpleasant than it ever had when she was with Adolph.

At least Niklas always finished quickly. She'd close her eyes and imagine herself elsewhere while he poked away at her, and maybe it wouldn't be too bad. The pawnbroker produced a purse from within his jerkin, loosened the drawstring, and then, as if Jarla's thoughts had summoned him, Dieter limped in the tavern door.

She gasped at his cuts, bruises and scrapes, torn clothing and dazed, sick expression. If he felt as wretched as he looked, it was lucky he still possessed the wit to hold his third eye closed.

She started towards him, and a hand grabbed her forearm from behind. 'I'm first,' Niklas said.

She pivoted, wrenching herself free. 'Not now,' she snapped. Niklas opened his mouth, presumably to object. 'Leave me alone!' The pawnbroker flinched, then snorted and turned away.

Jarla rushed to Dieter. Up close, his clothing and breath smelled of vomit. 'What happened?' she asked. He shook his head to indicate that he wasn't up to explaining yet, or that he couldn't do it in public.

'We'll go upstairs,' she said. She put her arm around him, guided him in the proper direction, then noticed the barman's glare. He wasn't happy with her for rebuffing Niklas or for what she intended now, either, because no money had changed hands. 'I'll pay for the room,' she told him.

It was scarcely worth paying for, just a tiny stale-smelling hole even more squalid than the stall in which she made her home. But it had a door to separate the occupants from the outside world, and a bed for them to rest on. Jarla sat Dieter down on top of the straw mattress, took him in her arms, and then he started to sob.

She rubbed his back and waited for him to cry himself out. It took a long time, but he finally stopped shaking and lifted his head from her shoulder. His eyes were bloodshot. He had ruddy blotches on his face and mucus on his upper lip.

She wiped his nose. 'Tell me what happened,' she said.

He hesitated, and she felt a pang of uneasiness. She was upset already, of course, profoundly upset to see him so distraught, but this was different.

He'd obviously run to her for comfort, and such being the case, she would have expected that, when the time came to explain what was wrong, the story would have gushed out like his tears. Instead, he had the air of a man calculating precisely what to say.

But surely that couldn't be so. He loved and trusted her too much to withhold or manipulate the truth. It was just that, in the wake of his ordeal, whatever it had been, he needed a moment to collect his thoughts.

'I–' He swallowed and began again. 'Mama Solveig's dead.'

'What?'

'We were going to call on some of her patients and a creature attacked us. Not another fiery snake, but something else out of Chaos. The Purple Hand must have sent it, too. I tried to fight, but my magic couldn't stop it. You see what it did to me. I thought it would kill me for certain, but it just cleared me out of its way, because it was really after Mama.'

Jarla felt tears start from her own eyes, heralding the bitter sorrow to come. She wasn't truly grieving yet. The news had shocked her numb. But she knew she would. Solveig Weiss had shown her more love and kindness than her true mother ever had.

'Did she suffer?' Jarla asked.

'I hope not. At the end, when… the beast finally sank its claws into her, everything seemed to happen quickly.' He started crying again, and this time, they wept together.

When that outpouring of anguish subsided, she murmured, 'I don't blame you for what happened, and I don't want you to blame yourself.'

To her surprise, he jerked back out of her embrace to stare into her face. The third eye popped open to study her as well.

'What do you mean by that?' he demanded.

'Just that I know you did everything you could to save Mama, and if you couldn't, no one else in the coven could have done it, either. So you mustn't hate yourself because the daemon or whatever it was got past you.'

'Oh. I thought…' He gave his head a shake, as if to clear it. 'You're right. I did my best, and I shouldn't despise myself for failing. Mama wouldn't want that.'

'No, she wouldn't. She'd want us to serve the god and take care of one another.' Perhaps because his manner was still strange, she suffered another stab of anxiety, 'You are going to stay with me and take care of me, aren't you? I've lost everyone else who really mattered.'

He sighed. 'Yes. Of course.'

DIETER CROUCHED IN the shadowy alley with the taste of Mama Solveig's blood and flesh in his misshapen mouth. Jarla's voice called his name repeatedly, the sound louder, nearer, every time.

She mustn't see him in his current monstrous guise. He recited the words intended to turn him back into a human being, but nothing happened. He tried again, and it still didn't work.

Jarla appeared framed in the entrance to the alley. She gaped at him. 'Dieter! You killed Mama! You ate her!'

He wanted to deny it, but a sort of inertia held him. He stood mute and passive, and then it was too late. She vanished, and a band of armed men materialised in her place. Some were Krieger's assistants, some were Mann's freakish followers, and the rest were the watch patrol Dieter had clawed his way through to reach his intended victim, up and walking despite their gory wounds.

They all charged Dieter, and he wheeled and fled before them. They cried his name as they pounded after him.

For a while he ran through Altdorf's benighted streets and alleyways, and then, abruptly, the city gave way to sun-lit fields of scarlet grass. Voices shouted his name from ahead as well as behind. He crested a rise and beheld Tzeentch's legions arrayed in a battle formation.

If he stayed where he was, his pursuers would catch and butcher him. If he ran onwards, the god's warriors would protect him, but it would mean joining their ranks to serve forever after.

He couldn't choose. He stood paralysed until guns banged, and the balls hammered into his torso. He screamed, and then the vermilion grasslands vanished.

Gasping, heart pounding, drenched in sweat, he lay on his back in darkness.

A nightmare, he told himself, it was only a nightmare. In reality, he wore his natural form, and he was still in Mama Solveig's cellar. Or rather, he supposed, it was his cellar now, so long as he paid the rent.

He took deep breaths, let them out slowly, and the tension started seeping out of his body. Then a voice said, 'Dieter.'

He threw off his covers and sat up on the cot. 'Who's there?'

For a heartbeat or two, no one answered, and Dieter wondered if the voice had merely been an echo of his dream. Then it repeated his name.

'I said, who's there?' Dieter called, and when the voice again failed to answer, he, too alarmed to take the time to light a candle in the usual way, rattled off a charm. A yellow teardrop of flame flowered atop the nearest taper, illuminating the infirmary, and, to a lesser degree, the shadowy spaces beyond. As far as Dieter could see, he was alone.

Mann had told of a voice that spoke from empty air. Had Dieter's lunatic scheme actually worked? 'Are you the Master of Change?' he asked.

'I watched you,' said the disembodied voice. It was masculine, with a shivering metallic undertone like the fading note of a gong. It sounded from one point, then another, as if the speaker were physically present and flitting around the room like a fly. 'I saw everything.'

Dieter swallowed. Saw everything? What did that mean? Was the Master, if this was really he, saying that he knew Dieter was a spy? That he'd watch him murder Mama Solveig?

Dieter rose from the cot. If he was in danger, he wanted to meet it on his feet. 'Just tell me who you are,' he said.

'I saw you quell the curse Adolph so stupidly unleashed. I watched you teach the others. I saw you rob the armoury and journey into the forest.'

Dieter felt marginally better. It only made sense that even if the Master of Change had the ability to spy on him, he wouldn't spend his every waking moment doing so, and by the sound of it, he hadn't been watching when Dieter met with Krieger, or did anything else incriminating.

'Then I hope you were pleased. Assuming that you are who I think you are.'

The voice laughed, which made the hint of vibrating metal more overt. The sound had a crazy quality as well, like the cackle of a senile old man finding humour where sounder minds saw none.

'Now why would you assume that?'

'Mama Solveig is dead. If the Master of Change wants to maintain governance over the coven she assembled, he's going to have to communicate with one of the other members.'

'But why would it be you, the new recruit? Why not someone who's served the Red Crown long enough that his loyalty is beyond question?'

Dieter didn't care for the implication that his own fidelity was not, but decided not to respond to it directly. Not yet, not unless he had to, for fear of making the situation worse. 'The high priest of the coven needs to be an accomplished warlock, and with Mama, Adolph and Nevin dead, and Jarla's skills so rudimentary, I seem to be the only candidate.'

'You're arrogant,' said the voice.

No, Dieter thought, I'm the sword of Tzeentch, his anointed champion. In the long run, likely more important than you. Then he faltered, appalled to catch himself embracing, even for an instant, the venomous lie the priest had told him.

But now was not the time to agonise over this further evidence of his psychic division and deterioration. Rather, he needed to show more respect. 'I don't mean to be arrogant,' he said. 'I bristle when I'm uneasy, and you rattled me by calling out of the darkness. Truly, I was only trying to answer the question you asked. But if that answer wasn't good enough, maybe this one will be.' He opened his new eye.

He thought that when he did, he might somehow catch a glimpse of the Master of Change even though the cult leader was apparently projecting his voice from far away. Unfortunately, he didn't. The only thing he saw that hadn't been visible before was a purplish shimmer crawling on Mama Solveig's worktable, the bundles of herbs hanging above it, and the thick brick pillars.

'Yes,' said the voice, 'the mark of the god. It means a great deal, and yet, not all of us who receive his favour are as thankful as we ought to be.'

'I am.'

'I hope so. My divinations suggest you're destined to accomplish much in the service of our lord. But I've found that prophecy by itself can prove a treacherous guide. A mage should never ignore his common sense.'

Dieter's pulse ticked in the side of his neck. 'And what does your common sense tell you?'

The voice laughed. 'Nothing conclusive, but it is troubled that in the brief time since you joined your coven, the mistress and four other members have died.'

'You said it yourself: it was Adolph's folly that killed Nevin and Maik and himself, for that matter. He forced me to strike him down. As for Mama, we assume the Purple Hand waylaid her. I certainly had no reason to do it. I liked her.'

'Yet even so, perhaps you coveted her position.'

Dieter shook his head. 'Adolph did. I didn't. Not while she was alive.'

'What about now?'

'Well, to be honest, yes. Who wants to be a common soldier if he can be a captain instead? So, if you truly doubt me, tell me what I must do to win your trust.'

'Fair enough. I intend to summon you to the next gathering of coven leaders. When you come, bring Jarla Kubler along with you.'

Dieter hesitated. 'I understood that no one but coven leaders ever attend such assemblies.'

The Master of Change chuckled. 'Then you were misinformed. Naturally, we bring lesser folk. We need them. When the lords of the Red Crown pay homage to our patron, it's only fitting that we offer a finer sacrifice than goats.'

'I'll gladly secure one. But Jarla is a faithful servant of the god.'

'Up to now, perhaps, but she's soft and weak. Better to send her to her reward before she fails us.'

'If you kill her, what effect will that have on the rest of our circle?'

'None, because they'll never know what became of her. She'll simply disappear, and then, not immediately but not long after, you'll show them new documents full of dark lore. It will prove you've been to see me, and I chose you to succeed Mama Solveig.'

Dieter struggled to think of another objection, but nothing came to him, or nothing helpful, anyway. It was useless to argue that murdering Jarla would be cruel and unjust. Devotion to Chaos was supposed to transcend all such petty considerations. Nor would it help to plead that he loved her, because that was exactly the point. The Master of Change was demanding that he betray her to demonstrate his absolute commitment.

Damn it, why was he even worrying about a whore, a Chaos worshipper, when the accomplishment of his mission might finally be at hand? He'd known from the start that if he actually succeeded in taking down the Red Crown, she was almost certain to burn with the rest of the cultists. He'd reminded himself again and again that she was expendable.

Yet he realised now that she mattered to him. Perhaps not sufficiently to sway him from his course, but certainly enough to make it bitter.

'All right,' he said. 'Just tell me where I'm supposed to bring her.'

'I'll guide you when the time comes.'

The mauve and violet shimmering faded, and Dieter sensed he was alone once more. His head started throbbing a moment later.

CHAPTER TWELVE

As HE FOLLOWED Krieger through the door, Dieter saw that the tavern was less busy than on their previous visit. Perhaps this evening's combatants had less of a following, although the broad-shouldered, leather-clad victor of the most recent contest looked formidable enough. Gripping his handler's outstretched hand, he clambered up out of the pit, and a few well-wishers babbled at him and slapped him on the back. Not dead yet but probably well on the way, leaving a trail of blood behind him, his opponent crawled feebly on the floor of the arena. Other spectators, apparently disappointed by the loser's performance, shouted taunts and insults down at him, or hurled chicken bones and empty bottles. One man unbuttoned his breeches to piss.

As before, Krieger bought two tankards of ale and hired the private alcove. Dieter dumped Mama Solveig's bag on the floor. Though he lacked all but a smattering of her knowledge of the healing arts, to provide himself with an income he'd continued treating the old woman's patients. Since he wasn't tainting the elixirs and poultices with the effluvium of Tzeentch's icon, he suspected that, on average, those who received his ministrations were faring about as well as they had before.

Krieger drew the curtain, took a chair, and said, 'Tell me that this time, you have what I need.'

'I'm making progress. I assume you know Solveig Weiss is dead.' Dieter prayed the witch hunter didn't know that Dieter himself had employed dark sorcery to kill her. In the long run, Krieger almost certainly wouldn't have pardoned that, even though it had been done to further his own ends.

'Yes.'

'Well, the Master of Change informed me he wants me to succeed her as coven leader.'

Krieger leaned forwards. 'When? Where did you meet him? Who is he?'

Dieter raised his hand to halt the barrage of questions. 'It was last night, and unfortunately, I still can't tell you much about him, because we weren't really in the same place. He was just a voice projected over a distance.'

Krieger grunted. 'Right. For a second, I forgot what a wary bastard he is.' His eyes narrowed. 'You said, you couldn't tell *much* about him.'

'Just that it was a male voice, with a strangeness in it.'

'Because he was using magic to make you hear it from far away?'

'Maybe, but I don't think so. I suspect that when you find him, you'll see that he carries the mark of Chaos like the raiders in the forest.' And like me, because you forced me into this. Dieter struggled to quash a sudden spasm of anger.

'It makes sense. It's another reason for him to hide as well as he does.' Krieger settled back and took a drink of ale. 'What else?'

'His manner was peculiar as well. For example, it was obvious who he was, and he needed for me to know if we were to converse to any purpose. Yet he refused to come right out and identify himself. And there were subtler oddities. I don't mean he's stupid, or addled in some overt and crippling fashion, but I had the impression he's not quite sane.'

'Well, he wouldn't be, would he, turning his back on Sigmar to wallow in forbidden magic and blasphemy. Such practices warp the mind as well as the body.'

Indeed they do, Dieter thought, and thus – again, thanks to you – I can't even trust my own ideas and impulses any more. He imagined casting the shadow binding on Krieger, dumping the witch hunter onto the floor, and stamping on him over and over again, relishing the snap of breaking bones.

'In any case,' Krieger continued, 'here's the important question: when and where are you supposed to meet him in person? Do you know yet?'

'Not really. It will be at the next assembly of coven leaders, but he doesn't intend to give me the particulars until it's nearly time.'

'Because he doesn't trust you?'

'Appar–' Dieter faltered.

'What's wrong?'

Something potentially disastrous. Most of the time, Dieter had no difficulty keeping his third eye closed. But on rare occasions, it sought to open of its own accord, and suddenly this was one of them. He fought to hold the lid down.

But he also needed to resume talking, to keep Krieger from perceiving that something was amiss. 'A headache's coming on. It's the strain. I told you at the start, I'm not the right sort of person for this job.'

'Nonsense. You're doing splendidly. Which means this will all be over soon, and then you can go home to your cosy house and stargaze to your heart's content. Now, you were explaining about the meeting.'

'Right.' The eye still wanted to open, and he kept struggling for control. 'Perhaps the Master will tell me where to go when it's time. Or maybe some form of enchantment will guide me step by step through the streets until I reach my destination. Either way–'

The world shifted abruptly, or rather, Dieter's perception of it altered in the subtle but unmistakable fashion he'd learned to recognise. The third eye was open.

Terrified, he felt his only options were to bolt or to strike down Krieger before the witch hunter could strike at him. He gathered himself to spring up out of his chair, then discerned that his companion hadn't reacted to the sudden revelation of his deformity.

Because he hadn't noticed. Nearly too late, Dieter realised that the new eye had only opened a crack, and his charm of concealment, dangling hair, and the paucity of light in the shadowy alcove kept Krieger from seeing it even now.

All right, Dieter thought, silently pleading with the eye, you win. You can look around, and pound my skull like an anvil after you're done. Just don't open any wider.

'"Either way"…' Krieger prompted.

Dieter took a deep breath. 'Yes. Sorry. Either way, it's not enough any more just to have a spy watching me. You need to keep a whole company of men ready to follow me the next time I draw the sign. That way, you'll have the strength to deal with the Master of Change and his lieutenants when I lead you to them.'

'I'll make the arrangements when we leave here. Which I suppose ought to be soon. We shouldn't spend any more time together than necessary.' Krieger reached for his ale, and a reddish, oozing phosphorescence shimmered into being on his hand and square, hearty-looking face, the outward manifestation, Dieter supposed, of a cruel and ruthless nature.

It was scarcely an encouraging omen, but he still pressed on with the remainder of what he'd intended to say. 'There's something else.'

Krieger sucked a fleck of foam from his lips. 'What?'

'If you knew about Mama Solveig, you must know about Jarla Kubler, also.'

The witch hunter smirked. 'Your trollop. Is she as tasty as she looks?'

'I'm supposed to bring her to the gathering as a sacrifice to the Changer of the Ways. That's how I earn the Master's trust.'

Krieger shrugged. 'Fine. Whatever it takes.'

'No, it isn't fine! She's an innocent, or nearly so, caught up in this madness through no fault of her own, and no threat to the Empire or anything else. When I reach the Master of Change's lair, I'll try to delay the sacrifice as long as possible. I want you to promise to attack as soon as you possibly can, and to let Jarla go free afterwards.'

A scarlet glimmer seethed on Krieger's scalp like an infestation of lice. 'If I were you, I'd concentrate on saving myself.'

'Give me your word, or I won't help you any further.'

'We both know that's a bluff.'

Was it? In truth, Dieter himself didn't know, but, staring into Krieger's eyes, he tried to appear adamant. 'You'd better think about it. Everything you want is nearly within reach. It would be a shame to let it all slip away.'

Krieger snorted. 'All right. As we're fishing for whales, I suppose I can afford to let a minnow slip out of the net. Just don't try to push or threaten me again.'

As THEY ROSE to depart, Krieger felt taut as a bowstring with eagerness. As the weeks dragged by, he'd begun to fear that Dieter was incapable of performing as required. But the wizard had come through, and now Krieger needed to put his followers on alert.

Then Dieter made a choking sound, and his knees buckled. He swayed and fell backwards, his head and shoulders billowing the curtain.

What ailed him? Was he poisoned? Dying? If so, it meant the end of Krieger's schemes. Alarmed, he scurried around the table for a better view.

Dieter's legs shook, and his heels pounded the floor. Krieger couldn't see the upper portion of his body, because it lay beyond the curtain. He swept the drape aside, shaking dust from its grimy folds in the process.

Dieter's upper body was shaking and jerking like his legs. His jaw worked as if he were chewing, saliva foamed from his mouth, and a grinding rasp sounded from his throat. His eyes stared at the ceiling.

Several people had noticed his condition. They gawked at him, but no one had yet come any closer, either to assist him or take advantage of his incapacity.

The wizard lifted his hands above his face, then started beating himself with the heels of his palms, right, left, right, left, over and over again.

He might do himself serious harm if not restrained. Krieger kneeled beside him and reached to take hold of his wrists.

He didn't expect the task to be particularly difficult. He was bigger and stronger than the wizard, and, to all appearances, Dieter wasn't truly conscious and didn't even know he was there.

But appearances proved to be deceptive. Dieter jerked his forearms away from Krieger's clutching fingers, then scrabbled at the witch hunter's face. The unexpected assault caught Krieger by surprise. He felt a flash of pain as the mage's nails tore his skin.

He flinched back to keep Dieter from clawing his eyes. The wizard sat up and reached for his face again. Krieger hooked a punch into the other man's jaw. Dieter's teeth clicked together, and he sprawled back onto the floor.

There he lay motionless, and, panting, his scratches smarting, Krieger studied him. It seemed to him that there was something different about the wizard's face, but he couldn't figure out what. He wondered if he should lean down for a closer inspection, and then Dieter groaned. His eyelids fluttered, and, moving like a sick old man, he tried to sit up.

Krieger shifted back to give him room. 'Are you all right now?'

Dieter lifted a trembling hand to his chin. 'What... what happened to me?'

'You threw some sort of fit. Started battering yourself in the face. I tried to stop you, and then you wanted to hurt me.' Krieger grinned. 'Luckily for me, you fight like a woman.'

'As I told you, I'm getting sick from the strain, the mere exposure to Dark Magic and blasphemy, even though I spurn it in my heart.'

'Just hold out a little longer, and then your harlot can nurse you back to health. Look, your bag came open when you fell. You'll want to gather up your medicines.'

HUNCHED OVER THE table in Mama Solveig's work area, Dieter scribbled an arcane formula on a slate, attempted to check it for errors, and his aching eyes blurred. As he rubbed them, it occurred to him that he didn't know if it was day or night outside the cellar. Nor was he certain when he'd last slept or eaten.

He couldn't neglect such basic needs indefinitely, or he'd make mistakes. But he begrudged the time required to attend to them. He was running a race, and he had to win it.

He knew how to do the work, or at least he hoped so. Magister Lukas had taught him the basic principles during his final year at the Celestial College. But the task consisted of a complex series of rituals, and a fumble at any point would oblige him to start over. Worse, it would ruin the irreplaceable materials needed to anchor the enchantment.

'Aren't you worried,' asked a familiar voice, 'that the Master of Change might be spying on you even now?'

Startled, Dieter jerked around in his chair. His cowl thrown back, his pupils reflecting the candle flame, the priest was standing at his side. Once again, Dieter wondered if the apparition was real or simply a figment of his diseased imagination, but only fleetingly. The question had come to weary him. Perhaps, as the forbidden texts proclaimed, it was a meaningless distinction.

'Go away,' he said.

'He told you he watches you,' the priest persisted.

Dieter sighed. 'He watched a gathering of the coven, and a mission to help Leopold Mann. He didn't say anything to suggest he spies on me when he has no reason to believe that something interesting is happening, and if he does, well, maybe he won't comprehend what he sees. In any case, as always, I have no choice.'

'Perhaps you don't,' said the priest, 'and perhaps the god who loves you will shield you from prying eyes. But why are you struggling out here when time is of the essence? Work in the shrine, in our lord's presence, where the magic will answer your call more readily.'

'No, because I don't have to. This spell derives from the pure Lore of the Heavens. It doesn't draw from the Changer's filthy texts.'

'But it could. Think how powerful the magic would be if you combined the two knowledges.'

'It will be potent enough as it is.'

'Then think of the precious hours you can save. Don't perform the Consecration of the Descending Sign, and the Attunement of the Eclipse. Use the Leper's Kiss.'

Dieter felt a jolt of mingled excitement and dread, because he saw instantly that the priest was correct. He could substitute a brief spell he'd discovered in the Chaotic texts for two of the lengthy preliminary rituals and be much further ahead. The shortcut could make all the difference.

He didn't want to work any more Dark Magic, or at least the true, rational, beleaguered part of him didn't. But at this point, polluted as he already was, did it even matter? It certainly wouldn't if his squeamishness cost him his life.

'You win,' he said, then saw that the priest had disappeared.

He rose, walked to the heart of the cellar, and revealed the shrine. Surfaces oozed and rippled with the intangible slime of Chaos. Tzeentch grinned a welcome.

He shifted the icon to the middle of the area, so he could tap into its power as easily as possible. Why not, he thought crazily, bitterly, clamping down on an urge to laugh. Why not, why not, why not?

JARLA'S EYES FLEW open. The sunlight outside made molten yellow threads of the cracks in the front wall of her room, just as it always did when the afternoon was bright enough. Her sweaty body lay in the hollow it had worn in her straw mattress. Plainly, the ordeal she'd just experienced had only been a nightmare. Now she was awake, and didn't even remember what had happened in the dream.

Yet even so, terror was slow to relinquish its grip on her. Her heart thumped, and she had the crazy feeling that if she looked around the room, she'd see something unbearable. When someone banged on the door, she gasped and flinched. Perhaps she'd needed something to goad her into motion, for in reacting, she broke free of her paralysis.

That didn't mean she'd shaken off dread entirely. The other members of the coven claimed they weren't afraid of witch hunters and maybe it was so. But, hard as she tried not to, Jarla sometimes imagined such avengers announcing themselves with an insistent knocking on her door, imagined that and all the pain that would follow.

She tried to answer and found her throat was dry. She swallowed. 'Who's there?' she quavered.

'Dieter! Let me in!'

She closed her eyes, expelled the last of her fear in a long, shivering exhalation, and excitement sprang up to take its place. Of late, she hadn't seen much of Dieter. He'd claimed he was busy unravelling the secrets of the god's sacred texts, but she'd wondered if he'd found someone he liked better, or decided a common whore was unworthy of his affections.

But evidently not, for when she opened the door, he took her in his arms, kissed her, and shoved her back down onto the bed.

He took her three times, and after each time, he held her close and they talked. It was the way Jarla had always dreamed lovemaking could be, and it was wonderful, or at least it was at first.

At the start of the third coupling, though, she had the odd feeling that it was essentially determination, not honest desire, that led him to initiate, and by the time the cracks in the wall stopped glowing, announcing the arrival of dusk, it seemed to her that they'd run out of things to say. He wouldn't stop chattering, though, wouldn't doze sated and content like a normal man. He repeated anecdotes he'd told before and questions to which he already knew the answers.

She remembered how guarded and strange he'd seemed in the wake of Mama Solveig's death. He seemed just as peculiar now, and she wondered with a pang of uneasiness if she actually knew him as well as she believed.

Yes, of course she did, and it was simply the mistreatment she'd suffered as a child and the anxieties of her double life that made her imagine otherwise. She wouldn't let such phantasms tarnish a golden interlude, or make her doubt the finest gift a grudging universe had ever given her.

She smiled at Dieter and stroked his cheek. 'I hate to go,' she said, 'but I have to work at the Axe and Fingers tonight.'

He caught her by the wrist. 'No. Stay with me.'

'I wish I could, but I have to earn my living.'

His grip tightened. 'No, you don't. I'll take care of you.'

She wondered if he truly meant it, and if he was earning enough to make it practical. 'I'd like that.' She hesitated. 'But, you know, even if you support me, I'll still need to do my work, because that's how I spy on the soldiers and serve the god.'

'But you don't need to do it tonight.' His fingers crushed her wrist like a torturer's shackle.

She tried to pull free, but couldn't. 'Dieter, you're hurting me!'

His eyes widened as if he truly hadn't realised. 'I'm sorry!' he said, and let her go.

She shifted away from him and rubbed her wrist. 'I think you're tired. Mama always said that communing with our lord exalts our spirits, but it taxes us as well. Now, I'm glad you want to take care of me, gladder than I can say, but we don't have to figure everything out this very instant. Let me go to the tavern, and you stay here and sleep. I'll come back as soon as I can.' She swung her legs over the side of the mattress and stood up.

He sprang up, too, and she realised that he was on the side of the bed nearer the door. If she tried to flee, he could intercept her. Wild, stupid fancies, for she had no reason to bolt, nor he, to hurt her, but for some reason she couldn't help picturing it.

'Do you trust me?' he asked.

She hesitated. 'Yes.'

'Then don't go. I need you to do something for me.'

Was that the secret reason for all your tenderness, she wondered? To make sure I stayed put until you were ready to make use of me? 'What?'

'To accompany me somewhere.'

'Where? Why?'

'If you trust me–'

'I do! But only if you're honest with me!'

Dieter took a deep breath. 'All right. The Master of Change wants to see us.'

That was so unexpected that for a moment, she wondered if he was joking. 'Have you been to see him already?'

'No. His voice spoke to me from out of the air, the same way he talks to Leopold Mann.'

'But he only communicates with coven leaders. Maybe he wants you to pick up where Mama left off, but what does he want with me?'

'Perhaps some other circle is in need of a leader.'

Jarla shook her head. With Dieter's encouragement, she'd been trying to think more highly of herself than she had hitherto, but even so, she was certain she'd make a wretched choice to direct a secret cabal of rebels and warlocks. 'That doesn't make any sense.'

Dieter's face twisted as if he was losing patience with her recalcitrance. At that moment, he reminded her of Adolph.

'You know I wouldn't let anybody hurt you,' he said. 'I've taken steps – I mean, all along, I've done my best to look after you, haven't I?'

Why had he referred to someone hurting her? Why had that possibility even occurred to him? 'Yes,' she said, 'you have.'

'And I always will. So let's do as the Master orders.' He grinned, a bleak and bitter rictus. 'It's not as if either one of us has a choice.'

'I'm sorry,' she said. 'Of course, I'll do whatever you say. I just didn't understand.' She struggled to give him a smile. 'Whether I'm going to the tavern or to meet our leader, I suppose I need to get dressed.' Her hand trembling ever so slightly, she reached for her shift, and he didn't stop her. He simply watched her for another moment, then started pulling on his own garments.

She didn't know what to do. She loved Dieter. Of all the people she'd ever loved, he was the only one left. The Cult of the Red Crown had given her a sense of belonging and significance.

Considered in that light, it would be insane to break with either, let alone both. Yet doubt and fear tugged at her more insistently with every passing moment, begging her to flee from whatever fate held in store.

As she laced the front of her gown, she watched for an opportunity, uncertain whether she truly meant to take it even if it came. Then Dieter pulled his shirt over his head.

At that moment, the garment covered his eyes and would hinder the use of his arms and hands. Jarla ran at him and shoved him stumbling backwards. She whirled, fumbled with the catch, and yanked on the door.

CHAPTER THIRTEEN

DIETER'S BACK SLAMMED against the wall. He pushed off it, recovered his balance, jerked his shirt down over his head, and thrust his hands out the ends of the sleeves. Some portion of the shabby old garment ripped.

The trailing folds of Jarla's skirt vanished out the doorway. Dieter realised he was lucky the door stuck. Otherwise, she'd have a bigger lead – although the situation was bad enough as it was.

He ran after her, out into the twilight. He hadn't yet put on his shoes, and the mucky surface of the rutted street sucked at his bare feet. Passers-by and vendors minding their stalls and barrows turned to watch the pursuit. Shovels and sledgehammers cocked over their shoulders, a quartet of filthy labourers grinned in anticipation of an amusing altercation.

Jarla either heard or sensed Dieter coming after her. She peered about, then oriented on a big, balding, black-bearded man seated on the bench of a cart. By the looks of it, he was just about to drive away.

Jarla evidently meant to beg him for help. Hoping to speak first, or to yell louder and drown her out, Dieter gasped in a breath and bellowed, 'Thief! Stop her! That whore stole all my money!'

'No!' Jarla cried. 'I never did!'

But she was dressed like a whore, and not entirely dressed at that, and perhaps that prejudiced the carter against her. At any rate, he smiled an ugly smile and said, 'The same thing's happened to me. Teach the bitch a lesson.' He called to his horse, flicked the reins, and the cart clattered into motion.

Jarla cast about, saw that none of the other spectators were inclined to help her either, and ran on. Dieter pounded after her, caught her by the hair, and yanked her off balance. She fell down in the mud, and he kicked her until she stopped resisting. Sobbing, she simply curled up to shield her most vulnerable parts.

He hauled her to her feet and marched her back to her stall. Some of the onlookers cheered ironically. He flung Jarla down on the bed and shoved the door shut.

As was so often the case of late, contradictory feelings and urges pulled him in two directions. He loved her, was ashamed of what he'd done, and ached to make amends. Yet at the same time, he yearned to go on hurting her, to punish her for defying him or simply for the pleasure it would give him.

He strained to suppress the latter impulse, and to his relief, it faded, although without making him feel as if his decent, rational side had truly assumed control. Rather, he had the odd feeling that the corrupted Dieter, born of dark lore and Tzeentch's touch, had simply opted to humour him.

If so, perhaps he'd done it to illustrate just how impotent Dieter's good intentions actually were, for it soon became apparent that none of his apologies or reassurances were having any effect. Arms wrapped protectively around herself, face ashen, tears sliding down her cheeks, Jarla just stared at him. Eventually he ran out of words, and then there was nothing to do but finish dressing and wait for the Master of Change to call them forth.

The summons came about an hour after night swallowed the city. A ball of purple foxfire appeared in the air near the door, then floated towards the panel, plainly indicating that it wanted Dieter to follow it out into the night.

He looked at Jarla and realised from her unchanged demeanour that she couldn't see the luminous orb. 'Get up,' he said, 'it's time.' He hesitated. 'If you try to run away–'

'You'll only hurt me again,' she spat. 'I understand.'

That flash of bitter anger showed he hadn't beaten all the spirit out of her, and he was glad. 'I know you won't believe this. You have every reason not to. But it really is going to be all right.'

The glowing sphere led them on a zigzag course through the darkened streets. He held Jarla's hand lest she try again to break away, while other folk trudged indifferently past. To Dieter, the passers-by appeared less than real. He had the insane but persistent feeling that as soon as he took another step and changed his angle of view, he'd see they were flat, like figures in a painting.

Trying not to be obvious about it, he glanced around, looking for some indication that Krieger and his men were on his trail. They should be – he'd left the mark before proceeding to Jarla's room – yet he couldn't see any sign of them. Mouth dry, pulse ticking in his neck, he told himself it didn't mean anything. He shouldn't be able to spot them, not if they were sneaking with sufficient craft to take the Master of Change by surprise.

Eventually the orb dropped and oozed through a rusty iron grate in the cobbles. Dieter sighed. He'd hated his brief stint as an assistant rat catcher, but it seemed he was destined to wade through the sewers one more time.

The grate wasn't locked or bolted down. The edges simply sat in grooves devised to hold it in place. Dieter stooped, lifted it, and shifted it aside. A stomach-churning stench wafted up from the darkness below.

Jarla winced. 'Down there?'

'It will be all right.' The statement sounded more absurd every time he repeated it.

He gestured for her to precede him down the ladder. Before he followed, he took what might be his final look at the sky. I'm still bound to you, he thought. I never stopped trying to be a worthy Celestial wizard, no matter how it looks.

One small mercy waited at the bottom of the descent: a walkway set above the sluggishly flowing filth. For the time being, at least, they wouldn't actually have to splash through the waste. Rats made a rustling sound as they skittered through the blackness.

He drew his belt knife and conjured a glow onto the blade to serve as a torch. Disdainful of the light, the darkness stepped backwards. The foxfire floated east, and once again, he waved for Jarla to take the lead. The ledge wasn't wide enough for them to walk side by side, and it would be unwise to place her at his back.

After a while, she said, 'We don't have to stay in the cult, risking our lives in a cause we can never win. We can run away together. I swear, I'll make you happy!'

'I'm sorry,' he said. 'But right from the start, it's all been leading here, no matter how I tried to abandon the path, and now our only hope is to try to find a way out the other side.'

The glowing orb abruptly made a right-angle turn and vanished into what appeared to be solid, fungus-spotted masonry. But when Dieter gingerly ran his hand over the wall, he found the edge where obstruction gave way to empty air. The hidden archway wavered into a blurry sort of semi-visibility when his fingers slipped inside it. The orb hung waiting on the other side.

Jarla took a deep breath. 'All right.' She started in.

'Wait.' Dieter peered back the way they'd come and still couldn't see any indication that Krieger and his men were on his trail.

Maybe they weren't. Maybe they never had been, and even if they had, they might well have lost track of him by now. The sewers were a maze.

But he had to assume they were behind him somewhere, and likewise needed to make certain they wouldn't miss the concealed doorway. Using the point of the glowing knife, he scratched an arrow on the stonework.

'What are you doing?' Jarla asked.

'Quiet,' he replied. He didn't dare explain for fear that someone would overhear. Of course, it was entirely possible that the Master of Change was employing sorcery to observe him at this very moment, but he simply had to hope it wasn't so.

'Now,' he said, 'go on.'

Beyond the threshold, it soon became apparent they'd exited the sewers for a different sort of warren. The floor was dry, with no depression to channel muck. The stonework was manifestly finer, with carvings ornamenting the walls. Yet the catacomb felt even fouler than the filthy, reeking tunnels that had brought them here, because the taint of Chaos lay over everything. Dieter perceived it as an oily, creeping shimmer.

Jarla likely couldn't see it the way a true magus could, but she sensed it, and despite her familiarity with the similar forces at play in Mama Solveig's shrine, she paled and swallowed as if resisting a pang of nausea. 'What is this place?' she asked.

Dieter inspected some of the graven symbols. 'Dwarfs built it,' he said, 'long before there was an Altdorf. But after they died out or abandoned it, another group occupied it, and cut their own glyphs alongside and atop the builders' original inscriptions.' He recognised many of the newer sigils from the forbidden texts. 'That second group served Chaos as we do.'

'I don't want to serve it,' Jarla whispered. 'I didn't understand!'

'Just trust me,' he pleaded, 'and keep moving.'

They walked on, and he sensed a stirring of arcane forces, visible only as a shift in the shadows that didn't quite fit with the motion of his light. The manifestation swirled around them like a whirlpool, and, unliving but aware in its fashion, seemingly examined them from all sides at once. Then a touch, ephemeral as a cobweb but somehow noisome as dung, dragged down Dieter's face. He stiffened, and, a moment later, Jarla cried out, no doubt alarmed and revolted by the same sensation.

'It won't hurt you,' he said. 'It's just a defensive ward. It had to make sure we are who we're supposed to be, but now that it has, it will let us pass.'

It did. But he wondered if Krieger could cope with such an enchantment, and do so with a minimum of noise.

Light flowered in the darkness ahead. Another fifty paces brought them to their destination, and the foxfire, its task accomplished, winked out of existence.

Peering about, Dieter found that the light of half a dozen scattered lanterns, inadequate though it was, sufficed to reveal that the long-vanished dwarfs had constructed a splendid temple to serve as the crowning glory of the complex. Interrupted by choir lofts and galleries, the walls of the sanctum sanctorum swept up and up to a vaulted ceiling. Unfortunately, the Chaos worshippers who came after had perverted and polluted this holy of holies even more thoroughly than they had the rest of the corridors and chambers. Made of the same congealed malignancy as the icon in Mama Solveig's cellar, a black image of Tzeentch leered behind an elevated red marble altar equipped with shackles, and runnels to drain away blood. A curved jewelled dagger lay atop it, waiting for someone to pick it up and stab and slice a sacrifice to death.

Robed in pink, puce and purple, in finer versions of the costumes Mama Solveig's coven wore to conduct their rituals, eight figures stood waiting in the vicinity of the altar. On first inspection, the Master of Change's deputies looked like ordinary men and women, yet as Dieter had guessed, the cult leader himself was a mutant so deformed that he surely lived his entire life underground. For, even cloaked in the most potent spells of disguise, he would have found it impossible to walk the streets of Altdorf undetected.

That was because the size and shape of his body were entirely wrong. He was fatter than any human could be without his heart failing, and because he was too immense to close his robe, Dieter could see that his lower body had fused together to become a bloated, sexless, worm-like tail with clusters of twitching fingers growing out of it. The appendage would hump and drag behind him as he crawled about.

Above the navel, an extra head, small as an infant's, drooling and weeping dark slime, lolled from the centre of a hairless, blubbery chest. The Master's arms were too long and possessed too many joints, and an extra one grew from the left shoulder. The upper head, positioned more or less where a head should be but off-centre nonetheless, was nearly all lipless mouth lined with square, stained teeth, the remaining features and the cranium itself squashed together at the top to create an appearance of imbecility.

Dieter had sojourned with Leopold Mann and his followers, but even so, the Master's appearance was grotesque enough to make him falter. Jarla sobbed, whirled, and took a first running stride towards the exit.

Dieter dropped his luminous knife and grabbed her. The blade clattered on the floor, and she thrashed, struggling to break away. 'Calm down!' he whispered. 'If you run now, they'll kill you for certain! I won't be able to stop them!' She kept flailing and kicking, and managed to jerk an arm free.

Then, however, the coven leaders rushed up to help him immobilise her, and of course she had no hope of prevailing against so many. They bore her to the altar, shoved her down on her back, and snapped the shackles shut around her wrists and ankles. She jerked on her chains, rattling them, wailed and sobbed, until, her hand lashing back and forth, a grinning female cultist slapped her into quiescence.

Dieter wanted to stop the abuse, but knew it would be suicide to try. He had to content himself with taking note of the key hanging on the side of the sacrificial stone.

He retrieved his knife, sheathed it, and approached the Master of Change. He dropped to his knees as he'd once knelt before Mama Solveig and the icon in her keeping. Up close, the mutant smelled like sour milk.

The Master put his right hand on top of Dieter's head. Portions of his palm bulged, pressing down, then receded, as if, beneath the skin, tumours were swelling and dissolving. 'I give you,' he said, the metallic shiver still underlying his otherwise human tone, 'the blessing of the Changer of the Ways.'

'Thank you, Master,' Dieter said.

'Are you ready to take the next step in your service?' the Master asked. 'Are you prepared to lead your coven?'

'Yes.'

'Then come with me.' The sorcerer led him before the altar, where Jarla lay shuddering, and the black draconic figure looming behind, then bade him kneel once more. The other cultists formed a circle around them.

Dieter realised with a stab of panic that they meant to anoint him a coven leader forthwith, and that the ritual would surely culminate in Jarla's murder. He'd hoped for some sort of instruction or examination first, something he could protract to give Krieger a chance to arrive. But that obviously wasn't how the Master wanted to proceed, and Dieter couldn't think of any way to deflect him from his course. He could only pray that the ceremony was a lengthy one.

As it turned out, the preliminaries, a series of chanted prayers and catechisms, did take a while. The obscene import of the declarations and the corrosive power radiating from Tzeentch's statue ground at Dieter's mind, churned his guts, and made his head swim. But he'd learned to endure such things, and so far at least, managed to prevent them from drowning his will and sense of purpose. Glancing from the corner of his eye, he kept on watching and listening for Krieger.

Who failed to appear.

'Now rise,' said the Master of Change.

Dieter stood up. Someone took his cloak and helped him into a vestment of tangled, sickly colours.

'Now take your place behind the altar.'

Dieter mounted the dais. Tzeentch leered down at him.

When Dieter turned and looked back at the Master and his lieutenants, he felt a sudden wild surge of hope, because a murky figure stood in the gloom at the rear of the chamber, where the light of the lanterns failed. But then he saw it was the priest.

'Now take up the blade,' said the Master of Change.

Dieter did that, too. The dagger was well balanced and looked razor-sharp. A tangible malice stirred inside it like a cat stretching.

'Can you feel the power in it?' the Master asked. 'It's an ancient, sacred instrument. It's sent souls beyond counting to feed and serve our lord. Now lift it up and strike.'

Her eyes wide, Jarla stared up at him. 'Please don't,' she whimpered, 'please don't.'

I don't want to, he thought, but even as he silently articulated the words, they abruptly felt like a lie.

How dare she beg him to risk his own life on her behalf when she herself had guided him to Mama Solveig and so bore responsibility for all that followed? When he was a wizard of the Celestial College and she was a despicable Chaos worshipper and a common whore? When, in all likelihood, any effort he made to save her would merely doom them both? For he couldn't prevail in a fight against the Master of Change and seven other warlocks too.

No, better to stick her in the heart and in so doing, at least preserve the hope of saving himself, especially when it would have the added benefit of putting an end to her constant whining need for reassurance. More than that, he realised that it would be like yanking out a rotten tooth. By destroying her, he would finally eliminate an aching, troublesome part of himself. What a relief that would be!

He swung the dagger high over his head, and as he drew himself up tall, he chanced to look out into the chamber once again.

All the spectators, cultists and phantom priest alike, were smirking at him with absolute confidence in their eyes. No doubt, at his back, Tzeentch was doing the same. They were positive they knew what he was about to do. Positive he didn't have a choice.

Somehow their gloating certainty shifted the balance inside him, twisting the anger he'd momentarily felt towards Jarla into a need for defiance. He threw the dagger over the altar at the Master of Change. He was no warrior, the curved knife wasn't meant for throwing, and it clanked down well short of its target. Still, the effect was salutary, as the cultists gaped at him in shock. It was a moment to savour, no matter what happened next.

'No,' he said, 'I'm not going to do it.' He lifted the key from its hook.

'You're insane,' said the Master of Change.

Dieter laughed. 'Absolutely. For weeks now.' He unlocked one manacle, then pressed the key into Jarla's hand. She could open the other shackles herself. He didn't want to take his eyes off the sorcerers for even a moment if it wasn't necessary. 'But even a madman can see this is stupid. How can the Red Crown ever accomplish anything if it slaughters its own adherents?'

'The whore is of no importance,' the Master said, 'except to provide a test for you.' Agitation made the fingers protruding from the worm-like tail twitch more rapidly.

'That statement is stupid, too,' Dieter said. Jarla sat up on the altar and started freeing her ankles. 'She does her part and is genuinely devoted to the god, which ought to make her more valuable than me. I'm a spy. I infiltrated your filthy conspiracy to bring it crashing down around your heads.'

The cultists goggled at him anew. Their consternation was so satisfying, so comical, that, for the moment at least, he didn't even feel frightened any more. Maybe a sane man wouldn't have reacted that way, but if so, he was glad to be crazy.

'So you see,' he continued, 'if you need a new coven leader, you should give the job to Jarla and sacrifice me. That's the way it makes sense. Although I warn you, you'll have more trouble chaining me to the altar.'

'Neither one of you is worthy to lead a circle of our lord's followers,' said the Master of Change, 'and accordingly, neither one of you can be allowed to leave here alive. Kill them!'

The cultists started chanting and sweeping their hands through mystic passes. Jarla scrambled down from the altar, and Dieter shoved her towards the edge of the dais. He wanted her to scurry around the periphery of the vault to the exit. If he could keep the enemy sorcerers occupied for a few moments, perhaps she'd have at least a slim chance of escaping. But he simply had to hope she understood, because there was no time left to explain, or for anything but combat.

He opened his third eye and glimpsed the multiple images that revealed an opponent's intent an instant before he actually moved. That might enable him to avoid an attack or two. He visualised the night sky, rattled off an incantation, and wrapped himself in his armour of light.

Darts of shadow streaked at him an instant later, but the corona leeched the virulence from them, and they stung no worse than pinpricks. He realised that by rights, the missiles should have flown before his protective enchantment was in place, but his foes hadn't worked their magic quickly enough. Perhaps, for all their power, they weren't accustomed to casting spells in battle, whereas he'd had a taste of it as a journeyman wizard, and grown grimly familiar with it again in recent weeks.

It was another small advantage. Perhaps he'd even be able to kill one or two of the whoresons before the others penetrated his defence.

He spoke to the air, and a blast of howling wind battered the cultist who'd slapped Jarla. It caught her in the middle of an incantation, and the half-born magic, escaping her control, opened raw, wet sores down the left side of her face. Another sorcerer sought to snare him in a binding, and he sent the dark, thorny coils leaping back to net their maker.

His foes spread out to flank him and no doubt get behind him if possible. He pivoted to strike at the ones on the right, and then, from the corner of his eye, glimpsed the Master of Change slashing his three hands through complex arcane patterns.

A thing resembling a huge black sea anemone, its shadowy substance made of dozens of fused, flattened, anguished faces like the countenances of the damned, wavered into being in the air above the altar. Several of its wire-thin tentacles whipped at Dieter. He tried to dodge, but they caught him anyway, stabbing pain around the edges of his face and lodging there as if they terminated in barbs or fishhooks. They jerked him up on tiptoe as though attempting to tear his own face away from the skull beneath for incorporation into the central mass.

He gritted out a counter spell, but it failed to wipe the hovering entity from existence. Heat seared his ribs; one of the sorcerers had managed to drive an attack through his protective halo.

It's over, Dieter realised. The warlocks will pick me apart while I dangle here struggling to free myself from the anemone. Krieger, you treacherous bastard, why didn't you come?

As though in answer to his silent reproach, gunfire banged, the reports echoing from the high stone walls. Someone screamed.

CHAPTER FOURTEEN

WITH HIS FACE angled upwards, immobilised, Dieter couldn't see anything but the dark anemone, but he assumed all the cultists had jerked around to defend themselves from the intruders. If so, then for a moment at least, they'd stop attacking him. Maybe he still had a chance after all.

Or maybe not. He threw darts of light at the flowerthing, but they didn't appear to damage it. He asked the wind to tear it apart, but the conjured entity withstood the blast. Meanwhile, the pain around the periphery of his face was excruciating. It made it all but impossible to cast spells with the necessary precision, and it seemed to him that the pull was growing stronger.

He croaked the call for a dark binding, nearly botching the cadence of the incantation but correcting just in time. The coils pounced at the anemone, and he sent them snaking and weaving among the petals, entangling the entire structure, then, with a sudden, savage exertion of will, yanked the complex knot tight as a hangman's noose arresting a condemned man's drop through the gallows floor.

The binding cut the manifestation to pieces. The myriad pieces screamed, and the petals started tumbling to the floor, only to vanish in mid-fall. The tentacles withered from existence as well, and the pain in Dieter's face, or anyway, the worst of it, disappeared also. Blood from the punctures along his hairline trickled down his forehead, threatening to drip into his eyes and blind him. He wiped it away and looked around.

As he'd surmised, Krieger and his minions had finally invaded the crypt, along with a flying fiery serpent like the one Dieter had encountered on the night he first met Adolph and Mama Solveig. The newcomers' pistols had done their work, smearing the air with sulphurous smoke in the process, and now the human intruders had switched them out for swords. The snake dived and struck.

Since Krieger had attacked by surprise, with the advantage of firearms, superior numbers and an infernal ally, he should have had no trouble massacring the leaders of the Red Crown. But in point of fact, it was unclear which side, if either, currently held the upper hand, because only a couple of the cultists had fallen. Perhaps the others wore protective talismans or possessed hidden alterations to their anatomy that had enabled them to withstand a volley of gunfire. In any event, they were striking back, with flares of dark power when possible, and fists and daggers when necessary.

Too much of the time, it wasn't necessary. Living up to his reputation for lethal skill and prodigious power, rattling off incantations, the Master of Change was conjuring supernatural servitors of his own to interpose themselves between the Red Crown and their foes. Dieter suspected that, like the spider-things Mama Solveig had evoked to test his abilities, the Master's creatures weren't real in every sense of the word. But they were tangible enough for one, a scuttling, crab-like thing the size of a table, to catch a witch hunter's leg in its serrated pincers and snip it out from underneath him. The man fell, and the crab cut and pulled the rest of his body apart.

Left undisturbed to produce such horrors in abundance, the Master would surely vanquish those who'd come to lay him low. Fortunately, Dieter, still standing between the towering black icon and the altar, was likewise well behind the defensive line of monstrosities, in good position to strike at the three-armed adept. In fact, the Master wasn't even looking in his direction and likely had no idea he'd freed himself from the power of the floating anemone.

Smiling, Dieter breathed the first syllable of a word of power, and something emitted an ear-splitting wail. When the Master heaved around in his direction, Dieter realised the source of the noise must have been the slavering infantile head growing from the warlock's chest, because the dripping yellow eyes of the twisted lump were glaring at him. It had somehow sensed his hostile intentions and shrieked a warning.

The Master snarled a rasp of a word Dieter had never heard before, and one of the conjured monstrosities forsook the defensive line to rush at him. Perhaps the ugly word was its name. The creature's round, writhing form was so bizarre and complex that at first glance, it baffled the eye. Dieter couldn't make out what it was, or whether it was crawling as fast as a man could sprint or rolling itself like a wheel.

Then his mind made sense of it, and he perceived it was a great tangled mass of arms and clutching hands. Perhaps the limbs all grew from a central hub, or maybe they simply attached to one another. Dieter couldn't see deeply enough into the shadowy crevices in the heaving, squirming mound to determine which.

He cast darts of light at it, but the barrage failed to slow it down. It leaped onto the dais and then, like a ball bouncing, flung itself on top of the altar. A dozen hands snatched at him, and he hurled himself backwards. The creature pounced after him. He scrambled to get behind Tzeentch's statue and use it for cover, but the entity lunged and cut him off.

Dieter kept retreating before it, off the edge of the platform and onwards, relying on the precognitive vision of his third eye to warn him which hands would grab and pummel next. He hurled knives of shadow, but they had no more effect than the darts of light. He wrapped the monstrosity in a binding, but, scarcely pausing in its rolling, slapping, scuttling advance, it gripped the jagged strands and ripped them apart.

Dieter felt himself starting to panic. He was already winded, and his glimpses of the future wouldn't keep him out of the creature's clutches once his reflexes slowed. He had to stop it forthwith, but how, when none of his spells appeared to have any effect at all?

He shouted at it with a voice like thunder, but that was no use either. It grabbed his ankle and jerked him off his feet. He slammed down hard on his back, and the entity crawled over him, countless hands gripping and pounding him. He realised that if not for his protective halo, they likely would have rendered him helpless in an instant.

The enchantment couldn't save him for long. If he was lucky, he might have time to attempt one final piece of magic. Twisting his head back and forth to keep any of the monstrosity's hands from covering his mouth, he gasped words of power, then scrabbled at the floor, his fingertips catching and bunching something cold and flat.

With his arms essentially immobilised, he couldn't actually rip the creature's shadow away from its corporeal form. But the mere effort satisfied the requirements of the spell, and the entity, no doubt suffering the shock and sudden weakness he remembered, faltered in its efforts to mangle and kill its prey. Meanwhile, a second such mass, made of darkness and accordingly vague in the ambient gloom, surged up from the floor.

The shadow creature threw itself on its counterpart, and the original let go of Dieter to defend itself against the assault. Tangled together, they rolled off him, and he jumped up and scrambled to distance himself from their portion of the battle.

Gasping and shaking, he cast about. Though more combatants had fallen on both sides, the fight still raged. Krieger had left off swinging his gory sword to bellow an incantation. His effort shredded the flesh of two of the Red Crown's conjured monstrosities. The serpent of flame hurtled down at the Master of Change, and he met it with a gesture of denial that stopped it as if it had slammed into an invisible wall. The relentless, ubiquitous discharge of unnatural energies brought chips of stone showering down from the ceiling and woke the graven images on the walls to jerky, repetitive life. Blades of gleaming copper-coloured grass stabbed up from the floor.

Bracing himself for his next effort, Dieter drew a deep breath. Then something smashed into the back of his head.

JARLA CROUCHED IN a small shrine, an alcove adjacent to the vault where everyone was fighting. A voice had started whispering from the shadows at the back of the space, and the statue in the centre, a representation of a robed dwarf carrying an orb and sceptre, cracked and crunched periodically. Maybe it was just getting ready to fall apart, but it reminded Jarla of an egg in the process of hatching.

She was afraid to stay where she was, but even more reluctant to venture back out into the open and the maelstrom of slaughter there. She wished that she'd tried to flee the temple when hostilities first erupted, but her instinct had been to bolt for cover instead, and now it was too late. With a band of dark-clad, well-armed intruders and a vile miscellany of Chaos creatures swelling the numbers of the combatants, she had little hope of slipping past them all.

So the only thing she could do was cower and watch, and more than anyone or anything else, she watched Dieter. She felt a reflexive stab of anguish when the thing with a hundred hands bore him down, and went limp with relief when he extricated himself from its clutches. The relief was short-lived. Mere moments later, a dark, hairless, shrivelled-looking figure with a whipping rat-like tail appeared directly behind him. Perhaps it had just come into existence, or maybe it used a trick of invisibility to creep up on those it wished to harm.

It cocked back a bony fist and punched the back of Dieter's head. Despite its emaciated appearance, it must be strong, because the blow threw him down on his belly. It immediately dropped to its knees on his back and gripped his neck in a stranglehold, lifting his head in the process. It opened a mouth lined with jagged tusks, and a white tongue as long as Jarla's arm slithered forth to lick the bloody wounds on Dieter's face.

Jarla tensed, her body preparing to flinch, for she was sure Dieter was about to die. He was plainly helpless, and the creature need only savage him with those terrible fangs or wrench and break his neck with its powerful, long-fingered hands to finish him off. But it didn't do either of those things. Not yet. Rather, it kept on throttling him while lapping at the flow of blood.

Such being the case, Jarla realised she might be able to save him.

But why should she risk herself? Why forsake her refuge, dubious though it was, dash out into the thick of the battle, and confront a Chaos creature? She comprehended almost nothing of what was happening, but she had heard Dieter say he was a spy. Surely that meant he'd deceived and used her from the start, and probably even expected her to die as a result of his machinations. He'd certainly

thrown her down in the street and kicked her into sub-
mission, then dragged her into this nightmare against her
will.

Yet in the end, he'd endangered himself to save her, and
of all the people she'd ever loved, he was the only one left.
If she lost him too, was there even a point in trying to preserve what passed for her wretched little life?

I'm an idiot, she thought, stupid as Adolph always said.
She drew herself to her feet and, trying to stride quickly
but quietly too, advanced on the blood-drinker and its
prey.

A stray flare of sorcerous fire blazed at her, and she
jumped out of the way. His leather armour hanging in tat-
ters, a lanky swordsman retreated across her path pursued
by a thing like a horned lizard stalking on two legs. He exe-
cuted stop cuts, and it slashed at him with talons as long
as fingers. Each was too intent on the other to notice Jarla.
She waited for them to pass, then scurried on.

Dieter's assailant shifted its grip from his neck to his
shoulders. In all likelihood, it had already choked him
into unconsciousness or worse. It drew the pale tongue
back into its mouth and bent to bite the prone man's
throat.

Realising she was out of time, Jarla sprinted. The creature
heard her coming, straightened up, and started to twist
around. She jabbed her thumbs with their long, painted
nails at its round black eyes.

Her right thumb found its target; it was like plunging it
into jelly. The left one missed and skated along the side of
the creature's face, scratching its dry, wrinkled hide.

She pulled her left hand back for another try, but the entity
struck first, a backhand swat that caught her under the jaw
and sent her reeling backwards. As she struggled to regain
her balance, the creature hissed and drew itself to its feet.

She retreated. It was all she could do. The creature stumbled, swayed, clapped a hand to its perforated, leaking eye,

and she dared to hope she'd incapacitated it after all. Maybe it wanted her to think that and relax her guard, for a bare instant later, it sprang. Startled, she froze.

A wind sprang up. It tore at Jarla's hair and clothing, but she was only at the edge of the effect. The blast of air had actually targeted her attacker. It caught the creature in mid-leap and tumbled it across the room to smash into the edge of the dais. Bone cracked. The apparition convulsed for a heartbeat or two, then slumped motionless.

Jarla pivoted towards Dieter, who was struggling to stand. She ran to him and helped him up. 'You summoned the wind, didn't you?' she asked.

Rubbing his neck, where the marks of the blood-drinker's fingers were still visible, he sucked in several rasping breaths before attempting a reply. 'Yes. The gods know how. I couldn't really even talk. When I pushed you away from the altar, I meant for you to get out of here.'

'I'm glad now that I didn't.'

'Keep yourself safe. I have to finish this.' Wiping and smearing the blood on his forehead, he fixed his three-eyed gaze on the Master of Change.

As MANY SPELLS as he'd cast and as much punishment as he'd absorbed already, Dieter was amazed he was still conscious. He could only infer that something, his mutation, perhaps, or even Tzeentch's favour, had granted him reserves of stamina no untainted human magus could match. Even so, he sensed he was reaching the end of them, but as he'd indicated to Jarla, he saw no choice but to keep fighting.

He took a moment to commune with the sky. He felt the wet weight of the rain pent inside the clouds, the restless winds, and, above them, the webs of force established by the positions of the planets and constellations.

At the same time, he observed the phantasmal slime and shimmer oozing and swirling through the chamber, sometimes adhering to surfaces, sometimes floating and billowing like mist.

Two powers, one filtered through the cleansing medium of the firmament and one streaming directly from the ultimate filth that was Chaos. One pure and one poisonous. He could command either, and knew that to have any chance at all against the Master of Change, he was likely to need both.

He rattled off a hybrid blasphemy of a spell he constructed extemporaneously. It was an insanely reckless thing to try, but, in his exalted state of consciousness, he was confident he was combining the words properly.

He swept his hand through the air as if throwing a ball, and splinters of light and shadow hurtled from his fingertips. He hoped that the Master's mystical defences, whatever they were, would prove inadequate to the task of stopping both sorts of missile at the same time.

The darts plunged into the Master's back, and he lurched around to face his attacker. The little head in the centre of his chest screamed in pain or rage, but the one set atop his shoulders showed no sign of distress. In fact, the enormous grin with those tombstone teeth stretched even wider.

The Lord of the Red Crown snarled words of power, and as he did so, his form split into two superimposed images, the first, the illusory one, moving just in advance of the second. The phantom thrust out its two left arms, and a colourless, rippling virulence streaked from its fingers. The precognitive vision warned when and in what vector the actual attack would come, and Dieter wrenched himself to the side.

Unfortunately, the edge of the effect must have grazed him anyway, or else its mere proximity was enough to cause harm, for his mind fractured, memory, identity and purpose splintering into terror and confusion. Already incapable of knowing precisely what he was doing or why, he visualised the configuration of the heavens at the time and place of his birth and shouted his own name.

His thoughts snapped back into focus, and he realised Franz Lukas's ward against psychic assault had saved him. His teacher had trained him to cast the spell as a sort of reflex, just as an expert fencer would parry a threatening blade without the need for conscious thought. Otherwise, it would have been useless against the very assault it was intended to defeat.

Dieter spoke to the air and the drifting, seething mist that was Chaos, imploring them to unite. He sent the result howling at the Master of Change.

The wind battered the warlock and tore the multi-coloured vestment from his body. The venom suspended inside it dissolved his flesh like acid. Blubber melted, baring gory ribs. The infantile head eroded to a featureless nub. The twitching fingers studding the worm-like tail burned away.

Yet the Master didn't collapse. Perhaps Tzeentch had marked and claimed him so completely that even a dose of Chaos in its most destructive form couldn't slay him. He screamed a word, and the wind failed. He shook a blistered, smoking fist, and an unseen force smashed into Dieter's stomach and knocked him reeling backwards.

The same force pounded him again and again. Despite the punishment, he managed a dark binding. He hoped to ensnare an invisible assailant, but apparently there was nothing tangible for the jagged coils to grab. They jerked uselessly shut on themselves.

Another blow spiked pain through his shoulder. It didn't seem to him as if the attacks were coming with extraordinary accuracy or science, but every one connected, and it would only be a matter of moments before they incapacitated or killed him.

He doubted he could cast another spell. He didn't have time, and the relentless assault would likely keep him from articulating the incantation properly even if he did. That almost certainly meant he was doomed, but still he struggled to think. To perceive. To find the way out of his dilemma.

He felt the wind awaiting his command. Evidently the Master of Change hadn't dissolved the enchantment that bound it to his will. He'd merely interrupted the flow of power, the way a slap in the face might startle and baulk a man, but only for a moment. Still, what did it matter when Dieter had already discovered that even a corrosive gale was insufficient to put the warlock down?

'The god's dagger,' said the priest.

Dieter glanced to the side. He'd lost sight of the robed apparition when the fight began, but the priest was standing beside him now. Despite the battle raging in the vault, he looked as calm as ever, and why not? Invisible fists weren't pounding him to death. It seemed likely that no one but Dieter could even see him.

'You felt its spirit when you picked it up,' the priest continued. 'Perhaps you can still feel it.'

Dieter realised it was worth a try. He couldn't see the knife any more. The dais blocked his view. But he reached out with his mind and sensed the same malevolence he'd encountered before. It enabled him to pinpoint the weapon's location.

Another blow rocked him backwards. He struggled to transcend the shock and focus his will. The wind screamed. The dagger spun up from behind the pedestal, then shot at the Master's head.

With all the power at his command, the warlock surely could have deflected the attack, but with his eyes fixed on Dieter, he didn't see it coming. Nor could the secondary head warn him, because Dieter had already succeeded in killing that part of him, anyway.

Bone crunched as the sacrificial instrument punched into the back of the Master's head, burying itself to the hilt.

The warlock pitched forwards, and after a moment, it became apparent that nothing was striking at Dieter any more. At the same time, he felt the knife's vicious jubilation at making a kill.

Dieter wished that he too could savour the victory, but since he and Jarla were still in danger, it was a luxury he couldn't afford. Gasping and swaying on his feet, he cast about, taking stock of the rest of the battle.

The fiery serpent was gone, but some of the Red Crown's conjured horrors had perished, too, and in the wake of their summoner's death, others now vanished, their defensive line disintegrating. Its loss would make it more difficult for the four surviving followers of the Red Crown to cast spells unhindered, and it appeared that Krieger wasn't the only fighter on the other side capable of working magic of his own. Another swordsman chanted a rhyme, and a retreating warlock's foot plunged into solid floor as if he'd stepped in a hole.

All in all, it seemed that the Master's death had turned the tide in Krieger's favour, and, reasonably confident of the witch hunter's chances, Dieter retreated, distancing himself from the thick of the fray. Battered and weary as he was, he urgently needed to catch his breath and settle himself for what was still to come. Jarla scurried out of a recessed space in the wall to join him.

It took about a minute for the last of the Red Crown to fall. Krieger was still on his feet, and so were half a dozen of his men. At least two of the latter were sorcerers. No one was casting spells at the moment – which had the beneficial effect of slowing the random Chaotic manifestations distorting reality throughout the chamber – but a violet glimmer, evidence of the forces they'd recently invoked, crawled on their lips and hands.

Seven against one was long odds, just about as hopeless a situation as the one Dieter had faced when he'd first defied the Master of Change. Jarla tried to embrace him, and he prevented her. He didn't want his movements hampered or his view obstructed. 'It's not over yet,' he whispered.

Krieger leered at the two of them. 'When did you grow the third eye?' he asked.

'A while back,' Dieter said. 'When did you cast your lot with the Purple Hand?'

The big man chuckled. 'I suppose that once I burst in here with a Chaos creature in tow, and my brothers and I started using magic, my true allegiance became rather obvious.'

'I should have realised early on,' Dieter said. 'It made no sense that, with all its resources, the Order of Witch Hunters couldn't find a more willing and capable spy than me. But you couldn't involve the entire order, could you? The honest witch hunters couldn't know anything about what your little circle of traitors intended if, at the end of it all, you were going to plunder the Master of Change's collection of grimoires for your own cult.'

'Cleverly reasoned,' Krieger said. 'That was the way of it.' He glanced at the man standing next to him. 'I told you he was sharp.'

'Apparently I'm not,' Dieter said, 'for I missed other clues along the way. The arrival of the first burning serpent gave me what I desperately needed: a second chance to win Jarla and Adolph's trust. The timing was amazingly fortunate – unless the people who were shadowing me observed my predicament and sent the creature to help me resolve it. Then, later, you had no interest in catching Leopold Mann and his followers. You claimed it wasn't your job, but, considering all the harm the raiders have done and the notoriety they've achieved, it's difficult to understand how any loyal servant of the Empire could be so utterly indifferent.

'But you didn't answer my question: how long have you served the Purple Hand?' Dieter didn't actually care, but he did want to prolong the conversation. It gave him additional time to control his laboured breathing and to recover a bit more of his strength.

'It's only been a few years,' Krieger said. 'When I started out, I was what you called an "honest" witch hunter.'

'What happened?'

Krieger snorted. 'What happened was that I was a man, too, with a man's appetites, and in one little flyspeck of a hamlet the peasants asked me to judge an accused witch who was also the most beautiful woman I'd ever seen.

'The evidence indicated she probably had dabbled in casting charms of the most trivial sort, but I had no reason to think anything awful would happen if I pretended otherwise. So I set her free, and she thanked me as we'd agreed she would.'

'And in due course,' Dieter said, 'something bad did happen.'

'Yes. She turned into a monster, slaughtered her entire village, and commenced a rampage across the province. It took a company of knights to bring her down.

'I winced when I heard about it, but at first I wasn't worried. No one was left alive to tattle that I'd investigated the bitch and declared her innocent. But then someone came to me with proof that he and his associates were in possession of the affidavit I'd written.'

'"Someone" being a member of the Purple Hand.'

'Yes, although I didn't find that out for a while. He told me that if I didn't do him and his friends the occasional favour – condemn a prisoner they wanted burned, or turn a blind eye to another's obvious guilt – they'd send the document to my superiors, and that would have been the end for me. I doubted my ability to convince a tribunal I'd made an honest mistake, and it wouldn't have mattered even if I could. The witch had done too much harm for the wretch who released her to evade punishment, no matter what the circumstances.'

'So you capitulated.'

'Yes, and over time, the favours became more frequent, and came to include crimes that had nothing to do with witch hunting. My new masters paid me in gold for my services, gradually took me into their confidence, and, discerning the aptitude in me, set about teaching me magic. They were drawing me in, you see. Converting me from a reluctant conscript into a true believer.'

'And it worked?'

'Of course. How could it fail? I couldn't deny the truth of the Changer's teachings, or resist the lure of forbidden secrets. I couldn't help delighting in the touch of Chaos and the working of Dark Magic.' Krieger grinned. 'Judging from the look of your forehead, you can't, either.'

'You're wrong about that.' Dieter decided he'd regained about as much of his vigour as he was likely to without actually lying down and sleeping the rest of the night away. 'We should talk about what happens next.'

'If you like.'

'I've given you everything you demanded of me, with the result that you've accomplished all your goals. The Master of Change and his lieutenants are dead. His library is surely waiting down here somewhere for you to take it for your own.' It hurt him to say as much, with the implication that he himself would never see it. Even now, in the most desperate circumstances, the craving for dark lore still gnawed at him. 'Now I ask you to keep your promises. Let Jarla and me go. Clear my name.'

Krieger chuckled. 'So you can return home with a third eye in the middle of your forehead?'

'Let me worry about that. All you need to know is that my deformity works to your advantage. I can't denounce you as a Chaos worshipper lest you denounce me for a mutant. Not that I'd bother to accuse you anyway. There was a time when I might have cared about your crimes, but

I've had such concerns beaten out of me. At this point I simply want to save myself.'

'It's good to hear you say so, and as you're willing to be sensible, I'll gladly honour our agreement. Why not?'

Dieter sneered. 'Why not, indeed? Except, of course, that you came to grief once already by allowing a person bearing the stain of Chaos to go free. Why would you risk it again, and have the threat that someday, for whatever reason, I might reveal the truth about you hanging over your head? Especially considering that you made the world believe I'm the Chaos worshipper. If you catch me – killing me in the process, of course – you'll advance your career as a witch hunter, which will bring additional opportunities to further the cause of the Purple Hand. Whereas if you declare that you were wrong about me, it will count as a mark against you.

'All of which leads me to suspect you're simply trying to cozen me into dropping my guard, to make it easier to kill me.'

'It would have been easier for you, too,' Krieger replied, 'if you could have found it in your heart to trust me one last time. Because I truly am grateful for your efforts, and I would have made your end quick and clean. You would have died happy, without ever realising that things weren't going to work out for you after all. But if you prefer to go down fighting, so be it.' He waved his hand, and his men started forwards. Jarla whimpered.

'I wouldn't,' Dieter said. He displayed the little clay figure with the same subtle flourish he'd once employed to pluck pennies from a child's ears.

Dieter was no sculptor, and the figure bore only a crude resemblance to its inspiration. The ambient gloom and the distance between him and Krieger should likewise have hindered recognition. But perhaps the witch hunter felt a pang of instinctive alarm when he beheld the doll, for he barked, 'Wait!' His minions halted their advance.

'That was wise,' Dieter said.

'What is that thing?' Krieger growled.

'It's you, Otto. Your future.'

'What are you talking about?'

'I said before that I should have deduced you were a Chaos cultist sooner than I did, and that's true, but I did realise before tonight. Since you have pretensions to magical skill yourself, you likely know that all true sorcerers catch glimpses of Chaos worming its way through the mundane world from time to time. This new eye of mine enhances that mode of sight.

'The eye opened a crack the second time we met at the tavern, and I saw an ugly glimmer crawling on you. At first, I imagined it was just an outward sign of a vicious, brutish nature, but then I realised it meant Chaos had taken you for its own.

'Once I understood that, it was easy to figure out that you were actually a follower of the Purple Hand, your pledges were worthless, and you'd deem it expedient to kill me as soon as I outlived my usefulness. If I wanted to survive, I needed a way of forcing you to honour our agreement.'

Krieger swallowed. 'So you pretended to have a seizure.'

'Exactly. Do you remember how I flailed and scratched at you? I did it to obtain a bit of your blood, hair and skin. I needed them to make this talisman.'

'Which is supposed to do what, exactly?'

'If I so choose, it will hurt you. I confess, I can't say precisely how. You might go blind. Or mad. Or catch the plague. You might suffer one calamity after another for the rest of your days. Suffice it to say, Celestial wizards understand the ways of destiny – that was why you chose me, remember? – and I've bound your fate inside this figure. Don't make me blight it.' Dieter spoke a word of command and pressed his thumb down on the doll's chest.

Krieger gasped and staggered. Dieter would have been happy to continue the torment for a considerable time, but he suspected that if he tried, the other cultists would shake off their uncertainty and move to interfere. So he stopped squeezing after only a moment or two.

'That was just to prove that you and the doll truly are connected,' he said. 'Don't make me do something that will have permanent consequences.'

His eyes wild, Krieger sucked in a ragged breath. 'I won't! I promise I won't! I'll proclaim your innocence as soon as we go back up into the city! I'll declare it right now, in writing! There must be ink and parchment down here somewhere…' He turned as though casting about for them, and his form divided into multiple images superimposed on one another.

The phantom moving ahead of all the others whirled back around with a small pistol in its hand. Evidently Krieger kept it concealed on his person as a weapon of last resort, and he was gambling that he possessed the speed and marksmanship to kill Dieter before his adversary could exert the power of the doll.

But thanks to Dieter's ability to glimpse the future, the ploy was doomed to fail. He waited another instant – dodge too soon, and Krieger might realise and adjust his aim – then sidestepped.

The several Kriegers collapsed into one. The little gun in his outstretched hand spat fire and banged just as Jarla threw herself in front of the muzzle. She thought she needed to endanger herself to shield Dieter, and since he'd been too busy watching the witch hunters to keep an eye on her as well, he hadn't discerned her intention.

She grunted and flopped backwards. Dieter tried to catch her, but, with the talisman filling one hand, couldn't grab hold. Jarla fell down on her back with a neat little hole above her heart.

He stared down at the body in astonishment. He'd mastered the tainted side of himself and refused to kill Jarla when she lay atop the altar. Instead, he'd unchained her, and fought the sorcerers of the Red Crown to give her a chance to escape. It seemed impossible that, after all that struggle, she lay dead anyway.

Then, abruptly, stupefaction gave way to fury. He bellowed and gripped the doll as tightly as he could. Responsive to his hatred even without incantations or mystical gestures to compel them, Chaos and some rarefied essence of lightning blended together, poured into his body, surged down his arm and burned in his straining fingers.

The clay figure burst into flame as if it were made of paper, then shattered into half a dozen pieces.

Krieger shrieked and dropped his gun and sword to paw at his face. It was a bad idea, because the flesh there had lost its cohesion, and a touch sufficed to dislodge it from the bone beneath. Gory scraps and viscous liquid streamed down like stew slopping from a ladle.

Krieger tried to extend a beseeching hand to Dieter, and it fell off his wrist. The witch hunter's left eye collapsed and slipped back into its socket as though some parasite ensconced inside his skull had sucked the optic into its mouth.

Krieger pitched forwards, convulsed twice, and then stopped moving entirely. The corpse bloated instantly, as though it had lain and rotted for days.

It was, Dieter assumed, the end for him as well. The threat to Krieger had been his only hope of forcing the Purple Hand to let him go. Now that he'd already carried it out, the remaining cultists had no reason to accede to his demands. Indeed, he'd given them additional cause to butcher him.

So be it, but, even though, in the wake of that last piece of magic, he doubted he had even a trace of power left, he'd do his best to make them work to avenge their leader. He drew breath, lifted his trembling hands, and only then realised they still weren't moving to attack him. Was it possible that Krieger's death, or the gruesome, unexpected manner of it, had cowed them?

Someone cleared his throat. Dieter pivoted to meet the gaze of a man who'd whipped him back in his cell in Halmbrandt. The ruffian had a long, scraggly caprine beard, a missing incisor, and blood from a fresh wound in his right forearm darkening his sleeve. He held a short sword in either hand.

'You said we could have the Red Crown's books and papers,' he said, the hint of a quaver in his voice.

'Yes,' Dieter replied.

'Then go. Go now, and we won't try to hurt you, all right?'

Fearing a trick, Dieter edged towards the exit, picking up his cloak and a lantern in the process. The cultists watched with malice in their eyes, but did nothing to prevent him.

It occurred to him that he was abandoning Jarla's body. The Purple Hand would either toss it in a sewer or simply let it lie and rot in the evil place where it had fallen.

She deserved better, but then, she always had. Dieter had deceived and exploited her from the start, and a proper burial, even if he could have managed it, was scarcely enough to make amends.

He staggered through the reeking sewers as fast as the darkness, slippery, treacherous footing, and his bruises, facial wounds and exhaustion would allow. He glanced back often to see if anyone was following him. As far as he could tell, nobody was.

At the foot of the ladder, wincing at the thought of the agonising headache that would soon follow, he closed his third eye. He pulled up his cowl as well, to obscure the unnatural organ and the bloody punctures on his forehead, cheeks and jaw, then set down his lantern and clambered up the rungs. Twice he nearly lost his grip, but not quite, and finally he crawled back out onto the street.

A spotted dog barked at him. Several boys glanced around in his direction, then resumed their game of kick-ball.

Dieter lifted his eyes to the heavens.

Even with the smoke, lights and rooftops of the city obscuring it, the beauty of the night sky clogged his throat and brought stinging tears to his eyes. He knew he should keep watching for enemies stalking after him, but as he rose and stumbled onwards, he only wanted to gaze at the stars and forget everything else.

'Well done,' said a baritone voice.

Dieter lurched around, saw the priest, and realised he wasn't surprised. Some part of him had expected the phantom to reappear.

Which didn't mean he was glad. 'What do you want now?' he wheezed.

The priest smiled. 'To congratulate you on your victory.'

Dieter's guts twisted. 'What victory? I just lost a woman who loved me and everything I was fighting to reclaim. Krieger was the only person who could have given me back my life, and I went berserk and killed him.'

'As you were supposed to. It's all a part of the Changer's plan. At the end, that was why the Purple Hand feared to fight you. Whether they realised it consciously or not, they sensed that the god would favour you, not them.'

'No!' Dieter exploded. 'There isn't any plan, and even if there is, I'm going to thwart it! I feel as though I've lost everything, but I haven't, not yet. Despite everything, I haven't lost myself, and by the sun and stars, I won't. I'll find a way to purge the sickness inside me and scour your master's filth from my face.'

'Excellent!' said the priest. 'Walk your road, learn your lessons, and we'll talk from time to time along the way.' He turned and disappeared. Overhead, a falling star sliced a long gash across the sky.

ABOUT THE AUTHOR

Richard Lee Byers has written over twenty novels, and countless short stories. A lifelong fantasy, science fiction and horror fan, he began his full time writing career in 1987 after working in the mental health field (he holds an MA in psychology) for many years. A resident of the Tampa Bay area of Florida, US, Richard spends much of his leisure time fencing foil, epee and sabre.

Step deeper into the action with the award-winning Warhammer Fantasy Roleplay!

The core rulebook provides everything you need to explore the gothic Old World and battle against the enemies of the Empire.

Warhammer Fantasy Roleplay

Core rulebook

1-84416-220-6

Buy it now from *www.blackindustries.com*
or by calling + 44 (0) 115 900 4144